RETURN TO THE DARK CORNER

THE DARK CORNER UNIVERSE
BOOK 2

DAVID W. ADAMS

CONTENTS

ISBN:
978-1-916582-37-8 [Paperback]
978-1-916582-38-5 [eBook]
978-1-916582-39-2 [Hardcover]

ECHO ON PUBLICATIONS

NOTE FROM THE AUTHOR

Firstly, I would like to thank you for picking up a copy of this revised, reformatted, and brand spanking new version of a *Dark Corner* book. I will never take that for granted and appreciate each and every one of you for doing so.

Let's cut to the chase.

This is not the first version of these books, as some of you may know. However, being an independent author comes with limitations, and for me at least, a great deal of impatience. When I wrote the original *Dark Corner* book, it was in the midst of the Coronavirus Pandemic, and the UK was in its first official lockdown. Go nowhere, do nothing, see nobody.

Basically my life in a nutshell, if you exclude going to work.

But I learned one day in my miserable and bland meandering through the days, that self-publishing had been on the rise while I looked the other way dreaming of having the time and money to be able to potentially have a crack at finally getting all of the stories out of my head. But better than that, was when I discovered there was a way to do it for FREE!

I was warned by several forums and articles that KDP, although an excellent resource compared to the previous nothingness, was also full of issues, pitfalls, and Amazon's usual greedy ways. You will make no money, nobody will see your book if you have less than 50 reviews, and nobody reads horror these days anyway.

Sadly, I must admit, that I was tempted to chuck the briefly stirred ambition of mine in the bin, and carry on going to work everyday during an outbreak so people could buy their 'essential' bathroom paint or Sharpie marker pens.

But it was my wife who encouraged me to continue. She had always written both poetry and fan fictions, but had never felt comfortable with the idea of the world reading her work. She was, however, incredibly persuasive, and after I reworked a story I started writing 20 years previously into what became the first story, *The White Dress*, I got bit by the bug. Over the course of 2020, I wrote ten short stories varying in severity, but overall quite reserved for horror, and resolved to get them published come what may.

Sadly, I couldn't afford an editor or proofreader, and my wife was also working full time and so simply didn't have the time to read for me. And so I decided to publish through a previously unknown, to me at least, website called My Bestseller. They were based in the Netherlands, and required you to buy an ISBN number or publish without one. However, while they offered expanded distribution, this did not include Amazon. I also discovered after purchasing an ISBN for that original version of the book, that it came at a reduced cost for one reason. The code was registered to the website. Which meant exclusivity.

Bollocks.

Exclusivity and not even on Amazon? No this would simply not do. I did however, make it work for a while, and in the course of three months sold a whopping two copies. I bought more than that myself!

Then came the time to explore KDP properly. I had published the book on My Bestseller without ever proofreading or editing it. I figured nobody was going to read it so didn't really worry about it. But one day, when writing the stories for the second book, *Return to the Dark Corner*, I went back to examine plot points that could be expanded.

Shit.

Errors, grammar issues, typos everywhere and more worryingly, plot holes. But it wasn't too late! Barely anybody had read it so I could fix it!

That's when I revised the book, and published through KDP, which came with free ISBNs! Jackpot I thought! But you must remember I was incredibly naïve and undereducated in this area. Exclusivity was a requirement again, but I didn't care. It was Amazon! Everyone uses Amazon! I even got suckered into Kindle Unlimited with the promise of more royalties. They really do know how to con you into things!

Anyway, since then, the *Dark Corner* series has grown and grown, even into producing several pieces of merchandise for the series such as posters and keyrings. The series concludes in the 13th book, a number I chose because I figured it fitting for something that began as a horror series primarily, although it became so much more!

And when the opportunity came along to work with Christian Francis to redesign, reformat and relaunch the series with a new uniform and polished look, I jumped at the chance. Christian put the shine to my stories that I had always hoped to achieve, and even redesigned the covers for me to give it a true 'series' look. I will be forever grateful for his generosity, hard work, and friendship, and am honored for these versions of my works to fall under the banner of Echo On Publishing.

So here we are, entering the *Dark Corner* once again. But I don't do things lightly. These are not simply redesigns of the exact same work. Oh no. My conscience wouldn't allow that! So every single book has an extra short story included to further expand this varied, fascinating and horrific universe. Consider it my gift of thanks to you all for sticking with me, encouraging me not to give up, and pushing me to do better.

As always, I encourage you to be kind, be healthy, and stay safe.

And thank you.

David W. Adams
28th November 2023

For Charlotte,
My proudest achievement in life has been our marriage.
Thank you for everything you have done to support me, and for being my
absolute rock, and inspiration.

We stopped checking for monsters under our beds, when we realized they were inside us.

— CHARLES DARWIN

PROLOGUE

A library can be a very intimidating building. Older towns and cities can be one of the lucky ones whose building of amazement and wonder happens to be hundreds of years old, packed full of stone architecture, or marble floors. A building in which memories and fantasy flow through the very walls, every brick and every beam.

This place was one of those lucky ones. Because this library had existed for over a century. It had the typical huge stone entrance, carved lions atop two pillars either side. Huge ornate ancient wooden doors.

The night had descended, lightning streaking the sky and the distant rumble of thunder overhead. Rain began to strike the woman's skin, cold and harsh. She rushed through the doors to seek shelter in the welcoming company of characters that she knew and loved.

The single librarian smiled at her as she walked past the desk. She seemed almost as old as the building itself, skin white, knitted cardigan hanging from her shoulders, glasses perched on the end of her nose, held around her neck by a chain.

The woman took note of how there seemed to be no-one around. The ceilings reached high into the air, archways towering above each leaded window, wooden beams stretching seemingly for miles, hanging in the air. The smell of the pages filled the place, and her senses.

She moved past the small children's section, toys still strewn across the floor from the morning activities. Past the biographies of the thousands of dictators, celebrities, and sportspeople who'd lived across the centuries. Past the educational section where so many had pulled all night study sessions, the emotion of fear and anxiety over whether they would pass or fail their exams.

The dim lights in the sconces cast her shadow along the stones in the wall as she noticed a large leather chair in the far left corner, beneath four towering oak bookcases in an L-shape, where there were no windows. There was no real light, just a very small electric lantern sat on the floor beside the chair. She knew this spot well. She'd been here before.

Last time, she had immersed herself in the contents of its literature and emerged slightly changed. As she moved towards that corner again, the thunder clapped louder, the lightning illuminated the roof through the huge ancient windows further along the wall, shimmering on the raindrops streaking down the glass. The lantern seemed to dim as she approached, and the books seemed to be calling to her.

More lightning, more thunder, the rain was now heavier as she reached for the same place she took the previous volume from. The hardback was cold to the touch, and heavy not just with its pages, but with the emotion and anticipation it contained. She turned the spine over and read the title, a smile spreading across her face, but a shiver down her spine.

As she took her seat in the huge chair, and raised the lantern to the small side table, she stroked the front cover, and gently opened it. The contents of the stories, listed, the titles excited her and terrified her as did the first volume. Nevertheless, she was eager, and opened the first story.

She had returned to The Dark Corner.

BONUS CONTENT

DARK THUNDER

It's not every day you see purple clouds, that much is for certain. Purple lightning, sure. But clouds? That shit ain't on the Discovery channel for sure. My real indication that something wasn't quite right, was the fact that the ground was vibrating, but there was no sound. For a moment, I wondered if I had slipped into a tornado in another realm or universe and happened to be currently located within the eye of the storm. But then again, my mind did always tend to wander to realms of fantasy. It was my teacher's favourite complaint about me back when I was in school. At least, the last time I was in school.

Being several million years old has its advantages. One is that of course, you see more things. More inventions. More technology. More weird and crazy shit. The downside is that although you don't age visually, unless I will it of course, you or at least I, age mentally. I have lost count of the amount of times I have been bored beyond belief, and felt so alone that I could scream. But then, who would hear me?

I have lived a billion lives, a billion ways and died a billion times. Watching over this planet, this realm, this existence within the multiverse can only entertain a being for so long. The humans and the beings on Earth disappointed me long ago. They see me everyday and yet they do not know it. Some feel that I walk beside them every day, when in fact I often walk among them.

Being seen as the original creation is tiresome, however. Wars in my name, violence in my name. And the ridiculous thing is... it's not even my fucking name!

I must confess at this point that your suspicions are likely correct as to my identity, but everything else you know of me is wrong. I did not create the Earth in seven days. I did not have a son with the virgin wife of another man. I did not then sacrifice that son, nor did I order the flooding of the Earth. All complete bullshit. They say history is written by the victors, but I cannot understand why my daughter having essentially won a war that never really started, would have me depicted in this way.

No. I don't suspect it was Lucifer at all. She doesn't have the contempt towards me, not at that level. She's always respected me despite our disagreements. No, this was much more likely the work of treacherous demons. Nevertheless, with no Heaven or Hell to watch over, let's just say I had to get creative. Earth is only one planet. The Sol System, as they call it, is only one tiny insignificant speck of existence. Why not try and create something again? I mean the universe was an accident, let's be honest. I'd just woken up in a vast emptiness, tired, scared and alone. Anyone would be angry. Wouldn't you? Smashing atoms together was just my way of essentially throwing a tantrum. But you're welcome anyway. You know, for your existence.

But this time, I thought, why not try and do something on purpose? I admit, it went a little bit askew with what I called Haldriana. I mean if you want an indication of how wrong it went, you only have to look at the name it's now referred to; Realm of Screams. I mean, these were meant to be beings of pure energy, light and wonder. It was an effort to create something more like myself. But of course I had no idea where I came from. As far as I was aware, before me there was nothing, but there had to be something to make me from. A real chicken and the egg thing. But, with no definitive... let's say recipe, well I fucked it up again. These poor ethereal creatures existed in pure pain. Unfathomable agony. But the worst part of it all, was they believed it was their purpose of existence. To go through such pain and distress and violence and torture, just to graduate from it eventually, and be free to explore their bountiful energy across time and space.

Their devised name was to be the Haldrians. Derived from the name of their realm, they would live in an ethereal state, but be free, should they choose, to take solid form by rearranging their molecules with nothing but their minds. It would allow them to learn and grow, and unlike the stupid creatures below, they would be aware of the existence of other realms right from the start. Now of course, they go by a very different name.

Pain Wraiths.

What a ghastly name for such a beautiful creation. Naturally, after this failure, I decided to rest a while. But then boredom crept in again. I ran through a few dozen lifetimes, learned nothing of consequence and returned to my non-corporeal state wondering what came next. I could not bring myself to destroy the Pain Wraiths, as they were now forging a purpose from their existence, and I didn't want to deny them that. So, I started smaller. I created a pocket universe of sorts. An endless ocean, with one solitary island in the middle. I say the middle, but being an endless ocean I suppose the middle is a little vague. The trouble was, when I came to deciding what kind of being I would try to create this time, I was interrupted by a tear in the fabric of space time, and BANG! Some disgusting creatures that were essentially angry clouds came bursting through and started drawing other creatures through, simply to eat. I'd made a secluded fucking restaurant!

So I gave up.

I have no human souls to nurture because there really is no point. I have no already deceased souls to keep me company because Heaven is long gone thanks to Lucifer's actions. And I now have no power of any kind. Heaven has been gone for too long, and without it, I simply float above existence, looking down on those below me.

This could be good though. This dark thunder over one of the more interesting American towns looks meaty. I'll enjoy watching this one unfold.

Shame I don't have any popcorn really.

FIELD OF BLOOD

The planes overhead were deafening, the rumble of the engines, the whirring of the propellers, the whistling noises of the bombs falling through the air. The bombardment had been intense.

There had been little to no response from the Allied forces, and the troops on the ground were being decimated. The remaining commanding officers were barking orders, but those orders were getting fewer and fewer, as the voices died out one by one. Now it was just a case of running as fast as they could to any safety they could find.

"RUN! All remaining troops retreat! Split into three groups, it'll make it harder for them to take us out!"

Daniel shouted the orders as there appeared to be no officers left, but nobody could hear him. The explosions and the eruptions of dirt and soil showering the soldiers, meant many were confused and disorientated as to what direction they were running in, several just seeming to run in circles. Many had abandoned their rifles to try and find cover, but there was no cover.

Tom was leaping over every dip and mound in the earth, determined not to get tripped up and to reach safety. Ahead of him, Sean was running alone, seemingly unnoticed, and Bobby, was running in zigzags to make it more difficult for the bombers to take an accurate shot.

From above, the field now resembled an assortment of ants, running in all different directions trying to avoid the concentrated light from the bully's magnifying glass. Bobby turned back to check on his other brothers and looked with terror as he stared back towards Tom. He started waving his hands to the side, and shouting, but Tom couldn't make it out. The whistling noise was getting louder, and he could just make out what Bobby was yelling.

"TOM! GET OUT OF THERE!"

Bobby stopped running away and started running back towards Tom. The whistling noise became deafening, and as Tom looked up he saw the shell heading directly for him. He pushed his legs and heart to the limit, throwing his rifle to the side and losing his backpack of equipment. No man could feasibly run across open ground with the amount of equipment the soldiers had been told to carry. Tom got within six feet of Bobby when the shell hit.

The ground blew up from underneath in the form of a mushroom cloud, sending earth and shrapnel flying in every direction, before emitting the ball of fire from the explosive charge inside. The men were scattered across the field, and as the noises faded into the background, Tom looked over and saw Bobby lying motionless on the floor in a pool of blood.

"War is hell. There is no glory in war. There is no winner or true victory. In the end, it will consume you and everyone you love. It changes you. Fighting to live with the actions you have taken, the horror you have seen, the bloodshed you have witnessed. There is no glory in that."

Bobby coughed the most severe fit he had up to that point, his eyes both black, skin mottled, beads of cold sweat on his brow. As Tom sat beside him, attempting to comfort him, unable to hold his hand, he spoke softly.

"There is no glory in defeat either Bobby. We can't let these bastards take our freedom. They will not take our land and they will not crush our spirit. God is with you, and I'm here with you. We will keep you safe tonight."

More coughing, a splattering of blood now emanating from Bobby's throat. Tom knew he'd be dead by morning. He knew most of them would be dead by morning. As Bobby lost consciousness again, Tom stood to walk away, leaving a rosary where Bobby's arm should have been. He turned and began walking the long walk down centre of the medical tent. The red mile, some of the soldiers were now calling it. Hundreds of beds stretched out, each with a wounded soul, gradually making their way into the light they had been deprived of in the last months of their lives. Most men tried to block out the moans and the painful cries, but not Tom. He listened to the sound of every man as he passed by. He prayed as he walked, wishing them all safe passage into the afterlife.

"NO! YOU! DEMON!"

Tom paused as one of the men shouted towards him, pointing a finger at his head, shaking. A nurse in the distance ran towards the sound and tried to calm him as he continued to protest that a demon was stalking him on his deathbed. Tom simply turned and walked away, heading back to the barracks.

"That much open ground is suicide. May as well just kill us now."

Daniel was furious, having been debriefed along with the rest of his platoon, on their next mission. Many shared his concern that it could be their final push. Despite the suggestion that the war was going well, there certainly wasn't that feel amongst the men. More were dying every day. There was a reason this conflict had been dubbed 'The Great War'.

Tom sat alone on his bunk, pondering the task that lay ahead of them. He could not see a resolution to the scenario they faced, and yet his faith remained strong.

"Quit the fucking prayers, church boy. No God is gonna save you. There ain't no God that would put his children through this hell."

Daniel had brought attention to Tom that he would have preferred to avoid.

"Leave him alone Danny. He believes what he believes."

Sean didn't believe in the wisdom of God either, but he certainly wasn't going to stop someone using whatever gave them comfort to get through this.

"You wanna pray Tommy, go right ahead."

Tom wasn't comfortable with the attention, whether it be positive or negative, but better to be protected than punished. Daniel snorted and shook his head.

"We all know there's no coming out of this, I'd rather go at those Gerry bastards with courage in my heart and knowing exactly what I'm getting into."

"War is hell."

Tom spoke to nobody in particular, but repeated the words his friend had spoken to him.

"What?"

"War is hell," replied Tom.

"No shit, mate," replied Daniel.

"Are you okay Tommy?" asked Sean.

"Just something that Bobby said to me, can't seem to forget it. The look in his eyes as he said it. Like he was talking directly to me."

"Well, who else was he gonna talk to, he's dying and you were the only one there."

"No, it was something else. Something *deeper*."

Daniel was momentarily captured in thought but snapped back out after a short period of silence.

"Well, come on lads, the enemy isn't going to kill itself. Get some rest. In the morning, we march to death."

The lights in the barracks switched out, and everyone lay down in their bunks. Tom was wide awake, those words repeating in his head over and over.

'*War is hell.*'

As Tom looked down at the wide eyes of one of his bunkmates, the burnt flesh clinging to his face, but barely, his mind was filled with those words and nothing else. His heart was pounding, his mind racing, the explosions and barrage of gunfire ringing out across the Somme.

This was not what they were promised.

They were promised a swift victory, they were promised this battle would secure vital land to turn the tide of the war in their favour. For the last two years, Tom had never questioned his superiors, and believed that he was indeed fighting for the freedom of his country. And that was of course true, but for every man who dropped dead at his side, another bullet of fear lodged into him, and he felt it increasing more by the second.

"Tommy! Hey Tommy! Get out of there! Enemy fire incoming!"

The faint cries from Sean seemed miles away. All Tom could focus on were the eyes of the man at his feet. He was flash frozen in time. The life taken from him in an instant, leaving his body still waiting to carry on the actions it was duty bound to do. The blood pooling in the mud reached Tom's feet, and he could vaguely hear a whistling sound getting ever closer.

Without warning, Tom was slammed into by an unseen force, sending him hurtling six or seven feet away through the air, landing in the mud further down the trench with a hard thud, smashing his face off the ground, and a heavy weight on top of him. As the shell hit the edge of the trench, the shockwave blew two dozen men off their feet, screams reverberating down the line.

Sean's groans were faint but close. As Tom returned himself to the present, he realised Sean was lying on top of him and couldn't move. He gradually rolled over, laying Sean to the side. As his eyes were able to focus on the scene before him, he could see Daniel in the distance waving men out of the section they were standing in, smoke filling the air, and the smell of charred flesh becoming stronger. Tom followed the trail of destruction, rock, splintered wood, scattered equipment, and then the blood.

A large puddle, surrounded by an impact splatter pattern… and a leg. As Tom turned back around to look at Sean, he realised the sacrifice his friend had just made to save his life. Sean was shivering, face dark with mud and blood, uniform soaked with red from the knee down, then nothing. He leaned in to Sean to try and do something. As he pulled a handkerchief from his pocket, Sean grabbed his uniform at the chest, scrunched it up and pulled him close to his face. With terror in his eyes, now bulging white against the red and brown backdrop of his skin, he whispered through hampered breath to Tom.

'*War is hell.*'

The grip released on Tom's tunic, and Sean fell back into the dirt, eyes remained open, staring at the grey skies above, no breath emerging from his now lifeless body. Tom reached over and closed his eyes.

Men were now fleeing over the top of the trench, several getting trapped in the barbed wire as they tried to escape. Others being picked off by gunfire, one by one. A thick heavy fog now coated the Somme, only the ground, stained red, was visible. Tom cowered at the edge, not wanting to leave the trench, but not wanting to stay. He pulled his silver cross from his pocket and held it tight. And then a strange feeling came over him. It was almost a sense of familiarity. The feeling that he had been in this situation before.

Of course, he had seen more than his fair share of battle since the war started in nineteen fourteen, but this was different. Even as he spoke his prayer, he knew he had uttered those words before.

"Dear Lord, please protect me as I leave this place. Guide me as I know you can and keep my brothers safe. Please Lord, guide me..."

"You know, he's not listening right?"

Tom snapped out of his prayer and looked around. There was nobody left in the trench.

"Up here Tommy."

Tom looked up and fell back at what he saw. Sitting in the open, on the edge of the trench wall, legs dangling beneath him, was Bobby.

"Bobby?" Tom asked, staggered, convinced he was seeing things.

Perhaps the rumoured mustard gas the Germans were said to be developing, had been launched, and he was hallucinating as he choked to death.

"What's the matter, Tommy? You look like you've seen a ghost."

Bobby smiled, as he reached into his pocket and took out a pack of cigarettes. As he lit one, a bullet soared through his head and lodged in the wall of mud opposite. He didn't even flinch. He pressed the cigarette to his lips and gestured the pack towards Tom.

"You want a smoke? Look like you could use one."

Tom shook his head.

"Suit yourself. Not much else to do."

"Bobby? How can this be you?"

Tom's eyes were now as wide as the man he had seen killed moments before. Bobby took several puffs from the cigarette and then threw it to the ground.

"I'm always here, Tommy. I told you last time. War is hell."

Those words again. Tom had not been able to think of anything else. But what did Bobby mean by 'last time'. The only time he had spoken those words were in the hospital. And there was no guarantee that Bobby had actually died yet. Far away, the sounds of Daniel screaming echoed across the battlefield.

"Always here? But you are in the hospital tent. Your arm? I saw you lose it! What are you talking about?"

Bobby sighed. Clearly his efforts were falling on deaf ears.

"I'll show you something, Tommy. Stand up."

Tommy moved back as tight to the trench wall behind him as he possibly could. He shook his head in disbelief at what this man was saying to him.

Bobby cocked his head to the side, and then sprang up to his feet. Bullets rained through him, screams still filling the air as men were cut down one by one. Explosions in the distance, and one much nearer sent waves of dirt and rock down on the trenches. Tom shielded his face from the debris, and something in his mind told him to move his left leg. As he did so, a huge piece of shrapnel pierced the ground where he had been resting that very leg. Coincidence, surely. But still, Bobby stood at the top staring down at him, hand outstretched.

"You're a smart kid Tommy, I'm surprised you haven't figured this out yet. This must be what, the fifth time now? Here, give me your hand, you have to get out of here."

Tom remained pressed to the wall, shaking his head.

"That's suicide, I can't go out there. Sean. Danny. They're gone. I'm afraid. I can't go out there!"

Tom trembled and slid down to the ground, burying his face in his hands.

"I can't do this! You're not really here!"

Tom was racking his mind for where this feeling of Deja vu had come from. He knew he'd said that prayer before. He also knew that the shrapnel was going to hit that very spot. And he also knew that Sean was going to die. But how?

Suddenly, as Tom's thoughts were trying to click into place, everything fell silent. No explosions. No screams. No gunfire. Not even the wind moving through the barbed wire. Tom slowly lifted his hands from his face, and gradually looked up to the trench edge.

Bobby was gone.

Tom slowly grasped in the mud to gain a footing and stood up, gradually edging his way forwards. The feeling of familiarity had ended. This was new. As he placed his hands on the top of the wall, he lifted his head to place his eyes in line with the ground above and stared out onto an empty battlefield. He scanned the horizon as far as he could through the mist and fog which remained.

"What is happening here?" he asked himself aloud.

He checked three times for signs of life, but when he found none, he gently pulled himself up into the open air, and stood fully up, squinting into the distance. The trench was now surrounded by thick grey fog, and vision was limited to no more than fifty feet. Still no life or sounds anywhere.

"Took you longer to get out of there than the last time. I guess that's not really an improvement, but we can work on it."

Tom spun around and Bobby was once again standing before him, holding out another cigarette.

"What is this?" asked Tom.

Bobby sighed and put away his offering.

"This is the Somme. This is the same place you just were, and where you are now, and where you will always be. The movie has just paused, that's all. It's waiting for you to figure out the ending."

The confusion was now overwhelming as Tom tried to piece together the mystery he was now going through, all the time terrified he was about to be gunned down by a covert shot.

"What movie? I don't understand. Where is all the gunfire, the soldiers, the explosions? Please, Bobby just tell me!"

Tom felt tears now roll down his cheeks, bumping over the dried mud on his cheeks.

"Tommy, what's the first thing you can remember?" asked Bobby.

Taken aback by the question, Tommy responded as expected.

"What do you mean, the first thing? What today, or yesterday, first thing from when?"

"Think hard and tell me what you remember from before I died."

Tom immediately formed to make a response, but nothing came out. His mind felt like it had frozen and there was a roadblock to his memories.

"I... I can't remember."

Bobby nodded and moved closer to Tom. He reached out and placed a hand on his shoulder.

"So, tell me, the first thing you can remember." Tom thought hard. The blockade remained.

"We were running through the fields, the planes above, you were ahead of me. There was a loud whistling noise, you looked up, and shouted at me to get down, you waved your arms, and then... Nothing."

Bobby nodded.

"And what do you remember after that?"

Tom thought hard.

"I... I remember sitting by your bedside, and you spoke to me."

"That wasn't aimed at you, Tommy. I was dying. I thought I could see shadows. I thought death was coming for me, and it was my final speech. You weren't there. You hadn't been there for weeks. None of you had."

"But we went to the briefing, we talked in the barracks, we slept through the night. None of that happened?"

Bobby smirked.

"It did happen Tommy. But it happened almost seventy five years ago."

Tommy staggered back a few steps.

"How do you know this?" he said in a very accusatory voice.

Bobby moved towards him.

"Because I've replayed this loop too. Only I figured it out. The day I ran to push you out of the way of that shell? I was the only one to make it out. You didn't."

"What? But Danny, Sean…"

"Danny was killed two weeks before charging across the open ground during a counter offensive. Sean died two days before you did when he pushed you out of the way of an incoming shell. He lost his leg and bled out in the trench."

Tommy could feel his breath becoming fainter, his heart was ready to burst.

"No. I'm not dead. I can't be. How can we all have been together if we died at different times?"

"Don't you see Tommy? We are all replaying the ways in which we died. Danny just died running across open ground. Sean just died saving your life and losing his leg. And this is where you died. Battle of the Somme, July twenty-first, nineteen-sixteen."

Tommy sat on the ground. Bobby moved to sit next to him.

"War is like a cancer, Tommy. It gets into your soul and rips apart everything you believe in. You're tricked by lies upon lies until you can't see past the killing. When I say that war is hell, that's because that is what it is for us. War is our hell. Doomed to repeat the battles and the pain and the death for all eternity. Eventually, you'll figure it out. You can make different choices, run out of the trench earlier, move your leg out of the way of shrapnel, but the one thing you can't do, is leave your fate."

"You… how do you know all this?"

"I told you that we've all been dead for seventy-five years. That's a long time of having Deja vu and piecing it all together. With each replay of my death, each reincarnation of the pain, I could remember things. I tried not going back for you, but the shell just landed closer to me, and the result was the same. The next time I tried deserting, but I was arrested and thrown back into the battle. Nothing I could do could prevent me reliving the same fate. So, I came to the inevitable conclusion. I was dead."

"That doesn't mean we're dead," complained Tommy, tears forming. "We could just be trapped in time!"

Bobby giggled.

"What are you laughing at?" Bobby giggled again.

"Tommy, look behind you."

Bobby pointed and Tommy turned around but was unable to explain what he saw. Around thirty feet in front of him, a large group of people were walking *through* the barbed wire. A woman wearing a red jacket, speaking to roughly twenty people, some of which were children, and gesturing with her hands attempting to emphasise her point. Tommy couldn't hear what they were saying, but their appearance alone was troubling enough.

"We are gone, Tommy. Echoes of the past. They are in the present. They can't hear us, believe me I've tried. But sometimes, they can *see* us. We are ghosts to them, just an apparition on the battlefield. Residual energy."

Tom shook his head violently.

"No, I won't accept that! Why can't you leave this place? What happens if I walk right up to those people and try to move out of the field? What happens if I try to leave?"

"You can't. I saw Danny try once. It didn't end well."

"Didn't end well?"

"Whatever force holds us in this place, whether it's supernatural, death or the Devil himself, it won't let us go. Danny nearly figured out the loop once, and in a panic tried to get in a jeep and drive away."

"What happened?"

Tom already felt like he knew the answer.

"Death came for him."

Tom was disturbed at that statement. Considering death had already come for Danny, how could it come again?

"Tell me."

"The sky darkened, the world emptied, much like it has now. And then a horned figure appeared in front of the jeep, flipped it over and smashed it under its enormous feet. Danny was crushed to death, only for his loop to start all over again. You can't leave. Nobody can leave."

Tom shook his head violently, even more so than before, gazing back and forth between Bobby and the translucent creatures that were walking along the battlefield completely unaware that they were treading in pools of blood.

"NO! It's not true. I am not DEAD!"

He gripped his rifle and charged out onto the battlefield screaming with every step, tears flowing down his face at a rate of knots. He ran through the group of people, leaping over the barbed wire, and continuing into the distance. Bobby stayed where he was, and as a look of grief took over his face, he faded away. As he vanished, he remarked one final sentence.

"You can't escape hell, Tommy."

And Bobby was gone.

Tom continued to run, pounding the mud, splashing through the puddles until he was completely emotionally and physically exhausted. He stopped and collapsed into the ground, and as he turned around, he saw that the group of people were still only thirty feet away.

He had gone nowhere.

All the running and he was exactly where he started. He looked behind him, and the trench was there, as if he'd never left. One of the group seemed to look at him. One of the women, squinting. Tom looked back and held up his hand. The woman held up her hand in response. A look of astonishment filled Tom's heart with hope. He clambered back to his feet and began running towards the woman.

Now with a more scared look on her face, the woman took a few steps back. She seemed distracted, the woman in red apparently calling to her, and she turned away briefly.

Despite Tom's best efforts, he was not getting any closer to the group. Then something stopped him dead. The group disappeared, and the wind began to howl. The wire in the fence began to twist and contort and loosen itself from the ground. The sharpened metal had now come to life, like some evil tentacles reaching up from hell itself. Tom was now terrified.

'*You can't escape hell.*'

He leapt back down into the trench and ran down its length as quickly as his exhausted legs could carry him, tripping and stumbling. He looked back and saw the wire fly over the top of the trench and down into the narrow passageways, picking up speed. Bobby was right.

He'd tried to leave and now death itself was coming for him.

Tom tripped over a discarded rifle and plummeted over the lower edge into a flooded section of the trenches. He pushed himself up out of the water as the wire rounded the corner. Now waterlogged, Tom was running out of steam, and he collapsed at the next junction. The wind howled like a tropical storm, and as Tom turned around, resigned to his fate, a strand of barbed wire burst through his thigh, and into the mud wall opposite. Tom screamed, the sound shattering through all existence, as another strand of wire shot through his stomach into the wall. Length after length of possessed metal pierced Tom's body, pinning him to the spot. As Tom coughed up blood through his mouth, which was now punctured with more wire, he could hear those words in his head one final time.

'*War is hell.*'

Tom's eyes snapped open, blinking away the sleep in his eyes. He'd managed to fall asleep, which was unusual for him. His skin was cold with the goosebumps of his nightmare. He couldn't remember the details, but now was not the time for dreaming. He looked up, and Bobby was still awake. His tourniquet around his arm was now as dark as the uniform he had been wearing. Tom signalled to the nurse to change it, but she didn't acknowledge him.

"It's okay Bobby. I'll pray for you."

He went to place a rosary where Bobby's hand should be but hesitated for a moment. Something in his head sensed he'd done this before. He shrugged off the feeling and placed the beads on the bed.

In the far corner of the tent, Bobby stood looking at Tom, and himself, shaking his head.

"You can't escape hell Tommy. You can only repeat it. Maybe next time you'll figure it out."

"What's the matter?" asked the guide.

Kathryn's eyes were fixed to one spot in the distance.

"Excuse me miss?" The guide continued to try and get her attention.

Kathryn was looking around thirty feet in front of her, where she saw, plain as day, a soldier running across the field, as if being chased by something. The figure didn't appear to be of the here and now, but briefly, she thought he had been looking at her.

"Miss?"

Kathryn felt a hand on her shoulder, and spun around, startled, to find the guide standing beside her and the rest of the tour group staring at her.

"Sorry, I just… never mind."

The guide returned to the group, and Kathryn looked back to where she saw the soldier, but he was gone. As she went to re-join the group, her foot caught something in the ground. As she knelt down, she saw what looked like metal sticking out of the mud. Kathryn pulled it out, applying some force to do so, and when the item was removed, she saw it looked like a bayonet attachment from a rifle.

Checking to make sure that nobody from the tour group was watching, she slipped it into her bag, and taking one last look towards the last sighting of the mysterious soldier, she ran off and re-joined the group.

When she caught up, the guide turned to her, and flashed a warm smile.

"Are you okay miss?"

Kathryn smiled back and nodded.

"Yes thank you. I've got what I came for."

FOOD FOR THOUGHT

The world always hungers, for one thing or more,
But some things that you look for, you should not explore.
When evil is present, you cannot escape,
And this story begins with a play of a tape.
The Earth was overcome with a medical need,
A disease had been growing and spreading its seed.
People were dying all over the land,
On dirt, overseas, on mountains and sand.
A new form of cancer was sweeping worldwide,
And it swept all our current medicines aside.
It was aggressive and violent and merciless, it's true,
It killed women and children and animals too.
Something had to be done to stop the spread,
Or before too long, everything on Earth would be dead.
The best scientists all competed rather than work together,
Through the days and the nights and through all kinds of weather.
Each one was determined to reach the cure first,
And end the unquenchable disease and its thirst.
The future of man was relying on the cure,
It was thought it may lie within something obscure.

Years and years passed, and still nothing was done,
It seemed as if this evil mutation had won.
Then one day in March, on a hiking expedition,
In the wilds of the Amazon, an idea came to fruition.
A retired scientist taking a well-earned retreat,
Found the answer to our prayers, growing at his feet.
A new breed of flower, bright, big and vibrant,
Could hold the key, the man racked with excitement.
A botanist by trade, seeking out that new life,
And finding new species, along with his wife,
Who worked at a university in Arizona,
She took the flower sample to her colleague in Barcelona.
They tested and tested and tested its properties,
There was no doubt this flower had healing qualities.
The vaccine soon followed, and millions produced,
The whole population signed up for the boost,
To their immune system, to be rid of the chance,
Of developing the cancer, and dancing Death's dance.
But in the rush of developing this magical cure,
They hadn't counted on something even more obscure.
Within the flower was a kind of bacteria,
Which with each vaccination was bringing much nearer,
A fate worse than death, and worse than the cancer,
And in time would birth evil, it had not been the answer.
Science is wonderful, and magical at times,
But when it is rushed, it leads to evil crimes.
For as more of the people were jabbed with the dose,
Something was happening doctors couldn't diagnose.
Mutations were happening in the blood of the patients,
More and more bodies were in the morgues, in the basements.
The funeral homes were piling them high,
As more of the population started to die.
But dead they did not stay, for the vaccine lay dormant,
The mutation within was simply abhorrent.
Death came for man, then man came with death,
And the dead all rose once more, with foul decaying breath.

They burst from the morgues, and funeral homes too,
Bent on hunger, only human flesh would do.
The best of the best had rushed and had failed,
And now the price they paid was survival derailed.
They raged through the streets, this army of undead,
In the hopes of scooping out what lies in your head.
Guns couldn't stop them, for they were not alive,
And the more flesh they ate, the more that they thrived.
Britain fell first, the rest of Europe soon followed,
The flesh was consumed and chewed as they swallowed.
Cries of help came from every country and all lands,
The humans had played into the new cancer's hands.
It couldn't have killed all humans alone,
It needed our arrogance, and now it had grown,
Into a mutant disease that turned us to zombies,
That ate and tore all the skin from our bodies.

It took just six months for the nations to fall,
But beneath the ground, survivors did call.
Nothing would take our world from us here and now,
And a blueprint was drawn to show everyone how.
The flesh eaters functioned on the noise of the screams,
Or the sounds of people awakening from very bad dreams.
The sound of a car barreling by,
And the noise of a plane crashing out of the sky.
So, the fighters decided to stay deadly quiet,
And sneakily make their move on the quiet.
They marched through the sewers at the crack of the dawn,
And assembled together on the White House front lawn.
They all moved barefooted along on the grass,
A few zombies down the street, heard no sound, and did pass.
The last of the humans, moved quietly down the street,
The plan worked, until something stuck one of their feet.
The scream was deafening, the blood flowing true,
The undead soon heard it, and back towards them they flew.
Shattered glass on the street had scampered their plan,

And now zombies feasted on that wounded man.
The others were spotted, shouting 'Run!' as they ran,
Their plan had been scuppered by one single man.
The irony is in this unfortunate tale,
The man who screamed out was the botanist male.
The man who started this terrible curse,
Had ensured mankind's future would only get worse.
The flesh eating lunatics came from every direction,
There was nowhere to hide for any sort of protection.
A handful of humans were all that remained,
And as doom closed in, their expressions were pained.
The growl of the throat that emerged from the dead,
Hung heavy in their ears, the symbol of dread.
They cowered in the street, awaiting their doom,
When from above, came an almighty boom.
The zombies distracted by the unexpected noise,
The Army had come with a troop full of our boys.
Gunfire rang out in a circular motion,
Survival in grasp, oh Lord what a notion!
But salvation was not on the soldier's minds,
Their orders were to search for a more valuable prize.
They leapt from the chopper, swinging blades through the necks,
Of the undead horde, their faces were vexed.
The zombies lay dead at the feet of these men,
Who wiped off their blades and prepared for attack again.
They moved towards the humans, whose smiles had faded,
And they noticed the street at both ends, barricaded.
The soldiers had no intention for them to live,
There was just one offering the humans could give.
"Please, we need help, we don't want to die,"
Came the voices of people as they started to cry.
The soldiers then paused, unsure for a moment,
Then their commands were repeated in their ears, no postponement.
They cut off the heads as they had with the undead,
And moved away as each body lay next to its head.
The soldiers turned back to the chopper then stopped,

As they'd killed the humans, their path had been blocked.
Fifty zombies between them and salvation,
Their cruel actions had now secured their damnation.
With only twenty soldiers against increasing undead,
The soldiers turned around and fled backwards instead.
They made it to the lawn, and headed down below,
But these zombies weren't dumb, in the sewers they'd go.
There was no escape from the hordes of undead,
And soon every soldier had an empty head.

As the zombies feasted on the brains of the living,
It had become clear that Death was not so forgiving.
Undone by our haste at being the first to a cure,
The human race had become no more.
And how do I tell you this frightening tale?
When the attempt to arrest our fate seemed to fail?
My friends I can say with a certain degree,
That those zombies are never going to munch upon me.
For I have the cure, and I'm sure it will work,
I just need a subject to test it on first.
I sit in my tower, right up at the top,
Many a night, I've wanted to throw myself off.
But I continued to work through the days and the nights,
I knew I could find a cure, and boy I was right.
From the top of the Eiffel Tower, an end is in sight,
At the end of that tunnel, mankind sees the light.
Tomorrow I capture a zombie attacker,
I'll distract their senses with a firecracker,
Then bag it, subdue it, and bring it up top,
And then all the madness will finally stop.
I'm safe here alone, with no-one around,
Hey wait just a minute,
What's that groaning sound?

EIGHT WAYS TO HELL

There are few images which truly conjure up unbridled fear, and paralysis. Some are so intense people simply cannot gaze upon them, because of the horror, blood, gore, simply a heightened level of distress. But the sight of a large spider crawling across the dead white flesh of a human being is one of those which both freeze time, and make that moment seem like an eternity.

The glass littered the floor of the office, glinting under the flickering, hanging lights of the ceiling. The steady drip of the tap from the sink, echoing around the now silent workspace. The scene which befell Max as he had entered the doorway had seemed to have been pulled directly from a scary movie.

It was only the fact that it was broad daylight outside, that had made it seem different. Those individual rays of sunlight piercing the gaps in the Venetian blinds, leaving stripes across the desk. Max hadn't moved from the doorway. He had extreme arachnophobia, and the only reason he ever agreed to enter this room was because he knew all of the creepy crawlies in question were safely locked away in their Perspex boxes.

Charles had even gone one step further, and every time Max had come to visit, he'd throw covers over all the boxes to avoid the feeling of Max being watched by dozens of eyes.

But right now, everything about that security had been taken away. Max was now in fear for his life, and yet he still couldn't move. As he looked at the quite dead face of Professor Charles Arlington, he saw movement in his hairline.

His pulse quickened, and a cold sweat began forming on his spine, and forehead. As the tarantula gradually crept into view, and scurried along Professor Arlington's face, Max's eyes bulged wide, and his fists gripped his side, turning almost as white as the deceased man lying on the floor. The thick wiry hairs on each of the spiders eight legs bristled against the follicles of Arlington's white beard as it moved across the figure. It's feet now applying pressure to the man's lips as it crawled without hesitation over and down the side of his neck, where it vanished from sight.

"Hey Max, what's the…"

A female voice came from behind the fear struck teen but was cut off immediately at the sight she was confronted with.

"Holy shit! What happened here?"

"I… I… Spider… down there…"

Max had found his voice, but not his legs, and directed Grace's eyes in the direction of the last known coordinates of the eight legged terror. Grace immediately pulled out her phone and called the police.

Security in the building was practically non-existent and if they had any hope of any CCTV footage, it was solely reliant on the building manager.

Grace gradually eased Max to one side, to ensure he was out of the room, and as she did so, she felt movement on her leg. She, like Max, was now frozen to the spot. Although not too affected by tropical creatures, she wasn't exactly a fan.

"What is it?" asked Max, to which he did not receive a reply. "Are you okay?"

Grace simply pointed down, and Max's eyes followed. On her right leg, moving up towards her thigh, was a red-knee tarantula. This was extremely worrying, and the distance between Max and danger was greatly shorter, but the true concern for him, was that this was not the spider he had just been watching crawl over the body of his tutor.

What was worse, was the slight sound of shuffling coming from under the broken containers.

The spider paused on Grace's leg at the sound of the noise, and turned, making its way back down before crawling onto the floor, and scurrying away towards the noise.

"Um Max?"

"Yeah?"

"Just how many spiders did Charles have in here?"

"At last count?"

"Yeah."

"Thirty-two." Grace's eyes bulged.

"And you come here why?"

"Charles is… *was* my friend. Just because I hate something, doesn't mean I hate the person who owns them."

"But why *here*? You could be tutored anywhere, and you choose to learn *here*."

"Charles doesn't… *didn't* like to leave them. Some of the species are incredibly rare, which makes them valuable."

Sirens sounded outside on the street, and the two took one last look at Charles Arlington, lying on the floor, before moving outside to let the police do their job. As they closed the door, a loud squeal came from underneath the cloth on the ground, under which six spiders were now feasting on a rat… and each other.

The clock hit one p.m. and the news channel began its hourly replay of the day's headlines. Max and Grace sat on the couch staring at the images on the screen for the fourth time that day, still traumatised by the events that had played out. The news anchor began.

"Good afternoon. More on our top story now, and former university professor Charles Arlington, was found murdered last night in his office on Fetherington Avenue. The discovery was made by two students who stumbled upon the scene when they arrived for their weekly tutoring session. Professor Arlington was a dedicated collector of rare species of spider and had previously discovered four new species whilst on a trip to the Amazon.

However, of the thirty-two species he had contained in his office, only thirty-one were recovered from various locations within the office. Still missing, is the newest discovery of Arlington's collection. The specimen which Arlington had named the 'Raven-backed Tarantula' was unaccounted for and is the presumed motive for his murder. The spider is believed to be worth up to four-hundred-thousand dollars, such is the rarity of the creature, and is highly deadly. Police have revealed the professor was killed by a knife wound to the chest, followed by a silenced gunshot to the head. Forensic investigators are still on scene to try and locate any DNA evidence. More on this as we get it."

Grace reached over and used the remote to switch off the TV. She was thinking how many people Charles had tutored privately, and who would want to murder him for a spider, however valuable it may be. It would take a dedicated scientist to even know its worth, and Charles certainly didn't know any of those.

"Hey Max, you okay?"

"Yeah, I just can't believe someone could do that."

"Me too, I'm still trying to process it. Charles only tutored ten people right? Out of those ten, it was just me and you who are accounted for, nobody else has an alibi, right?"

Max nodded.

"So, who else in our little group could have killed him? I mean honestly, I don't see any of them doing it, it just wouldn't be..."

Grace cut herself off, as her eyes were fixed on the black of the TV screen. Max followed her gaze, and once again felt the cold sweat making its way down his back. Crawling down the TV screen at a rather slow pace, was a black widow spider.

Unmistakable markings, Grace had seen the one in Arlington's office many times. It reached the floor and moved towards them across the carpet. Both Grace and Max lifted their feet up onto the couch, the only measure of defence they could muster. As they did so, the spider stopped. Max couldn't quite tell what it was doing, but it was almost as if the spider was staring at them. He could feel every one of those black beady eyes on his skin, but not in a scary creepy way, almost like some sort of visual hug, like a loved one would give you from across a room.

"What is it doing?" asked Grace.

"I don't know, but do you feel like it's looking at you?"

"Yeah, and it's creepy as fuck."

Things were about to get creepier, as from underneath the TV stand, Max could make out a black mass moving in the shadows. As it moved into the light, the two of them shot bolt upright, standing on the couch, backs pressed to the wall, for what had emerged from beneath the unit was a small army of black widow spiders, marching almost in formation, and as they reached the first spider, they all stopped.

"Are they *all* staring at us?" Grace managed to mouth to Max.

He nodded and said nothing.

"What do you want?" she asked the hoard currently poised on the carpet.

Almost in response, all the spiders began moving again, but not towards the teenagers, towards the door. As they all disappeared beneath the gap and out of the house, Max and Grace climbed down from their positions, and looked out of the windows to see the spiders moving down the street in a thick black line.

"Do you get the feeling we should follow them?" Max asked.

"Yeah, Harry and Ron tried that in *Chamber of Secrets*, and that didn't exactly go to plan did it?" Grace replied sarcastically.

"Somehow I doubt there's a twenty-foot spider waiting somewhere in town. Believe me, I'd have noticed that one."

"You hadn't noticed the four hundred spiders under your TV though, did you."

"That's because they weren't there before!"

They both looked out the window again, and the spiders were now only visible in the distance.

"I don't know about you, but I am not following spider armies of any size. Let's just get an exterminator in here and check into a hotel for the night."

Max went into his room, checking all surfaces before entering.

"Oh, come on Max, there's no more spiders in here. What if they were trying to tell us something?"

"I don't wanna know what they were doing in here, I'm glad they're gone, and I am not sleeping here until I know there aren't any more!"

Grace could hear him on the phone to an exterminator, who clearly didn't believe that Max had fallen victim to a black widow army, and neither did his mother, who he called next. She heard a raised voice, and then the sound of Max giving in before he emerged back into the room.

"So?" asked Grace.

"My mother says I can't afford to go to a hotel, and the exterminator said there was no way that number of black widows could be in this country let alone in one house."

"So, I guess, you're sleeping with the lights on?"

"I'm not fucking sleeping at all."

Max awoke the next morning with a jolt. Although eventually drifting off the night before, an icy chill had now come over him, and he felt like he was being watched. He checked, but the window was shut tight, and duct taped for good measure. There was no way anymore spiders were coming into his house while his mother was away. He'd tried his best to stay awake, but around three a.m. he nodded off, torch still poised in his hands. But this was unsettling.

It was seven-thirty, light was peeking through the curtains, but the room was dark. Almost like a shield was preventing the daylight from coming in at all. As he breathed out, his breath emerged as if he were in a freezer, a cloud forming before his face. As his eyes focussed on the cloud coming from his mouth, he saw eyes beyond it.

As his own eyes readjusted, he realised he was staring at a face standing in his closet, looking back at him. As he looked into the eyes of Professor Arlington, he grasped wildly for his phone, not taking his eyes off the man for a moment. His breathing intensified, more clouds appearing in the air, and when he couldn't find his phone he quickly looked down at the bed covers, located the phone and looked back up.

Arlington was gone.

Max's eyes searched the closet for the man he knew was dead, and yet somehow he'd been in his room. Wondering if he was going crazy, he looked back at his phone, punched in Grace's number, and hit the call button.

"You fell asleep didn't you?" came the accusing tone of his best friend.

"Grace, listen. I just saw Charles in my closet."

"You what? Are you sure you weren't dreaming? I knew you couldn't stay awake all night."

"LISTEN TO ME! I woke up, the room is ice cold, and I mean *ice cold*, and as my eyes focus, he's there staring back at me from the closet. Please, I need you over here now."

"Yeah, okay, don't panic I'll be right there."

Grace hung up the phone, and Max put his down, and placed his face in the palm of his hands. But the room was still cold, and as Max looked up, he felt eyes on him. He slowly turned his head to the side to be met with the face of Charles Arlington, sat on the bed, looking deep into Max's eyes.

"Ch… Charles?" asked Max tentatively.

Arlington's eyes bulged with fear, and his mouth opened wider than a human could ever hope to stretch, and from the black hole of his jaws, hundreds upon thousands of black spiders flowed forth like a plague, spilling onto the bed covers, running all over the walls, piling onto Max. Waterfall upon waterfall of tiny legs and eyes swarmed the room.

Max screamed a sound so terrifying it may as well have pierced the sound barrier, he flailed his arms, scrambled for safety, batting the eight legged demons off of him, but he was now wading in a sea of arachnids, fear his only source of movement, and as he gripped on to the door frame, he gained footing, and ran down the hallway as fast as he could, the walls now teeming with spiders chasing him down like a relentless tidal wave, until he reached the front door, and burst out onto the street, still screaming, and swiping his arms all over his body. But then he stopped.

Every neighbour was out on their drive looking at him, and that's when he noticed, there was nothing on him. No spiders on his clothes at all. He looked back in through the open front door, and there was nothing there. No black widows crawling up the walls, no tarantulas scurrying across the carpet. Nothing. Max felt a hand on his shoulder and screamed as he leapt and turned around.

"Hey, hey! It's me! What's going on?"

Max turned away from Grace and looked back towards the house, but all he could do was point. The neighbours gradually went back inside, still confused as to what they had just witnessed, and despite Max's protests, Grace walked into the house.

"I don't care what you believe, I saw what I saw! I'm still having flashbacks, and I can still feel those fucking legs on my skin!"

Max still had not recovered from the events of the morning. He refused to go back into the house, so Grace had agreed to go into town with him to try and take his mind off it.

"I don't think you've gotten over his death, and your stress levels are making you see things."

"You saw the black widows, you wanted to follow them, so how am I the only crazy one?"

Grace couldn't argue with what she saw. Chances are, if you both see something, it's highly unlikely that you're both crazy.

"Okay fine, but what does it mean?" she asked.

Max stopped and thought for a moment.

"Okay, we find Arlington dead in his office, he collects spiders, one is missing, and he was murdered too, right?"

Grace nodded.

"Then we see an army of spiders come out of nowhere, seemingly look at us, and then move off down the street like they want us to follow them, right?"

Grace nodded again.

"Then, we decide not to follow them, and I have my delightful encounter with the ghost of Arlington in my bedroom and the entire contents of the arachnid kingdom, right?"

Grace nodded a third time.

"So, what if they're trying to tell us something? Something about who killed him? It's been four days since the murder and the police have nothing. What if Arlington is trying to tell us who killed him?"

Grace pondered this for a minute or two, and decided it was

certainly a logical explanation for the events that had occurred, even though the events themselves were something out of a work of fiction.

"Okay, let's assume that you're right. What do we do now? Max? Are you listening, or still figuring this out?"

Max was staring beyond her.

"I think it just figured its own way out," he replied and walked towards the street corner. "Look."

He pointed at the abandoned Pizzeria in the corner plot, and in its window were hundreds of spiders moving down the glass. As Grace and Max approached, they moved down the window, across the brickwork, and along the edge of the building on the floor in a thick black line, once again.

"Should we follow them?" Grace asked.

"Well, we didn't last time, and look what happened."

Max started after the herd of arachnids, and Grace followed, both keeping their distance.

Three streets later, the spiders made a hard left, and disappeared over the edge of the pavement, spilling into a set of stairs set back under the entrance to an apartment building. The whole time they had been following the trail, not a single person had noticed the spiders. It had been as if they weren't even there.

But as Max and Grace reached the stairwell, they could see a faint light through the window below street level. Max crouched down, pressing himself against the stairs leading to the front door of the building. In through the window, was a metal table, almost like one you would find in a morgue. On that table Grace could make out five or six containers, each containing some sort of exotic creature.

Alongside them was an empty specimen case. She looked over at Max, and he nodded, and they both climbed down the stairs to the area below. The spiders which led them here were now gone, but Max did not feel like they were alone. They gazed through the glass but saw nobody inside. The door to the building was locked, and while Grace was pondering how they could get inside, the army of spiders reappeared and made their way up the door and poured into the lock. Max looked at her in disbelief, and as she looked back at him, she saw Charles standing behind him.

She froze, Max looked confused, and as the door clicked open, Max made his way towards it, before turning back to also face the professor. They both remained still, and surprisingly, Max spoke to him.

"You aren't going to spew spiders at me again are you?"

Grace gave him an 'I can't believe you're arguing with a ghost' look but was more surprised when Charles gave an answer.

"No, Max."

"What is happening?" Grace asked him.

"Go inside. I cannot enter unless you do."

Charles' voice was horse, and his eyes filled with both sadness and anger, his fists balled at his side, just as Max's had been upon discovering the body. The pair turned and moved through the now open doorway, and when they looked back, Charles was gone.

The narrow corridor led directly to the room they had seen from outside, and they very cautiously moved into the room, making sure to hug themselves against the cabinets in case anything was loose.

It seemed like a medical room, very clean, very sterile, what looked like chemistry equipment on the far counter, beakers, vials, even a Bunsen burner. Moving around the morgue table, Grace could see three doors at the far end of the room, one labelled 'WC' and two others, one of which was open. Upon seeing the open door, they both stopped moving. A voice could be heard from inside. A man cast a shadow through the doorway as he moved back and forth across the light source from within.

Grace motioned to Max that they should move towards the door, and they shuffled until they were in a small alcove to the side of that door, and between it, and the 'WC'. They listened intently to the voices from within.

"Come on, you know this is legit. Where else are you gonna find this species. You said you wanted it, so I went and got it! What more do you want?"

"Look, you took actions that reflect very badly on the whole deal. You killed the man! You were supposed to knock his ass out, take the bug and run! The buyers are getting real uneasy about the heat surrounding this buy, Al."

"You need to make this happen Jason, I can't have this thing here for much longer. And what was I meant to do? He came into the room when I was carrying the thing out. I thought if I smash the place up he'd leave, and I'd run out. It's not my fault he decided to cut it rough."

"It is completely your fault! You stabbed him, and then shot him! What the hell was that?"

"It wasn't my fault! He came at me, I grabbed a piece of glass, and he jumped me. I thought he was dead, and as I went to leave, he grabbed me, so I did what I had to do."

"Look Al, I'm doing everything I can to make this sale, but you need to convince the buyer that they aren't gonna get their collars felt by the boys in blue. Now make it happen.

Max and Grace pressed themselves back into the alcove as far as they could, as the man's footsteps moved towards the door. He burst past them into the room, and slammed another, smaller Perspex box onto the table. As they watched from the darkness, the man tipped the smaller box into the larger empty one, and then moved towards the sink. Now sitting in the final case, was the Raven-backed tarantula.

Cornered, and with nowhere to go, the pair decided to make their move, and crept out of the alcove while the man, Al, was watching the screen of his phone with his back turned to them. They could see the glint of a firearm in the back of his trousers. This was incredibly dangerous, and Max was shaking a little. They felt their way along the cabinets, and were just six feet from the exit, when Max caught a glass beaker on the counter of chemistry equipment, and as it rolled and fell smashing to the floor, he and Grace stopped dead in their tracks. Al spun around aiming at them with his gun.

"Who the fuck are you?" he asked, curious, but finger poised on the trigger.

"Nobody, wrong house, we're really sorry."

Grace tried to make her voice sound as pathetic as possible, but Al didn't buy it.

"Don't bullshit me, little Missy! Now I'll ask you one more time. Who the fuck are you? And why are you in my apartment?"

Max had nothing to say, and as Al raised the gun up until it was aimed square at Grace's head, he caught movement from the corner of his eye. He had to stall the man.

"You killed my friend," said Max, garnering him a surprised 'what the hell are you doing' look from Grace.

He subtly jerked his eyes in the direction of the window, and Grace followed the direction and when she saw Charles standing in the window, she knew exactly what he was doing.

"Your friend? What the spider guy? He brought that on himself."

Al slightly lowered the gun, not entirely sure what to do next, but trying to maintain control over the situation. Behind him, in the window, Charles remained, and from beneath his jacket, hundreds of different tarantulas, and spiders, began flowing onto the floor, spreading out.

"You killed a man in cold blood, and for what? A dumb spider?"

It was Grace's turn to divert attention now. The spiders moved along the floor in such numbers, they fell over themselves as they moved towards Al.

"That's no dumb spider, it's going to make me a fortune. And your spider catching friend was the only one with a specimen anywhere in the world. His loss, my gain."

Al felt more powerful following his words, and tightened his grip on the gun, once again pointing it directly at Grace's head.

"Leave her alone asshole," Max shouted out, which led to the gun being turned on him instead.

"Yeah, should probably kill you first right? I could have some fun with your friend here."

Al looked Grace up and down, much to her disgust. But his sickly grin was short lived, as the spiders began moving up his leg. He looked down to see an army moving across the floor, and stumbled back into the other cabinets, and aimed his gun into the black mass.

"What the hell!" he shouted and began firing shots into the spiders, scattering them everywhere.

As Max and Grace took cover back in the alcove from the gunfire, Al continued firing blindly, shattering the glass beakers, and three of the Perspex containers on the table. Al kept shooting until he ran out of bullets, and then his gaze caught Charles. His mouth was now wide with fear, and he threw the gun into the spider army and turned and ran for the door. As he reached the doorway, the door slammed in his face. Al tried the door and then began trying to shoulder barge it as Charles moved through his army towards Al.

Max and Grace watched on in horror and disbelief.

Al turned around to be met face to face with Charles. The spiders now moved up Al's entire body and onto his arms, lifting them and pinning them against the door he had been trying to escape through. The dim light shone off their fat bodies and caught the bristles on the hair of the tarantulas.

"Wh… What do you want with me?" Al asked through trembling vocal tones.

Charles' eyes turned black, his arms slowly raised to his sides, and as his mouth opened wide, Max knew what was coming next, and closed his eyes. A loud roar emanated from deep within Charles' chest and thousands of black widow spiders flew forth from his mouth and directly into the mouth of Al, pouring down his throat drowning out the screams. Charles' roars got louder and louder, and the lights began to flicker, as the spiders continued to flow into Al's body. His eyes rolled back, as his body convulsed, and the widows began pouring out of his nose and ears. His body shook violently as if it was being hit with a million volts of electricity, then there was one final roar and the light above the table exploded sending the room into darkness.

Max and Grace held each other as the room fell almost silent. They could hear the sound of scurrying in the distance, and a figure slumping to the ground. As Grace pulled out her phone, and turned on the torch, they both stood, and shone it in the direction of where the violent act had occurred. Al's body was slumped against the door, eyes black, dark veins either side of his eyes, nose and mouth. A slight disturbance in the darkness, caused them to look towards the window, and they saw Charles walking past, outside. He stopped, turned, smiled, and then walked away, fading to nothing as he left the scene. Sirens in the street jolted the pair back to reality, and they could see several people's feet stood on the pavement, people looking down. The gunshots had alerted the people in the building above. As the officers made their way down to the apartment, Grace and Max prepared to try and explain what they had just witnessed.

"And finally, tonight, the body of suspected murderer Alan Brent was found this evening in his apartment, after it appears the rare tarantula he stole from former professor Charles Arlington, escaped and bit him as he attempted to sell the specimen on the black market. Witnesses say they had spotted the body from the street and went inside only to find the man was indeed deceased. Officers confirmed the DNA found at the scene of the murder matched that of Brent and put this down to a tragic accident. In a bizarre twist, the body of Jason Simpson was also discovered tonight in similar circumstances. It appears after checking Brent's call history, that Simpson was the chosen vessel to sell the rare spider onto its new owner. The tropical pet shop owner was found on the floor of his store, below the cases containing the common tarantulas he had for sale. Police are baffled as to how the spiders were able to attack him, as none appeared to be missing.

Officers now suggest the case is closed, but we will bring you any updates if we get them."

Max flicked off the TV and smiled as he sat back down.

"I still don't believe what I saw," Grace commented.

"Well, I'm not sure I do either. I'm pretty sure nobody would believe us if we tried to tell them."

"Yeah, not sure if a couple of nineteen year olds decided to go national with a spider demon ghost story, we'd be free to wander the streets."

"Makes you think though, right?" asked Max.

"About what?"

"If things like that exist, what other ghostly, weird things exist?"

Grace thought for a minute and pulled out her phone.

"Let's Google it," she said. "Oh, hey look, my Aunt's haunted museum just opened, wanna check it out?"

Max read the advert, and decided it was worth a ninety-minute bus ride.

"Yeah sure, I don't have anything better to do with my weekend. Besides, I've always wanted to see a real pirate medallion!"

BOY IN THE BLUE LIGHT

The glow from the laptop screen pierced the darkness with its unflinching and dominating light. Who needed actual light bulbs when most teenagers now have several time consuming devices to light a room for them. The blue light had certainly pierced the mind of Joe Pine. His eyes were transfixed to the comments flowing in to his screen, like a waterfall of evil cascading down through his mind and into his stomach, churning it up as it hit the rocks.

Joe wasn't what you would call an unconventional teenager. In fact, he hadn't done anything out of the ordinary during his entire life.

There had been no accidental slips of the tongue, no embarrassing scenarios, not even being either educationally gifted or deprived. He was neither a nerd, nor a bully. He had never searched for the limelight or attention but had also never shied away from it. He was the perfect guy in the middle. Normal. Completely unassuming.

And yet through the magic of the internet, he had become front and centre. The girls were the worst, and usually came up with the most vicious insults. They had taken their little clique and gone through every person in their class in some way or another, whether that was berating them for no reason, sleeping with the popular guys, or just making things up because they were bored. Most were able to shrug it off because it only lasted a few days. But not Joe. Joe had tried so desperately to not draw attention to himself, but his mental health was not as strong as some of the others in his class. And everything he was reading on the screen each night, he was taking personally, and taking it to heart. Tears began to fill his eyes as he read the latest barrage of comments appearing in the chat room.

COURTNEY : I mean what's with his hair? You'd think he could put in some effort, I mean is he trying to go for the 'who gives a shit' look?

FRANKIE : Lol! I know right? And there's something about his face. I mean I can't quite place what it is, but I just wanna slap it. Or maybe cut it off so I don't have to look at it!

COURTNEY : You're such a bitch but yeah I totally know what you mean.

FRANKIE : Did you see him looking at me the other day? It was like he was hungry, and I was a Krispy Kreme! I mean eeewwww! Like I'd ever go near that!

COURTNEY : That's so gross! Could you imagine!

FRANKIE : I really don't wanna imagine Courtney, I'm pretty sure I can make myself sick without thinking of his gross body all over me!

Pete has joined the chat.

COURTNEY : Haha, yeah too true. What's that freak even doing in our school. Surely there's a remedial school for weirdos like that.

Nikki has joined the chat.

NIKKI : Probably wouldn't take him. I mean if I were a headmaster or a principal, I wouldn't want that in my school either!

COURTNEY : Hey Pete, you think we should prank him

tomorrow, been kinda slow this week, and I could do with a good laugh!

PETE : Hey girls. Yeah I would, but I don't really wanna touch him. Might be like some sort of alien. Grab him and his skin melts and I catch some sort of weird disease!"

Shane has joined the chat.

PETE : Hey Shane! I vote you stuff this little douche in a locker tomorrow!
SHANE : I would but I value being disease free!

Joe felt the tears roll down his cheek, the churning in his stomach becoming more intense, the poison spreading through his mind. He had done nothing to these people, hadn't even spoken to them more than the odd occasion, and yet here they were, tearing down his walls, and ridiculing him, just because they were bored. They could not possibly have any idea of the effect they were having.

FRANKIE : Okay guys, I have to go. I need a dozen showers to wash this conversation off me!
SHANE : Want any help with that?
COURTNEY : Lol!
PETE : Damn Shane, go get it!
FRANKIE : Yeah I think I'll pass, took me a few showers to get rid of you the last time! Besides, don't wanna be having fun, with the thought of this weirdo still hanging around my brain! Laters!

Frankie has left the chat.

SHANE : Yeah might do the same, that kid creeps me out. Swear he's queer or something. The way he stares at me is disgusting.

Joe began to shake with sadness and fear, and for the fourth night in a row, the more comments that flowed in, the more he began to unravel. He was worthless. Nobody wanted him around. What is the point in being noticed if they only notice you to belittle you and to make fun of you. He felt worthless. Nobody cared if he was here or not. They wouldn't notice when he was gone. What difference would it make to them? They would just move on to the next target.

If only he could show them how evil they were to people. How much they instigated dread in their victims until it ate them from the inside. The world wide web had become a tool for worldwide hatred.

Joe only wished as he consumed the last of the pills from the bottle, that he could somehow use it to get even. So that these people would never harm anyone else. As the offenders logged off the chat room one by one, Joe slumped onto his keyboard, and as the blue light faded from his view, the final comment appeared in the chat.

COURTNEY : With any luck, he'll just die and get it over with!

Frankie was your typical cheerleader type. Head full of guys and shoes, and not much else. She was less a *typical* cheerleader, and more of a *stereotypical* cheerleader. She'd only been at Fairmont College for a year and a half, but she got right to the top of the social pyramid when she slept with the captain of the swim team. If you can't fake your way to the top, then why not fuck your way up there instead. It was an approach several of the girls had taken, more often than not, to encourage nerdy little guys to help them do their homework to keep up the illusion that they were smart, and still get good grades.

That day however, she wasn't doing so good. The cheer was one of the worst she'd choreographed, and she couldn't even get the steps right herself, so how she was meant to get a room full of girls to follow was a mystery. Finally giving in, she called for an end to the practice session.

"Okay ladies, let's call it a day and try again tomorrow."

Several of the other girls gave her a scathing look, as they felt they had been the ones getting the steps right.

"Frankie, why are we stopping when you're the one getting it wrong?" asked one of the braver girls.

Frankie stopped in her tracks and marched over to the girl.

"We are stopping, princess, because I say we are stopping. And if you don't wanna spend your future doing my laundry, and waiting tables, then I suggest you do as you're told! Now all of you get out, and use your own showers, I don't wanna see any of you in the gym ones, you deserve to go home smelling of shame!"

The other eight girls slunk out of the gym, swearing, and cursing behind them as they went.

"Fucking bitch, who does she think she is?"

"I know, but don't piss her off, I need this."

"Fine, but I'm showering at your house, because there's no way I'm going home smelling like a tramp."

As the last girls left the gym, Frankie made her way to the changing rooms. She approached her locker, opened it, and picked out her phone. Sitting down on the bench, she slipped off her shoes and socks, and glanced down at the screen.

'Two unread messages in group chat.'

She opened up the chat and read the messages.

ANON10155 : Not feeling so hot Frankie?

Frankie looked confused but read the next message.

ANON10155 : Maybe you should take a cold shower. Or a dozen.

"What the fuck?"

Frankie typed a quick response but didn't get chance to hit send before another message came through.

ANON10155 : That is how many showers it takes to forget things right?
FRANKIE : Who the fuck are you?

No response.

Frankie threw her phone down into her bag and started to get undressed. As she lifted her shirt over her head, she heard a noise from the showers.

"Hello?" she enquired. No response.

"If any of you bitches are in here, I swear I'm going to kill you, so get the fuck out!"

Frankie's phone beeped.

ANON10155 : What's the matter Frankie? I thought you liked company in the shower.

Frankie dropped her phone to the floor. She stood up and started to cautiously move around the room.

"Shane? Is that you? It's not funny."

As she moved into the showers, she could see nothing. Nobody was there. She was indeed alone. As she turned to head back to her locker, behind her, one of the showers turned on. She stopped dead in her tracks. Staring at the water now flowing, and the steam rising from the heat, she turned three hundred and sixty degrees, but again, could find nobody. She cautiously walked up to the shower, the spray just catching her arm, causing her to flinch at the heat, and she switched it off. In the distance, she heard her phone beep again. Walking carefully back to her locker, she picked her phone up from the floor, now sporting a sizeable crack down the screen. A new message.

ANON10155 : Sorry, was that too hot?

Frankie was now fully freaking out, and started scanning the room for cameras, but found none. She felt like shouting out again but decided against it. She felt like an idiot, like she was part of some massive prank, so typed her response instead.

FRANKIE : Why don't you go fuck yourself and leave me alone. Whoever you are, you're not funny and I'm done with this shit.

As she hit 'send' another shower turned on, and as she jumped up startled from the bench, she caught her calf on a jagged nail sticking out from the side of the bench.

"Son of a bitch!" she shouted, as she looked down and saw the blood began to trickle.

Another message.

ANON10155 : I bet that hurt. You might wanna clean that up.

Convinced she was being watched somehow, Frankie quickly finished undressing, switched to her normal clothes, threw her phone in her bag, and ran out of the locker room. Moments after the door closed behind her, the shower switched itself off.

Frankie marched through the corridors and pushed the double doors open to the courtyard. A couple of guys from the football team wolf whistled her, but she ignored them and headed for the car park. The messages were whizzing through her mind. Who had been watching her and how, and not only that, but who was this anonymous texter? She fished in her bag for her keys, but as she did so, her phone beeped again. She stopped dead in the middle of the car park and cautiously took out her phone.

ANON10155 : Better watch out, Frankie.

Anon10155 has left the chat.

Frankie read the message again. As she contemplated it's meaning, she heard a familiar voice call out to her.

"Hey Frankie! There's my girl!"

Frankie looked up and saw Courtney running towards her. She waved her hand in response, and waited for Courtney to arrive, sliding her phone back into her bag.

As Courtney jogged across the road, there was a sound of a loud horn blasting, the screeching of tyres, and the sickening thud of body on metal, as Courtney was completely wiped out by the school bus coming to pick up the last of the kids from after school activities. Screams echoed around the grounds, as people ran from all directions to see what had happened. Frankie stood deathly still, eyes bulging with fear, unable to look away from the scene before her. The front of the bus was blanketed with chunks of human flesh, the blood dripping down the now smashed windscreen, and the human pancake that was Courtney, in a crumpled heap on the floor.

As Frankie managed to bring her hand to her mouth, still trembling, her phone pinged again.

Anon10155 has re-joined the chat.

ANON10155 : Told you to watch out.

Anon10155 has left the chat.

"I'm telling you, something killed her!"

Frankie had spent the last twenty minutes trying to convince the others that something was responsible for Courtney's death but was being met with increasing negativity.

"Look, she walked out in front of a bus. There's nothing supernatural about that, she was just stupid," replied Shane.

"Then explain to me, these messages from this anonymous person, huh?"

"Yeah, the messages that don't exist. Real smooth way of making us believe you," replied Pete. "Look Frankie, I know what you saw was upsetting, but you're gonna have to admit that what you're saying is a little far out there."

Frankie placed her head in her hands and rubbed her eyes. Lifting it back up, she seemed resigned to the fact that she wouldn't win this argument. And perhaps they were right. She had been seriously stressing about the cheerleading routine.

"Fine. Look, I'm gonna go home, and try and get some sleep. I'll let you know if I hear anything about the funeral arrangements."

The guys nodded, and they all parted ways, Pete and Shane heading towards the cinema, and Frankie towards her home. She had decided not to take her car to meet with the guys because after what she had seen the previous afternoon, she still wasn't comfortable behind the wheel.

Her phone rang in her bag, and when she plucked it out, a small smile spread across her face. She answered the call.

"Hey Nikki."

"Hey Frankie, how are you doing?"

"I've been better, but I just had a chat with the boys, and they seem to think I need some sleep."

"Yeah, they're probably right, you haven't gotten much rest since it happened."

"I know. I just sat up awake all last night, thinking about the locker room, and the messages, and then kept seeing Courtney's face as the bus hit her. That's all I can think about."

"Hey, listen Frankie. I just wanted to give you a quick buzz and ask you, who is Anon10155?"

Frankie stopped dead in her tracks, and her smile faded to fear.

"What did you just say?" she asked in a heightened voice.

"This guy just messaged me online, and his user is Anon10155."

"What did he say to you? Think. This is very important."

"Well, I'm thinking it's Shane or Pete playing a prank, but the first message said, 'nice outfit'. I thought that was weird, because not to be too graphic, but I'm not actually wearing anything but my robe, I just got out the shower."

"Nikki, where did you get this message?"

"On the group chat for the class, where we all talk. Can't you see it?"

Frankie moved her phone from her ear and opened the group chat session, but there was no message there. She put the phone back to her ear.

"Nikki, there's nothing there. It says you're online but no messages."

"That's weird because I got another one a few minutes before I called you. That's why I called."

Frankie felt a lump in her throat.

"What did the message say?" she asked, not wanting to know the answer, but craving it at the same time.

"It said, call Frankie, and tell her it's a nice night for a movie. And then they left the chat."

Frankie's eyes bulged in fear as they had the day before, and as she spun on the spot, there was a huge explosion from the shopping complex, sending glass and metal flying through the air, fire rising from the cinema like a mushroom cloud, the sound of people screaming at the top of their lungs.

"Frankie? Frankie? Hello? What's going on?"

Nikki's voice was distant in her ear, and she couldn't see or hear anything past the crackling of the fire, and the pieces of debris landing on the ground.

Six people are now confirmed to be dead following the horrific explosion which tore through the Silverton Shopping District yesterday evening. The cause of the explosion is still unknown, but the bodies of all those involved have now been formally identified. Nineteen-year-old Shane Watson, eighteen-year-old Peter Hulme, nineteen-year-old Martha French, and three eighteen-year olds Danni Johnson, Valerie Witton and Caroline Sanderson were all identified by relatives this morning.
In a bizarre twist to this tragic event, all those who died were students of nearby Fairmont College, believed to be on a night out. Firefighters and Police continue to investigate the cause, and we will of course bring you any updates as we get them.

Frankie sat tucked up on her bed, hands gripped on to her knees, as she watched the news report. Her mother had wanted to take her to see a psychiatrist, but she'd refused. She was now afraid to leave the house. Every time she encountered someone, some manner of disaster had struck. In the last forty-eight hours, she had lost three of her best friends, and half of her cheerleading squad. And her phone had been locked in her dressing table drawer since she had gotten home the night before. There was a knock on her door.

"Hey, thought you could use some company."

Nikki moved over to the bed and sat beside Frankie. She reached out a hand, but felt the vibe was not right, and so quickly retracted it.

"You weren't answering your phone, so I got worried. Your mother said it was fine to come over."

Frankie rocked back and forth, not making any eye contact with Nikki, but keeping her gaze fixed on the drawer containing her phone.

"You know I was right." she spoke.

"Look, Frankie, I don't know what is happening here, but there is definitely something wrong, that much I can admit."

"I told you all, something killed Courtney, and nobody listened to me. Now Pete and Shane are dead too."

Nikki moved back slightly, unsure if her friend was fully in control of her faculties after the events of the last two days.

"You didn't kill them, Frankie. You know you're not responsible for their death right?"

Frankie shook her head.

"I am responsible. If I'd have pushed you guys and made more of an effort to find out who the fuck this Anon10155 was, then maybe there'd be four of us here instead of two."

"Have you told this to the police?" Frankie shook her head again.

"What, and have them commit me to a loony bin? No chance. I'm not crazy.

"You know, the messages I got from this guy, vanished too. How is that possible? I thought our whole conversation in that thing is backed up?"

"It is. And you're not meant to be able to create anonymous users either, for safeguarding reasons. So, somebody somewhere is fucking with us."

"Is there any way we can find out if somebody is deleting the chats?"

Frankie thought about it for a moment, and then remembered that Pete was using a kid named Mark to help him with his homework. He was smart, worked in the computer lab most of the time.

"Maybe that kid, Mark, could tell us."

"It's worth a shot right?"

They both nodded.

"Okay, Nikki, pull up Facebook and look this kid up."

Nikki pulled a disappointed face.

"Ah shit, my battery died. Guess we will have to use your phone."

Nikki received a look that said, 'not a chance', and gestured towards the desk instead.

"Or, you know, maybe just use your iPad."

Frankie leapt from the bed, with a much more active feeling than she'd had in two days, but as she picked up the iPad, the battery went from ninety-six percent to seven percent.

"That's weird," she exclaimed. Nikki moved to meet her.

"What's up?

As they watched, the battery indicator on the screen of the iPad dropped to one percent, then jumped to seven percent. But the creepiest action was as the battery percentage moved up to eight, and the battery icon was replaced by a question mark, before the screen shut off entirely.

"You saw that right?" asked Frankie in an exasperated breath.

"Yeah. What the hell was that?" replied Nikki.

They both looked over at the drawer, as they heard a ping from inside. The pair exchanged glances, neither of them wanting to examine the contents of the drawer. Gradually, Frankie edged closer, and eased open the draw. The phone was face down, but the glow of the blue light was visible around the sides of the device. She gradually picked it up and turned it over.

'*One unread message.*'

"Are you gonna read it?" asked Nikki but got no response.

Frankie moved her finger across the screen to unlock the phone and opened the group chat.

ANON10155 : Mark can't help you now.

Anon10155 has left the chat.

The funeral of anyone is a trying and emotional time. But a mass funeral is horrifying. The parents and board of the college had decided given the short time between the tragic deaths of several of their students, that it would be a good idea to say goodbye to all of them together and celebrate their lives. But Frankie was not there.

In body she was standing with everyone else, Nikki at her side and her mother behind her, but in her mind, she was in the chat room. She was replaying the messages over and over in her mind. How was this happening, and who was doing this to them. The words of the priest passed her by completely, and she stared into the eight holes in the ground, until she felt a gentle pull on her arm, indicating the service was over. Everyone started to head to the wake which was being held at the school in the gym, but Frankie held back. Nikki noticed and stopped too.

"What is it?" she asked.

"I don't know. I just felt like I had to stop here."

Nikki looked down at the gravestone.

"Did you know him?"

"Nope. I have no idea who he was."

"Come on, let's go."

The pair continued their way, and behind them, the eight coffins were slowly lowered into the ground.

Firefighters have determined the cause of the explosion in the Silverton Shopping District, was the result of faulty wiring in an advertising board in one of the cinema screens. The fire spread below and reached gas canisters and fireworks which were being kept in a storage room under the cinema for the upcoming fourth of July celebrations. An investigation is now continuing to determine who is responsible for the faulty wiring, and how it was able to spread so quickly, undetected by the building's fire suppression systems.

As the news update rolled on, Nikki and Frankie were perched on the couch, trying to figure out who they could contact to help them. There had been no chat messages in two days, and that was becoming more and more concerning. The possibility that Frankie had somehow imagined all of this was becoming more real, despite Nikki's presence.

"You want a coke?" Nikki asked.

"Yeah sure, thanks."

As Nikki left the room, the news bulletin continued, and it made Frankie sit up and take note.

'And to end our programme tonight, we look back at the tragic event this time last year, when Fairmont College student Joseph Pine, sadly took his own life. With all the recent sadness that has befallen the college of late, Joseph's mother, and driver of the Fairmont school bus, spoke to us earlier today.'

"Hey, what's this about?" asked Nikki as she sat back down.

"No idea, never heard of the kid," replied Frankie. The news report continued.

'Mrs Pine, how have you found the last year?
"The last twelve months have been some of the hardest times in my
life. Joe was a good kid, never got into trouble, never got himself
involved in anything untoward. We still don't understand why he
did what he did to this day. All he had to do was come to us."
And how have the recent events in Fairmont stirred up these feelings?
Weren't you the bus driver the day Courtney Christiansen died?
"Yes, and I find it very disturbing. The people involved were those
who tortured my son."
How do you mean ma'am?
"My son was bullied day and night on a chat room online meant for
study sessions between students. The night he died, the entire
conversation was geared towards bullying my poor Joe."
Mrs Pine declined to continue the interview after showing obvious
signs of distress, so we left this bizarre coincidence behind for the
time being. Today's programme is in memory of Joseph Pine.'

Nikki and Frankie sat there in shock. They gazed at the TV for a few moments, and then Nikki spoke first.

"I can't believe it." Frankie shook her head. "We killed him. It was us."

"I didn't even remember him. I could swear I've never met that kid in my life."

"We killed him."

Frankie was fixating on the outcome of that fateful night when her brain clicked into gear for the first time in her life. She scrambled over to the coffee table and pulled a piece of paper out from the drawer at the bottom. She grabbed a pen and began listing the letters of the alphabet.

"What are you doing?" asked Nikki, but she was silenced by Frankie's finger signalling her to wait.

When she was done, the two of them sat back and looked at the piece of paper. Each letter of the alphabet had its numerical order written above it. The numbers above J, O and E were circled.

"Ten, fifteen, five," murmured Nikki.

"Anon10155," confirmed Frankie.

The two of them sat on the floor thinking and trying to come to terms with what this all meant. Frankie grabbed her phone out of her pocket and opened up the group chat and cycled back through the chat logs until she came to those from a year ago.

JOE P. : Hey does anyone have time to run through the physics assignment with me please?

FRANKIE : So, who's up for the movies this weekend?

COURTNEY : Yeah, sounds great! Got this kid doing my homework for me so I should be cool. He's okay, just flash him a boob every so often, and he keeps coming back!

FRANKIE : You're so bad!

JOE P. : Seriously guys, I need help with the last two questions, anyone else finding it difficult?

PETE : You fine ladies want some company?

SHANE : Yeah, we could make it a foursome. Or just go see the movie ;)

FRANKIE : Lol, you are so not getting a foursome!

COURTNEY : Besides, if we invite Nikki, it's a five-way!

NIKKI : Sounds like a blast! Might need some drinks in me before that happens though!

As Frankie read back the messages, she realised. Joe had always been in the group chat, and in every chat they had ignored him, and pretended he didn't even exist. She read through page after page of chat and became more and more horrified at the scale of what they had done. The number of messages they had ignored numbered in the thousands. And then she came to the final chat recorded to mention Joe. Frankie's eyes welled up at the final message sent in that session.

COURTNEY : With any luck he'll just die and get it over with.

A tear moved down Frankie's face, and as Nikki read the chats, she too began to feel horrified.

"What did we do?" she asked, as Frankie sat beside her slipping into more and more bouts of tears.

"We killed him! That's what we did!"

Frankie's sadness and regret was now in full flow. Nikki on the other hand began to slip back into denial.

"I mean, I was barely ever in that chat, I never said much about him, it was you guys that really started it off!"

Frankie paused between breaths for a moment and turned to her friend.

"What? You are as guilty as the rest of us! We all did this to him, and we are all suffering because of it!"

The pair were cut off from their argument by both of their phones pinging with message alerts. Then another one, and another, and soon the messages were flowing in faster than they could read them.

'I can't believe these bitches did that to this guy!'

'It must take a special kind of scum to treat someone like this.'

'People like this don't deserve existence!'

'What a waste of blood, skin and organs.'

'Clearly beauty doesn't get you brains. Or FEELINGS!'

The messages continued and continued, with barely three seconds between them. The news report from Joe's mother had clearly stirred the pot, and the barrel of the gun of abuse was now aimed squarely at

Frankie and Nikki. A chill ran through both their spines as the next message appeared.

'With any luck, they'll just die and get it over with!'
"Okay, I need to go."

Nikki stood up and walked out of the house, picking up into a run as she headed home. Frankie sat in the middle of the carpet, tears still streaming down her face as the barrage of abuse continued. She put her phone face down, went upstairs, and collapsed face first onto her bed in a flood of tears, the phone still alerting her to new messages in the background.

Nikki burst through her front door and headed straight for her dad's liquor cabinet. It was locked, but she picked up the TV remote, and hurled it through the glass. As she reached in, and grabbed his whiskey, she sliced her wrist on the broken glass.

"AH GODDAMMIT IT!" she screamed.

She marched her way into the kitchen, blood now dripping at an alarming rate. She grabbed the first aid kit, and wrapped the biggest bandage she could find, tightly around the wrist. The blood slowly began to seep through, but she grabbed the bottle of whiskey anyway, opened the bottle and upturned it into her mouth.

She placed the bottle back on the counter, half of it now gone, and took a deep breath. The combination of the alcohol and the blood loss was now causing her to feel weary and unsteady on her feet. Her phone alerted her to more messages and as she looked at the screen, alongside the messages was a private message request. Squinting through her eyes, she accepted the request and opened the message.

ANON10155 : That's a nasty cut you have there, Nikki.

Nikki began getting angrier again, and launched the bottle of whiskey at the wall, sending glass flying in every direction, including back at her. She began furiously typing a response.

NIKKI : Why don't you go bother some other ghosts you dead loser! Nobody gives a fuck about you! We didn't then, AND WE DON'T NOW!

She planted her phone firmly on the kitchen counter and glanced at the bandage now dark with blood. Her phone alerted her to a reply.

ANON10155 : To be a ghost Nikki, you have to be dead.

That made her stop and think. Joe was dead. They knew it, they'd seen it on the news, they had even re-read the chats from the year before.
Another message.

ANON10155 : Why don't you take a nice relaxing lie down on the sofa, Nikki.

Nikki could barely stand by this point, and staggered across the broken glass to the lounge, barely hanging on to her phone. As she collapsed onto the sofa, her phone pinged again.

ANON10155 : Now isn't that much…

"Better."
The voice came from behind Nikki, and before she could react, a knife flew across her throat, slitting it from ear to ear, blood violently cascading out of her skin, her garbled cries for help and gasps of breath both to no avail. The sofa turned crimson red, and her body convulsed, but was held firmly in place. The bandage was ripped from her wrist, and the knife found its way to the other wrist, slicing it open to match the first, each movement causing another jolt in Nikki's gradually waning body. As the final signs of life left Nikki's bloodstained body, the knife, held by a gloved hand, found its way into Nikki's right hand.
"Sleep well."

The blue glow from the laptop screen filled the room, as Frankie gazed at the chat room filling up with more contributions from students across the land.

STEVIE : I can't believe these whores aren't behind bars!

DANNY : I know. I'd kill them myself if they ever did that to my brother.

VERONICA : Pretty sure that stupid bitch Frankie is gonna get kicked off the cheerleading squad now. Finally, someone with real talent can step up!

STEVIE : Haha! Yeah right! I mean what were the school thinking, putting a murderer in charge!

VERONICA : I don't know, but that bitch deserves to die for what she did.

Andreas has entered the room.

ANDREAS : Hey guys, is this the place for bitch bashing? Personally, I'd hang those whores from the trees and fuck their corpses!

VERONICA : Hey, I'll help you tie the nooses!

STEVIE : OMG! You guys are hilarious!

Frankie's eyes welled with tears, but no emotion spread over her face. She watched hundreds more comments flow into the chat and reached for the glass of vodka. As she downed the last of the pills from the bottle, and washed it down with the vodka, she felt her head get heavier and heavier. And as her head slumped onto the keyboard of the laptop, the blue light created a shadow on her wall, and from outside her house, Joe's mother looked up at the window and saw the shadow.

"All for my baby boy."

She took one last look at the chat room on her phone, before signing out and closing the app, placing her phone back into her bag. She placed the bag of blood soaked clothes into Frankie's trash can, closed the lid, took one last look up at the house, and walked down the street towards home. As she moved back towards Nikki's house, she could see the red and blue lights flashing, and the sounds of screaming coming from inside, and felt a smile spread across her face. As she moved beyond the chaos, and approached her own house, she opened the front door, went inside, and sat down on the couch, picking up the remote to flick the TV on.

Her phone pinged an alert, suggesting a new message. She picked up the TV remote again, flicked off the TV set, and placed the remote back on the coffee table on top of the maintenance manual for the advertising units. As she swiped her phone open, she had a text message. Opening the message, she read it and smiled once again.

Joe
Thanks Mum. Now I can rest.

SAPPHIRES & GOLD

17th November 1611

"I'm not entirely convinced by that Captain."

"You may not be convinced, my dear friend, but the fact remains that it is a possibility."

"That is indeed true, however, do you have the evidence to support your fears?"

"I have… reservations about revealing my sources for this information. All I am prepared to say, is that I need you to do this for me, for I fear that all we have gained will be too much of an attraction for my enemies to resist."

Antonio pondered the words of his Captain for a moment or two, and when pressed for an answer, finally gave his reply.

"Very well Captain. I will indeed undertake this journey you wish of me. However, as I am sure you are aware, I will need a ship."

Captain Peter Easton was not short of potential vessels for any voyage, but this one required skillful planning. It would have to be either an unassuming looking ship to avoid attention, or a heavily armed vessel to defend itself from any potential threats.

"Of course, the *San Sebastian* is off the table," surmised Antonio. Easton smiled and nodded.

"Quite off the table. Although perhaps there is…"

Easton was cut off from the sound of his name being bellowed from the deck.

"Trouble?" asked Antonio.

"When is it not trouble?" replied Easton.

The two pushed back their chairs and ran up the steps to the deck, where they were greeted by the entire crew gathered at the railings.

"Captain! There's a ship! And it is adrift!"

The deckhand was clearly excited. Most of the crew had been with Easton since the beginning of this voyage, including Antonio Vergara. The Captain had never steered him wrong, and he was as loyal to Easton as a man could possibly be. However, the timing of this discovery, did create an element of suspicion at the timing of such a discovery given the details of their conversation.

"Calm down men, I am aware of the ship."

The crew looked at their Captain with confusion, and Antonio approach him with much of the same.

"You knew of this vessel Captain?" he asked.

"I was made aware of rumours, but I did not know for certain that she existed. She is something of a myth."

"May I ask to the nature of this myth?" asked Easton's first mate. "Once we are onboard, my friend. We must inspect her."

Easton barked orders to his crew to pull the *San Sebastian* alongside, and prepare to board, and they scrambled to their stations, busy with excitement, and the always lurking fear of being chastised or as had previously been the case with a select few, the threat of being thrown overboard. As the crewmen busied themselves, Antonio ran his rough, work-hardened hand across the mahogany rail of the Captain's prized capture. He could not take his eyes from the bow of the nearby vessel.

The figurehead appeared to be a large green snake of some kind wrapped around the figure of a woman, her eyes painted black, the hull of the ship itself was black to match. As the *Sebastian* moved closer, Antonio could make out the detailed green lines along the top of the hull, running parallel to the deck, which appeared to be of pine construction. The mast was also light in colour, but the sails, whilst erected, were torn, and the green fabric flailed in the wind.

"She's a beauty, isn't she?"

Easton had not moved from his colleague, but Antonio had been so focussed on the ship, that he had forgotten his mentor was stood next to him.

"That she is Captain. Do you know her name?"

Easton smiled and nodded.

"She's the *Sapphire Serpent*."

The moment he stepped onto the *Serpent*, Antonio felt something unsettling. He couldn't quite place what that feeling was, but something was not quite right. Easton on the other hand, was elated. The smile had not left his face since he set foot on the pine deck and had already instructed his men to search the ship, and that task was well underway.

"Come with me, Antonio. It's time we had a discussion."

The Captain gestured for the first mate to follow him, and he did so without saying a word. None of the crew were anywhere near the two of them, and yet Antonio felt as if he was being watched. Easton led him to a large ornate set of double doors, black wooden frames, and distorted glass panels, clearly designed to give privacy. This must have been the Captain's cabin.

His Captain led him inside and closed the doors. The room itself was incredibly baron. No trophies or displays of wealth. Very little furniture. All that appeared to be inside was a mahogany desk, with a sapphire green finish on top, a chair to match, and a small set of table and chairs, perhaps designed for dining. In the far corner, was a bed with green covers and blankets, the blankets themselves, still in disarray as if recently disturbed. Easton sat where the ship's Captain would have sat and gestured for his colleague to sit in the adjoining seat.

"Antonio, this ship is a mystery. However, since I first heard of its potential existence from Lieutenant Pike, I knew I wanted it."

"How did he come to know of it, Sir?"

"He believed that he had seen it whilst on a mission with the British Navy before we had become colleagues, but as he was drunk at the time, he didn't like to put too much faith in what he had seen. I knew we were passing this way, so I had the men adjust course slightly to see if we would come across her. And we did."

Antonio was captivated by every word and craved more. He wanted to know why the ship was such as prize, why it was a myth, and perhaps the answer to why he felt like he was walking through someone else's home.

"Please, Captain, continue."

"The *Sapphire Serpent* has no known birthplace, no officially recognised crew, and nobody knows what country she represented. All that is known is her ability to lose her crew. We don't know how old she is, but whenever she has been spotted, she has always been empty."

Antonio's anxiety levels began to increase. *She had always been spotted empty.* What is the significance of that? Easton continued.

"When Pike spotted her, he claims she was travelling fast in the other direction. Upon enquiring, the legend of the *Serpent* is long lived and varying in detail. Some say they have boarded her, and then been chased off by the spirits of a long dead crew. Others have claimed to have killed her crew but sent her on her way because the treasures she holds are cursed. We are interested in her for the very reason I intend to send you to Nassau, my friend."

Antonio raised his eyebrows in question, and Easton continued.

"I need the bulk of my haul hiding away in secret, and the *Serpent* is not only rumoured to have an extensive haul of her own, but the hold to contain much more. We could transfer our own captured loot to add to the *Serpent's* loot and sail them both to Nassau. I would not trust anyone else in all the known world with this mission, Antonio. You have become a loyal first mate, and a loyal friend."

"Sir, I am honoured."

"No honour among pirates, my friend," replied Easton with a smile.

The pair laughed amongst themselves, before they heard someone calling for the Captain.

As Easton and his friend made their way down to the hold, they were stopped in their tracks by the sheer shine from the gold, reflecting the sunlight from the deck above. Easton couldn't take his eyes off the haul, and after lowering his hand from his eyes to protect him from the glare, Antonio too was captivated.

"Captain, sir, the hold is full," claimed the deckhand. "There are two other chambers in the rear of the ship with the same amount of treasure again!"

"Excellent!" replied Easton. "Men, we are going to be very rich indeed."

18th November 1611

The crew were divided. Some were excited at the prospect of the mission, others were angry they were not part of transporting what many saw as their money to what they believed, was the other side of the world. One in particular took offence that Antonio was placed with the trust to Captain the *Sapphire Serpent* and spoke out with violent anger.

"And just what the fuck qualifies this dog to sail around the world with my money!" he bellowed.

Antonio shrunk back slightly, unsure himself, and still wary that eyes were watching him from the Serpent. He looked back over at the ship, but saw nothing, and was snapped back to attention by a tankard narrowly missing his head and bouncing off the wall and into the sea. This clearly angered Easton.

"You will remember your place, Cullen."

"Why don't you just admit that you don't trust us?"

Cullen was now pushing his Captain beyond reasonable levels. Antonio was expecting the man to be chastised, but Easton remained conservative.

"Should I not have reason to trust you, Cullen? I have never hidden anything from you before, men. You are as aware as I am, that our enemies are massing. This ship is a jewel in our empire, but there are those who wish to take it away. Would you rather die on your pile of gold, or live long enough to spend it?"

The question seemed to irk more of the crew. They had not contemplated death, but now some were growing suspicion that they may not finish this voyage. Cullen spoke up again.

"I'd rather take my share of both ships now and take my leave of you both."

The crew, although split fifty-fifty, knew that this was a mistake on Cullen's part, and several of them shrank back. The Captain smiled and approached Cullen, stopping a couple of feet away. He took off his tricorn hat, and held it to his side, the other hand behind his back.

"You are as entitled to your share, as any other man onboard this vessel, Cullen. You have all shown as much loyalty to me, as my first mate. That is why I will allow you to board the *Serpent* and accompany Antonio as his first mate."

The decision took Antonio and the crew by surprise. They had fully expected the man to be on his way to Davy Jones' Locker by now. Cullen himself seemed to be taken aback too.

"You are... you are certain Captain?"

Easton nodded.

"Your conviction is impressive. I want that kind of attitude guarding our treasure on its long journey south. Please go aboard the *Sapphire Serpent* and make her ready to sail."

Cullen was completely disarmed by this, but agreed and took his leave of the Captain, and hurried across the planks and onto the *Serpent*. Antonio approached the Captain with confusion.

"Captain, if I may ask, what are you doing?"

The crew seemed to share his trepidation, particularly those who were going with him. Easton simply smiled, and handed his tricorn to Antonio, before moving past him, and up to the edge of the deck. Over on the *Serpent*, Cullen was climbing the mast to attempt to take down the damaged sails, eager to get away.

Easton drew his pistol from his belt, aimed directly at Cullen, and as the man looked down to see his Captain, Easton pulled the trigger. As the lead shot pierced Cullen's skull, blood splattered across the green fabric of the sails, and as his body fell to the deck, from the *Sebastian*, the crew could see the pine deck turning red. Easton turned back towards the rest of the crew and spoke.

"Any more questions?"

20th November 1611

As he watched his Captain, and his friend sail away, Antonio couldn't help feeling that he would never see Easton again. There was a sense of finality about this journey, and if he was being honest with himself, the distance that would be put between them, would tempt him or members of his crew, to spend some of the treasure themselves. Feelings of this nature though would need to be put to rest, however, because they had a long journey ahead of them.

As the *San Sebastian* faded into the distance, Antonio turned away and headed down onto the main deck, where the last of Cullen's blood was now being cleaned up. Easton had never been one to cross, even when he was under the employ of the English monarchy, but especially when it came to his haul. Antonio was now the Captain of a mythical ship. He still had no knowledge of why there never seemed to be a crew on this ship, and no knowledge of where the immense loot in the hold had come from. It was clearly decades of wealth, perhaps from the multiple crews' exploits, but clearly none of it had ever been spent.

As the splash of Cullen's body hitting the water in the background echoed around the deck, he entered what were now his quarters to assess where he was. His belongings had been transferred over from the *Sebastian* to pad out the cabin a little, but there was still a lot of space and a lot of dark corners. As he glanced at his map on the desk, he was taking in the length of the voyage to Nassau. This would be his longest single trek on any vessel, and he was now suddenly responsible for a huge amount of gold, and twenty men. As he sat at his chair, the door knocked.

"Come in," he responded.

The door did not open. It knocked again.

"I said come in," replied Antonio once more.

The door still failed to open. Antonio gazed upon the door, and there was a definitive figure stood in view of the glass panes. However, when the door knocked again, the hands of the figure did not move. They remained squarely at its side. Antonio did not offer entry this time but stood up from his chair and gradually moved towards the door.

As he did so, the knock came again, but harsher than the previous three. Again, the outlined arms of the figure did not move. As Antonio reached for the door handle, the glass pounded almost to breaking point, causing him to stagger backwards, and his heart to pound.

Gathering his courage, he grabbed hold of the door handle and yanked open the door, to find nobody on the other side, and his crew busy at work on deck at least thirty feet away.

He gazed around the deck, but saw nobody in the immediate vicinity, and certainly not near enough to have run away as the door opened. Again, convinced he was being watched, he closed the door carefully, and waited for a moment.

Nothing.

Antonio turned around and his heart leapt into his mouth. Sat in his chair was the figure of a man, wearing a tricorn hat much like Captain Easton's hat, but wearing a tattered green coat, sporting a long tangled black beard. Antonio could hear an unfathomable noise, as if someone had left a tap running. He was frozen to the spot, but as his eyes gazed down towards the feet of the figure, perched under his desk, he could make out water running down from the figure.

A sharp movement and the feet sprinted from under the desk, and when Antonio looked back up, the figure had gone. He backed up and felt for the door handle, and when he gripped it, he turned it, and gradually eased the door open, his eyes darting around the room searching for the demonic presence that had sat in his chair. Seeing nothing, he turned to leave, and came face to face with the figure. Water poured from his cold, dead mouth onto the floor, his skin barely clinging to his face, and his breath icy cold on Antonio's face.

"*Este barco está condenado.*"

As the sentence passed over Antonio's terrorized face, the figure stepped closer, and then charged right through him, knocking him to the ground. As his eyes began to close, he could hear voices from his crew in the background, and could make out blurred men surrounding him, and as he passed into unconsciousness, he heard that voice in his mind once more. *Este barco está condenado.* This ship is doomed.

Focus was beyond Antonio's reach. He could make out the moon, bold and glowing in the night sky, and various figures moving around the deck, but could not create a clear enough image in his mind. He felt solid wood beneath his feet, and the rock of the ocean, the sea breeze on his face, but clarity of his eyes continued to elude him.

He took one step forward, and fell to his left, catching himself on the railings. The wood was cold to the touch, as if coated in ice. Antonio retracted his hand quickly and held it to his chest.

His eyes began to focus more, and he could see there was indeed frost on the wooden banister. As he moved his gaze slowly around the deck, he could see that there were not only figures moving around, but also outlined figures on the deck. He squinted, and managed to improve his vision, and his eyes came to rest on the body of a man lying in front of him. The victim's eyes were wide open, his throat cut, the wound wide, blood soaking his clothing, and the deck on which he lay.

Looking further ahead, Antonio saw countless more bodies, all eyes wide open, blood soaking the deck where they lay, some with throats also cut, others with wounds to their chest.

As he moved forward, he stepped cautiously over the bodies before him, in the direction of the men moving, who he still couldn't clearly see. His feet slipped in the thick red liquid beneath his boots, but as he got closer to the men in question, the view became clearer. He watched as one of the men lifted another into the air with one hand, and ran his sword right through his stomach, the man's eyes bulging in pain, blood trailing from his mouth. The sword was removed from the victim, before being thrust through him a second time. Then a third, and a fourth.

The same scene was being played out all over the ship. Men slaughtered and butchered as Antonio watched. As the sword was withdrawn from the now dead deckhand for the eighth and final time, the murderer stepped back, his back still facing Antonio. The victim, remarkably remained stood upright, as if balanced by some mystical force. The killer then raised his sword again, and sliced it across the throat of the deckhand, sending more blood spilling onto the deck, and the figure twirled around, collapsing in a heap. Antonio looked at his body in horror. But as Antonio brought his hand to his mouth, the eyes on the body opened wide and he mouthed words to Antonio.

"This ship is doomed."

Cold sweat was now flowing down his back, but Antonio couldn't take his eyes from that of the dead deckhand. He didn't even feel the sword run him through at first. The pain was delayed, but when it came, it was excruciating. He looked down at his stomach, to see the metal thrusting in and out of him, six, seven, eight times. He managed to gaze upwards, where he was met by the killer of the deckhand. But his eyes were empty. No light, all black. The figure stepped back, Antonio fell to his knees, and looking down at his stomach, he could see a pool of red surrounding him. As he looked back up, his mind blinded with agony, he saw a flash of metal as he felt the blade slice through his throat, and he collapsed to the floor.

As Antonio lurched up from the floor, he screamed a deafening roar, sending several of his men back on their heels.

"Captain, please, it's okay!"

The man tried to calm Antonio down. As he regulated his own breathing once more, he recognised his first mate, Doyle staring back at him.

"Where, where am I?" Antonio had completely lost sense of his surroundings.

"You're in your cabin, Captain. You fell and hit your head, but you are alright. We need to get you into bed, so you can rest."

As Doyle and three other crewmen lifted Antonio to his feet, he saw the figure of the Spanish Captain standing in the doorway, like a guardian of hell, and as Antonio slipped back into unconsciousness, the figure mouthed the same words again.

"Este barco está condenado."

23rd November 1611

Antonio had not slept for two nights. He lay awake in his hammock, staring at his own chair, convinced the spirit of the Spanish Captain would return. He felt the presence around him almost constantly and had restricted himself from the rest of the crew since he had awoken on the floor of his cabin, almost two hours after his encounter with this harrowing figure.

During those two hours, he had experienced visions that shook him to his very core. He had chosen not to discuss the sight of the murders, or how incredibly real the whole situation had felt to him. He had felt the sword plunge into him over and over and had heard the tear of his skin as the blade cut his throat. But none of it was real.

Doyle had continued to take charge of the *Serpent* while his Captain remained isolated and had kept him regularly informed on their progress through the doorway. They were now just two weeks from Nassau. Two more weeks and Antonio would never have to see or be present onboard the *Serpent* again.

Needing water, he climbed down from his hammock, and headed for the table opposite, and slumped down in one of the chairs. As he poured himself a cup of water, he heard a rumbling near his desk. He paused, before taking a drink. The rumbling occurred a second time. It appeared to be coming from the drawer in the desk, and Antonio moved to investigate, taking his water with him. As he reached the other side of his desk, he could see the drawer itself vibrating, moving with no outside force. As he approached it, however, the rumbling stopped. Antonio reached down and opened the drawer and sat inside was a book. As he held the book in the moonlight, he could make out a scrawled signature on the cover.

Augustin Pereyra

Spanish, and most likely the individual's diary. Being of Spanish decent himself, Antonio opened the book to see that it was indeed a journal. It was the journal of a Captain. He read several entries, revealing nothing particularly remarkable. A near miss with the Royal Navy, a misunderstanding between his first mate, and the wife of the cook.

However, the next entry made him sit down in his chair. He focussed on every word.

7th September 1463

I was forced into an unsatisfying situation, from which my soul may never recover. I have done unspeakable things during my voyages on this ship, but never have I felt the pain that I feel this night.

The attack on the Serpent was an unsuccessful one, and we prevailed, as I knew we would. My men are strong of heart, and skilled with the blade. I did not doubt our victory.

My first mate Cesar led the assault on the Cortana, and we slaughtered their crew. Their hold was bulging with gold, and we took it all. But unbeknown to me, Cesar had come across a small family on the ship. A woman and her two small children. As I was overseeing the transport of the gold to the Serpent, he remained on the Cortana. The children attempted to protect their mother, and their possessions, and Cesar beat them out of the way.

I heard their cries from the deck and ventured after the sound. As I walked in, he shoved the first child back, plunged his knife into the boy's chest eight times, then slit his throat, the body falling to the floor. Something stirred inside me, and yet I did nothing. The woman pulled a cross from a chain around her neck and plunged it into Cesar's shoulder. He cried out in pain, ripped it away from the woman, and as he beat her, she prayed to the Gods in her native language.

The second child screamed, and Cesar moved to the boy, and repeated the assault of the first child. Eight stab wounds and a slit throat. At the sight of her two children dead, the woman began chanting. Her eyes burned red, her clothes bloodied and torn, but the words continued.

She stared through me, I could feel her words resonating through my soul. I felt cold in my chest, and ice in my veins. Cesar moved back towards the woman, and completed the circle of violence, the woman screaming her words through gargled blood as her life began to leave her body.

As Cesar pulled away, I looked at her crumpled, battered, beaten body, and I felt tears roll down my cheek. I did nothing. I am a monster. She twitched with the final signs of life, no longer living, but not quite dead. She looked at me for help, and I did nothing. Cesar walked past me, leaving the woman squirming amongst the bodies of her children. I closed the door to the cabin and locked it. Her gargled screams had echoed around the ship, and still the words I could not understand continued, and as I lit the spark leading to the gunpowder barrels, I felt her presence on me.

I watched as the Cortana burned. I heard the screams through the flames, and I could see her face when I closed my eyes. And now she is here. I feel her pain, and yet I feel empty.

Antonio felt tears of his own slide down his face at the brutal imagery depicted in the journal before him. There were tear stains on the pages, almost two centuries old. The pain and despair of both the woman and the Captain resonated through the paper. Antonio took another sip of water and read the next entry.

We are cursed men. This ship no longer has a purpose. We have sailed for thirty-two days with no port in sight. Our hold bursting with treasure but dwindling on supplies. Cesar is dead. I keep seeing the face of the woman everywhere. She is in my cabin. She is at the wheel. I have even seen her in the crow's nest. She will not leave me alone.

Several of my men are dead. They clash with each other, and paranoia rules this vessel. My men claim they have seen the woman and her children, panic grows in their hearts. I cannot face them. I brought this curse upon them. I have the guilt of a thousand men. I killed Cesar with my own bare hands, full of rage, in the hopes to put things right. It did not quench this demon thirst.

We should have made Nassau fourteen days ago. All I see before me is open ocean. I feel my fate has been sealed.

A noise from the doorway disturbed Antonio. A gentle knock at the door.

"Come in."

The door swung open, and he could see that Doyle was standing before him.

"Please, Doyle. Sit down."

Antonio gestured to the seat in front of him. Doyle did not move.

"Doyle?" asked Antonio.

He stood from the desk, laying the journal on top of it, and moved towards his first mate.

"Doyle?" he asked again.

As he got nearer, Antonio faced a disturbing sight. Doyle's eyes were wide with fear, his shirt darkened.

"Doyle?" Antonio asked a third time, a quiver in his voice.

Doyle collapsed to the floor, and Antonio raced to help him. As he turned him over, he saw that his throat had been cut, and he had multiple stab wounds in his shirt, now soaked red.

Another noise came this time from the deck. Antonio, lay Doyle to the floor, and moved out of the cabin. He could make out a figure at the very front of the ship, standing up on the front of the bow, looking back at him.

"WHO ARE YOU?" he shouted.

The figure did not respond.

Antonio moved closer, now striding with rage, and as he got closer he could make out the face of the figure. It was not that of the Spanish Captain, who he now presumed to be Augustin Pereyra, but that of a woman. Antonio stopped.

"You are her."

The woman said nothing. She glared into Antonio's eyes, her own were black. No light in them, much like those of the monsters in Antonio's vision. Red surrounded them, and her mouth was white, no colour in her lips.

"I'm sorry for what they did to you," he offered.

The woman's lips trembled with emotion, before her mouth flew open and she let out a scream which knocked Antonio to the ground and left him scrambling to cover his ears. When the scream stopped, he looked up and the woman was gone, but in his place, stood one of his deckhands. He was holding a sword, dripping with blood. His eyes were full of agony, his face stained with tears. He looked directly at Antonio and mouthed those fateful words he had heard before.

"*Este barco está condenado.*"

He raised the sword, slit his own throat, and tumbled over the bow and into the water.

6ᵗʰ December 1611

The situation on the *Sapphire Serpent* had rapidly deteriorated. The ship should have only been a matter of days from the port of Nassau, and yet the murder of Doyle had created mistrust in the crew. Several had camped down in the hold to ensure the treasure was not disturbed. Of the twenty men Antonio had left the *San Sebastian* with, only fourteen remained.

Doyle and the deckhand had died the night Antonio discovered the journal, and four more had killed each other as they fought over unseen forces plotting to steal their share. There were now more dark stains on the once pine deck than there were clear patches. Each man was now so consumed by either fear or rage that they had stopped mopping up the blood. Antonio himself had remained in his cabin for much of the trip, only venturing out to take food from the galley, and always armed.

The vicious nature of the weather had also created a turbulence which seemed to be feeding the evil aboard the *Serpent*. With every flash of lightning and crash of the sea, a wave of anger shot through the crew. Many of them were now targeting their Captain as his explanation of the death of his first mate wasn't exactly realistic. The only members of the crew who remained on his side were the cook and his ward.

Antonio had called them into his cabin to discuss their situation when lightning struck the back of the ship, blowing the window of Antonio's cabin out, and sending shards of glass across the room. The rain was now pounding the desk and soaking everything in sight.

Antonio opened the drawer, grabbed the Spanish Captain's journal, and retreated to the far corner of the room with the chef and the young boy.

"Captain, there is growing unease within the other men. They feel that we are far off course, and they lay the blame with you," explained the chef, Pavel. "I fear before long, they will make an attempt on your life.

Antonio had feared as much, but his mind was consumed by the images of the woman, and the captain. They haunted his dreams and his every waking moment. He was Captain of a cursed ship, with its cursed loot, and there was no telling where they actually were.

"We should make Nassau in a matter of hours, and then everything will be as it was. We will be rich men, and Captain Easton will join us, and everything will be right."

Antonio has started rocking back and forth in his chair, eyes devoid of concentration, the words of Pavel, resonating only briefly, as the figure of Augustin reappeared at the window, seemingly unaffected by the wind, rain, and crashing waves coming through the vacant window panes. It was clear that Pavel could not see Augustin, but the face of the young boy transformed into terror. The shadowy, decaying figure raised his arm, and pointed his grey finger directly at the boy. Antonio switched his gaze to the boy, who was now stood up and gradually moving towards Augustin, eyes still full of fear, but seemingly drawn by an invisible force.

"Clemence, what are you doing? Come back here. Clemence?"

Pavel called after his ward, but the boy was undeterred. As he approached the figure of Augustin, he grabbed hold of Clemence, and leapt through the open window, taking him into the dark depths of the ocean.

"CLEMENCE!" screamed Pavel and launched towards the window, but it was too late.

As he looked over the edge into the waters below, the boy was long gone. Pavel glared back at Antonio, now rocking in his seat again.

"What did you see?" he said accusingly.

"Augustin came for the boy, the way the woman came for him."

Antonio spoke almost in a trance.

"What are you talking about! Who is Augustin? What took Clemence?"

Pavel was now shaking Antonio by the shoulders but couldn't break his trance like state. Turning away, he made his way towards the door, attempting to come to terms with what he had just witnessed. As he opened the door, he turned to face Antonio once more, and simply shook his head.

"You are not the man to lead us to salvation."

As Pavel finished his sentence, the length of a blade pierced the back of his throat and erupted through his mouth. Antonio broke from his small mental prison and flew across the room towards the open window, where he cowered amongst the broken glass.

Pavel's body trembled with convulsions, as the blade was removed, and he dropped to the floor. Behind him, six men stood, all with blades drawn and they circled Pavel's twitching body. They each raised their swords and plunged them over and over into Pavel's now limp body. Antonio counted. Eight times each. Forty-eight plunged blades. Always eight wounds, and the final throat slit. The latter was delivered by the lead offender before they looked toward their Captain.

Their blades dragged along the ground beside them leaving a trail of Pavel's blood as they scratched into the dark wooden floor. The wind howled upon Antonio, the rain soaking him to the bone, seemingly with every flash of lightning, the six men moving a step closer to him. The fear was real now. Antonio was about to meet his end. The candles flickered violently, barely staying lit amongst the tropical storms. As the men advanced and reached the desk, they all raised their swords, and Antonio placed his hands over his head.

Then all went silent. The wind ceased. Antonio looked behind him, and the storm was still raging, the sea throwing the *Sapphire Serpent* around like some sort of doll. But there was silence. He looked back towards the desk but could see nothing.

Darkness had taken over the cabin, all the candles were extinguished. Antonio could hear whispers in the void but could not make out what they were saying. He stood to his feet and leaned forward to feel for the wood of the desk. He placed his hand upon it, but the surface felt *wrong*. He lifted his hand and squinted to look at his palm. The moonlight cast just enough light to see that the palm of his hand was thick with dark red fluids. The blood dripped from his fingertips, and his heart felt like it stopped.

Then, as if it had never happened, the wind crashed through the open window, and lifted Antonio up and over his desk crashing to the floor with a thud. He crawled to his feet and fumbled for a way to light the candle in the lantern nearest the door. This, however, was not needed, as the candles re-illuminated themselves, and the scene before Antonio was a torrid one.

The six men who had killed Pavel were now lying on the floor in their own blood, all with eight blade wounds to their chests, and their throats slit. Standing over the bodies was another man, whom Antonio recognised as one of his older deckhands, Ezio. Ezio was looking down at his feet, blade dripping with the blood of the six men laying before him. When he looked up at Antonio, his face was not his own. Eyes were dark, breathing harsh and raspy. He raised his blade to his own throat.

"Este barco está condenado."

Antonio turned away as the sound of blade on skin, followed by the gurgling sound of a man choking on his own blood had become too frequent a noise on his ship. When he heard Ezio's body hit the ground, he turned back. Sure enough there were now eight bodies on the floor. Antonio burst from his cabin, sprinted across the slippery battered deck, and into the galley, where he locked the door, and cowered on the floor behind it.

"This ship is cursed… this ship is cursed… this ship is cursed…"

14th December 1611

Antonio sat with his feet dangling over the edge of the plank, as the *Serpent* bobbed up and down amongst the waves. His eyes were focused on his blistered bare feet, where he had rubbed the skin raw with his own fingers. He looked up at the sky, sun shining brightly, bathing him in warmth. But he didn't feel the warmth. No amount of suns in the sky could bring the warmth back to his body. His eyes were red, purple bags hung from below them. His hair was frayed and windswept, and his clothes were torn and bloody.

The *Sapphire Serpent* should have made Nassau over a week ago, and there was no land in sight. Antonio had come to terms with the fact that he, like the crews before him, were bound to wander the seas on this cursed ship. All the treasure in the world and no way to reach land to spend it. He took one long look at the ocean below him, before standing up and turning around. As he hobbled back towards the main deck, his sword dragged behind him, scratching the wooden plank, and drawing a red line of blood in the scratches.

As he reached the main deck, he strolled between the bodies of the remaining five crew members, each with eight stab wounds, and a slit throat. The same as the children, he thought. Seemed a fitting end for those willing to crew a ship of the damned.

Antonio climbed the short flight of steps to the wheel, and placed his sword on the ground. As he took the wheel, he saw the woman standing in the crow's nest. She raised her hand and pointed towards the sword laying on the ground beside him. He glanced down at it and thought how friendly the blade now looked. He reached down and grasped the handle. This was finally it. His release from the horror that had eaten him from the inside out. He watched as the steel from his blade glinted in the sun and raised it towards his throat. He closed his eyes and smiled.

"NOOOOOOOOO!!!"

A demonic, scream of death erupted from beside Antonio, and shoved him to the side, knocking the blade from his hand, and him to the floor along with it, cascading down the stairs to the deck below. As he spun around in the direction of the wheel, he saw Augustin yanking the wheel all the way to the right, and the ship veered to starboard sending Antonio sliding down the deck back towards the plank. Another scream, this time from the crow's nest above.

The ship bounced violently, as the underside of the *Serpent* hit something below the waves. The plank sheared off the ship, and Antonio rolled along the deck and overboard through the gap left by the plank, spearing his ribs on the jagged wood that remained. As he tumbled into the ocean, he was crushed by the hull of the ship, a wave of red erupting below the surface.

Another jarring motion, another scream from the sky as the woman disappeared, and Augustin along with her. And with one more almighty crash, the bow of the *Sapphire Serpent* impaled itself into a large rock formation, crashing through limestone, and granite, coming to rest half in and half out of the cluster which formed a small rocky island.

Below the waves behind the ship, Antonio gradually fell into the darkness, his eyes closing as he descended. As he faded from view, another smile crept across his face.

29th October 2018

As Kristin stumbled down the side of the island formation, she saw the Caribbean Sunset. Or at least, what remained of it. The hull was gone, sunk below the waterline, with just a few pieces of burning wreckage left floating on the surface. Carlos had clearly not intended to them to escape.

Another few moments of scanning the ocean, and she spotted a smaller craft, anchored off the far edge of the island. She cautiously moved down the side of the rocks, the wind now getting very powerful, and the clouds beginning to move across the sky. She reached the sea, and prepared herself to leap into the dark waters, knowing what she had faced inside. Taking a deep breath, she leapt into the abyss, narrowly missing several outcrops below the surface. As she kicked her way back towards the surface, she turned and saw the faces of the men that had accompanied her here. Hanging motionless in the depths were the empty eyes of Steve, Alex, Frank and Arthur.

And lower down, was the figure of Carlos, held down by undead hands. Behind those hands were the faces of two men. Kristin turned away and kicked her way back into the night air, and swam her hardest to Carlos' boat, not looking back again, whilst below the waves, Antonio and Augustin kept their grip on Carlos.

RED SNOW: CABIN FEVER

The sound of the door closing for the final time was like a dagger to the heart. As the key turned in the lock, and the barrels clicked, the task was complete. Duncan looked up into the grey sky as the snow continued to fall. He closed his eyes feeling the icy sculptures land softly on his skin and melt, joining his tears as the moisture moved down his face. Looking through the window of the toy store once more, he smiled at the children stood near the artificial Christmas tree, as they had every year since he opened the store on the site of the old children's hospital. They waved to him, a look of sadness on their faces. Duncan waved back, and as he walked away from the store front, the children turned and moved away, fading back from vision, leaving the store dark and empty.

"Dad, you really need to stop harassing me, it's making me wanna go and join the army. I might get less grief."

Duncan's daughter, Grace, was beginning to lose her remaining patience with her father.

"It's bad enough you're making me leave my friends behind, but taking my phone away?"

Duncan didn't pause and continued double checking his suitcase. Grace continued staring at him, and when he didn't respond, she tapped him on the back, and he jumped clear of the ground with a shock.

"Jesus Christ Grace!" he protested, holding his chest. "Don't do that!"

"I've been talking to you for the last twenty minutes, Dad. Did you seriously not hear any of that?"

"Any of what?"

"Give me my phone back, or I'm moving in with Max."

Grace held her hand out, and put the other on her hip, waiting for her father to give in.

"Fine, but can we please get the last of the boxes into the car?"

Duncan closed his suitcase, and carried it down the stairs, Grace following behind with the last box of her belongings. She was not on board with this move. Since the store had closed, Duncan had not been making a lot of sense. He'd spent the first few weeks talking about 'the children' and the last couple of months applying for every job possible.

Grace had had an intense few weeks herself, but her father was not really interested. He'd become detached from his family more and more. The toy store had been his life. As she heard her mother coming home, she picked up the pace.

"Hi Mom," Grace offered, but she got an immediate question response.

"Where's your father?"

Nobody wants to pay attention to me, clearly, Grace thought.

"He's putting the last of his stuff into the truck. The removal guys have been waiting for an hour. He keeps double checking everything."

Daniella sighed. Duncan was bad enough when it came to the finances, or the stock levels for the store, but on the few occasions they had moved house, he had been like a man possessed. He had to have every item packed a certain way, and if anyone touched it afterwards, he would open it up, and check it again. She was certain he suffered from some form of OCD, but he refused to be tested. He wasn't a fan of blood or needles and was convinced both of those things would make an appearance, and cause him to pass out.

"Okay honey, thanks."

Daniella gave Grace a quick hug and sent her out to the truck with her box. She took one last look around the house. The living room fireplace, where Duncan had proposed to her on Valentine's Day. The kitchen where she'd gone into labour with Grace and had to run down the street to the toy store to get Duncan. She moved upstairs to the bedroom where she had told Duncan they should take a break. She thought about that moment for a while. Work was becoming too much, and she wasn't getting any attention at home. Grace was hanging out more and more with her friends.

Daniella thought about the first time she had cheated on Duncan and remembered how guilty she had felt. The second time, it felt easier, but somehow hollow. And on the third occasion, when Grace had come home early and caught her, that was the end. Duncan had taken the news quite well, all things considered, and the neighbour with whom she had been involved with, had moved away quickly.

Daniella decided a break would be best for them to see if they still had a relationship worth saving. After the incident though, Duncan had come to realise what he had been neglecting, and Daniella had realised how much she still loved him, and they managed to reconcile. Even when the store was going through the early financial issues, they managed to make it work, but when the new Silverton Shopping Complex was completed, profits plummeted, and people stopped shopping at the small independent stores. They had put everything into trying to save the business, but to no avail. Finally, they made the decision to say goodbye to it, after eighteen years across various locations, and start afresh.

The truck beeped its horn outside, and Daniella was snapped out of her memories.

"Alaska, here we come."

Grace thought her home town had always seen its fair share of snow, but that was nothing compared to Alaska. White hills as far as the eye could see. Not the worst view from a bedroom window. Shame it was only temporary. She heard her father come back into the cabin.

"Okay, so the house won't be ready for another two weeks, so all our stuff is going to have to go into storage."

"Are you serious?"

Grace was not happy. She wanted to get settled as soon as possible to try and forget how far away they had been forced to come. Her phone beeped, and as she looked down and saw Max's text, she smiled, and felt a yearning for home.

"This haunted museum your aunt has opened is awesome! Really wish you were here. xx"

She typed a similar reply, and then addressed her father.

"Dad, why couldn't we have just stayed where we were until the place was ready? We didn't even need to be out of there until next month!"

"Look, Grace, I have to start my job in three days, and I really would rather not have to have a long distance relationship with you and your mother and try and sort out the logistics of moving while trying to settle in to a new place. I need you guys here. I need you."

Grace felt a tinge of sadness. Her dad had become a lot more affectionate since him and Daniella had patched things up. His face was fixed, and his eyes were welling up a little, so she moved to give him a hug.

"Okay Dad, whatever you need, we're here."

"Thank you sweetheart."

"Okay, so what about this place?" asked Daniella.

Duncan perked up and reached into his pocket, pulling out a piece of paper.

"We've got this place for the next three weeks just in case there's another delay with the house. The only requirements are that we check in once a week with the landlord in town, and if we need the road ploughing, we call this number, and they'll come right out regardless of the time or day."

Grace and her mother chuckled.

"What?" asked Duncan.

"We never had to be ploughed out of our old house," replied Grace.

Duncan smiled.

"Well, when in Alaska."

Daniella walked into the kitchen. It was a very large size, given the temporary nature of the normal residents. You could easily have thrown a large dinner party in there. In fact, the whole cabin was of a sizeable nature, and given how remote it was, that should make it feel more comfortable, she thought.

"Dad, how far is it to the nearest neighbour?" asked Grace.

Duncan looked at his map he'd picked up from the removal truck.

"Erm… about seven miles. No… eight. Eight miles."

"Must be about the same distance to a cell tower, because I got nothin'."

Daniella re-entered the room, tapping an unresponsive smartphone. Grace then immediately panicked and checked her own phone. One bar of signal. Not a lot, but enough to get a text through to Max.

"I've got one bar, Max text me."

"You need to forget about Max," Daniella replied. "That boy needs to get his life back on track."

"Mom, if you'd seen a dead body and a bunch of spiders, then you'd be disturbed too."

"You saw all that, and you're… normal," her mother replied.

"Thanks for the confidence."

The door knocked, and everyone looked towards it.

"Are we expecting company?" asked Daniella.

"Not that I know of," replied Duncan.

He moved to open the door, but before he reached it, he was stopped by the sight of a face at the window. Pressed against the glass, fogging it up with breath, was a middle-aged man, with white beard, and piercing blue eyes. His stare was intense and directed at Daniella.

Duncan opened the door and looked around the frame towards the mysterious man.

"Excuse me? Can I help you?" asked Duncan.

The man didn't move but continued to stare through the glass at Daniella. She became very uncomfortable, and moved towards Duncan, and out of the man's line of sight. The man finally broke his gaze, leaving a fogged up patch on the glass, and gradually walked through the snow back to the front door.

"You the new family?" asked the man in a very gruff, low voice.

"Well, yes. I'm Duncan, this is my wife Daniella, and our daughter Grace."

Duncan gestured at each of the women in turn, whilst observing the intense stare the man gave to each of them.

"Garrett."

The man offered his presumed name, and then placed a damp hand on Duncan's neck, causing him to flinch back a little.

"Nice to meet you, Mr Garrett," replied Duncan, removing his hand, unsure of where this was going, or what to say next.

"Watch yourselves."

Garrett spoke with a threatening tone, but didn't appear to make a threat himself.

"Excuse me?"

Duncan's interest was now flared up.

"What do you mean by that?"

Garrett's gaze now switched to Grace. His eyes followed her from her feet to her eyes, but he seemed less interested than he was in Daniella. She stepped in, uncomfortable with the atmosphere and the way the man was examining her nineteen-year-old daughter.

"What exactly do you want here?" she stated.

Garrett looked back towards Daniella before providing her with more detail.

"There are... people here. Newcomers don't last long. Watch yourselves."

"What do you mean newcomers don't last long?" asked Duncan.

Garrett didn't break eye contact with Daniella but responded to Duncan's question.

"You just be careful."

Garrett turned and began walking down the driveway towards the narrow road that led towards town. Confused, and a little disturbed, Duncan closed the door, and walked towards his family.

"What was that all about?" Grace asked.

"No idea," replied her father. "Honey?" he said, looking at his wife, and trying to wipe the sticky fluid from his neck. "You okay?"

Daniella was looking out the window. Garrett was stood in the tree line, looking back at her.

"Yeah. I'm fine."

"No, not that one. I don't like that one. Let's get this one."

"But it's full fat, get the zero sugar one at least."

Duncan watched the two women in his life arguing over which yoghurt to buy. He had missed out on this kind of thing when he was running the store, and it was only now that he was realising that he probably missed out on much more. When he opened the store, Grace was only two years old. Now she was almost twenty. And yet he could only remember a handful of her birthdays, and the last time he could remember going Christmas shopping for her presents himself, he was buying her a My Little Pony playset. Time moved so quickly.

But now he would make it up to them. This was their chance at a fresh start. Grace had opted not to go to college or university, and instead took classes she felt would help her get a good job. She knew her dad had grown up without much money, and she'd always wanted to help out, but now the store was gone, she'd felt she needed to contribute more than ever. Duncan didn't want her to feel the burden of having to support their family. That was his job. Which is why they had made the move.

Duncan had been offered the chance to join a large marketing firm in Valdez, based near the port. Having done his own marketing and run his own business for almost two decades, they'd snapped him up. It was quite a journey from their current temporary lodgings near the Thompson Pass, but it would be worth it when they finally moved into their new home. The women caught him staring at them, and as Duncan's smile got wider, they both became more confused.

"Erm, Dad, what are you staring at?"

"Oh nothing, just appreciating the benefits of sugar free yoghurt."

The snow was really coming down, and the sun was all but gone, when the family left the grocery store.

"Damn, how long were we shopping?" asked Grace.

Duncan smiled and opened the door to their rented pickup truck.

"It doesn't matter, we'll get back to the cabin before the snow blocks the road."

"I hope so, I wanna try out the hot tub," replied Daniella.

She gave her husband a cheeky smile, and kissed him on the cheek. Grace was not impressed and rolled her eyes.

"Can you at least wait until I've gone to bed and put my headphones in?" she pleaded, to the amusement of her parents.

They all shut their doors, the car park now bathed in near darkness, thick grey clouds covering the moon, the only light shining onto the snow coming from the few working street lights. Duncan started the truck, switched on the lights, and activated the windscreen wipers. As the snow moved from the window, the three of them jumped. The headlights were casting a beam directly over three men and a woman, all standing directly in front of the truck, staring back at them.

"What are they doing?" asked Grace.

"I don't know honey. Let's just get out of here."

Duncan put the truck into reverse, but the rear wheels were now stuck in a small snow drift.

"Dammit, I don't think I brought the chains."

"Let's quickly check the back seats," offered Daniella.

All three of them searched under the seats and in the large storage compartment beneath the rear bench, but there were no chains there, just blankets.

"Erm… Dad?" asked Grace, who was now looking back out the windscreen.

"Yeah sweetie?"

"They're gone."

Both Duncan and Daniella looked up and sure enough, the gang of strangers were gone.

"Okay, then let's get out of here."

Duncan slipped his seat belt over his shoulder and clicked it into place. As Daniella went to do the same, she turned to the side and was met by the face of the woman stranger staring right back, her face mere inches from the glass. Daniella screamed and leapt back towards her husband.

"What the fuck?" shouted Duncan.

He turned to his own window, to see one of the men. The other two were pressed against the two rear windows, staring at Grace.

"Drive Duncan!" shouted Daniella, and her husband obliged, slamming the vehicle into drive, and his foot to the floor.

The tyres span, snow flying from the rear of the truck, and he drove over the pavement, and out onto the main road, the four strangers staring at them from the parking lot. As Grace looked back, the group seemed to vanish in the blink of an eye, and while her eyes searched the perimeter of the store, she spotted the woman running into the trees behind the trolley bay.

There was further movement in the trees, but then they moved out of range, the truck sliding across the road as Duncan tried to get out of town as fast as possible.

The red and blue lights illuminated the whole section of road and shone through the large snowflakes now falling in the pass, making it appear as if fairy lights were cascading down from the sky. Grace thought about how beautiful it looked. Very in tune with Christmas.

Her and Daniella watched through the windscreen as the police officer was giving Duncan his breathalyser test. Evidently, there is only so much wayward driving you can do, even in the remotest parts of the country before you attract the attention of law enforcement. As funny as this was to watch, neither Grace nor her mother could shake the feeling of unease at what had occurred back at the grocery store.

As Duncan struggled to walk in a straight line in the snow, Daniella felt a tap on her shoulder, and turned to see her daughter resting her head on the back of her seat.

"Mom, what is going on in this place? Everybody's acting so weird." Daniella nodded in agreement.

"I know. Almost feels like something is wrong here, but I can't figure out what. And why everyone has such a fetish for staring at people."

"I know! I've had more people checking me out in the last twelve hours than I have in the last two years!"

"Me too. And not in a nice way."

Grace leaned back in her seat and chuckled as her father stumbled in a snow drift. As the police officer helped him back to his feet, Grace spotted movement in the tree line. As she squinted through the snow, it looked like a pair of red eyes was staring back at her. She couldn't make out any distinct figures or shapes, but then the number of red dots increased. She could now make out eight distinct red lights in the forest.

"Mom, do you see that?" she asked.

Daniella squinted through the snow.

"See what honey?"

Grace looked back and the dots were gone.

"Nothing. Never mind."

The truck door opened, and the cabin lit up, as Duncan climbed back inside, now soaking from his dip in the snow verge.

"He thought I was nuts, but I wasn't drunk so he's letting us go."

"It's been a while since I saw you trying to concentrate that much," Daniella chuckled.

"You try walking in a straight line in a blizzard!"

Duncan restarted the engine, and as the police car vanished into the distance, in the opposite direction, Duncan steered the truck back onto the road, and headed towards the cabin. Grace stared out the side window, watching the trees blur past. Feeling slightly travel sick from the image, she turned and looked out the back window, and as the truck turned a corner, a figure walked out onto the road behind them. Grace couldn't make out who it was, but the eyes were clear. Two red piercing eyes watched the truck move away, and in the blink of an eye, they were gone.

Duncan couldn't remember the last time he had put shopping away. The fact he was in a completely strange kitchen helped him though, because there was not yet a correct place for anything to go, and therefore no way Daniella could yell at him for putting things in the wrong place. He smiled at the thought of that. In marriage, he thought, little victories were important. Kind of like when he'd been forced to mow the lawn one weekend and found a wallet on the curb containing a wad of cash. Little victories.

"So, are we still up for that dip in the hot tub?" enquired Daniella with a cheeky grin.

Grace rolled her eyes again.

"I'm going to bed, knock yourselves out," she said. "And that's a genuine suggestion by the way. Anything to keep the noises down."

As she disappeared up the stairs, Duncan offered his wife an enticing glance.

"I am if you are?" he replied, the pair wrapping their arms around each other.

"You finish putting the groceries away, and I'll go and change into something suitable."

They shared a brief kiss, before Daniella walked around the corner and Duncan could hear her moving up the stairs. What an evening this was going to turn into. He wasn't even thinking about the group of strangers at the store. He was in a log cabin, in a snowy remote part of Alaska, alone with his family, and his wife was about to climb into a hot tub with him. Life was good.

The lights from the cabin lit up the area around it, casting a milky glow over the snow outside. The image was reminiscent of a typical winter card scene you might find in a multipack of Christmas cards. The lights on the tree shone in the lounge window, twinkling reflections in the truck windows. From the trees in front of the house, a series of red glowing eyes were watching. Those eyes were fixed on the view of the windows upstairs.

Grace was sat on her bed, headphones in, laptop open, bobbing her head to whatever tunes she had settled on for the night. The TV was on in the background, but she wasn't paying any attention. In the next window along, the eyes watched as the light flicked on, illuminating the master bedroom. Daniella walked into view, and as she walked past the window, she unbuttoned her shirt, and allowed it to slip to the floor. A low grumbling noise came from one of the sets of eyes. As Daniella let her skirt fall, drool landed on the snow. The eyes seemed to glow harsher, and heavy breathing intensified, like a wolf stalking its prey.

Daniella removed her black lace bra, and walked over to the bed, and fumbled in a suitcase. The eyes began spreading out, and the snapping of branches was audible in the silence of the surroundings. One of the pairs of eyes remained, fixed on the bedroom view, as Daniella slipped off her underwear, and moved into a white bikini. As she closed the suitcase, and walked out of the room, switching the light off as she went, next door, Grace felt as if she was being watched. She turned to look out of her window but saw nothing but the twinkling of the Christmas lights on the truck.

The eyes were gone.

The water bubbled away nicely as Duncan relaxed with his beer. The snow falling made the scene almost magical, and the steam gave the whole ambience an Icelandic quality. And yet the image he was focussed on the most, was the gorgeous thirty-nine year old woman opposite him. He'd been incredibly lucky to snag Daniella back in college.

She'd been dating her lab partner for six months when Duncan transferred to Fairmont, and he knew as soon as he saw her that he wanted her. After her boyfriend pulled an Arty Ziff outside a local nightclub, Duncan had happened to walk by, and pulled him off her, and damn near knocked his teeth through the back of his skull. They became an item soon after, but their relationship was so physically intense above all else, that Daniella soon found herself pregnant, which ended their education, and career prospects.

It was then, that Duncan decided to open the toy store. But gazing at his wife now, all those primal feelings came rushing back. If the water wasn't bubbling already, it soon would be.

"How the hell do you manage to look so damn sexy?"

"That's your pick up line?" replied Daniella. "What happened to your mojo?"

"Well, I thought about going with something along the lines of 'Girl, you look so fine, I wish I could plant you and grow a whole field of you!'"

Daniella burst out laughing.

"Ah, The Fresh Prince. Good choice. But I'm afraid if you keep enjoying this sweet life and drinking those beers, you're gonna be more Uncle Phil than Will Smith."

Slightly offended by the remark, but still enjoying himself, Duncan smiled.

"Well then I'd better get some exercise, hadn't I?" he asked, putting down the beer, and sliding towards his wife.

She too lowered her glass of wine and moved towards him.

"I guess so."

Their lips met, and they wrapped their arms around each other as they kissed. The bubbles tickled Daniella's feet, and she giggled. Duncan laughed in response, but then reached for a remote control.

"Oh, it gets better," he said.

And with a press of a button, the entire hot tub changed colour, casting a deep purple across the water, gradually changing to a turquoise colour, a deep blue, and then cycling back to purple.

"Oh wow. Now that's romantic," replied Daniella.

And the two embraced again. A loud crack from the trees behind them made them stop for a moment.

"Did you hear that?" asked Duncan.

"Yeah. It must be a squirrel or something," replied Daniella.

"I need to remember we're in the wild up here. Only noises I'm used to are screaming kids, drunks, and exploding movie theatres."

The pair giggled again thinking about their old lives. "Well, speaking of wild…"

Daniella reached behind her head, and unfastened the top of her bikini, letting the material fall away from her chest, and creating a very interested look on Duncan's face. She moved closer, and the two kissed, more passionately and intently than before, as they felt each other amongst the bubbles.

Another snap from the woods went unheard, as the pair were now completely engrossed by each other. As the red glowing eyes moved down through the trees, they fixated on the image before them. From around sixty feet away, the eyes made out the sight of the hot tub.

They watched as Daniella rode her husband in the water, the purple illuminated liquid spilling over the side. Duncan's lips caressed his wife's breasts, and the animal urge within the owner of the red eyes grew more intense and began its descent down the snowy forest towards the house.

Grace flicked through her Spotify play lists, but the battery on her phone was now next to zero. She checked for messages, but her signal had faded.

"Great. Not even one bar now. Thank you Alaska."

She stood up from her bed and placed her headphones on her dresser. As she searched for her phone charger, she heard what sounded like a glass breaking downstairs. She stopped and moved onto the landing.

"Mom? Dad?" she spoke into the dim light.

Then she heard giggling from her parents, so she figured they were still 'enjoying' themselves, and headed back to her room, when something else caught her eye.

She had a direct view from the landing of the driveway, and the front of the truck. As she gazed at the vehicle, she noticed the front tyre on the driver's side was flat. Still, more giggling came from downstairs, and desperate to avoid any possible chance of hearing her parents having sex, she went back into her room, and made a mental note to tell her Dad in the morning. As she sat at the dresser, she plugged in her phone, and set her laptop to charge beside it. Looking in the mirror, she gazed at her own reflection, and began a conversation with herself.

"Well Grace, you let the one guy you liked get away. You're nearly twenty years old, but can you make your own life decisions? No, of course not. You need to follow your parents around the country. And why? Because you're too damn sensible."

Grace sighed and looked at the clock. Ten thirty.

"Well, I guess I should shower and then head to bed. May as well get used to talking to myself, because fuck knows who else there is to talk to."

She walked into her en-suite bathroom and flicked on the light. Not bad for a log cabin. In fact, it was nicer than her own bathroom from home. This could work. Nice looking bath. Pretty shower curtain. Nice big window, letting in the crisp night air. She reached over and closed it. Maybe they could make this work after all. She took off her sweater, and threw it back into her room, landing on the edge of the bed, and turned towards the shower. Unbuttoning her red check shirt with one hand, she reached for the shower curtain with the other, and pulled it back.

Her scream echoed through the cabin and pierced the edge of the woodlands. As the man grabbed her by the throat and lifted her from the ground, Grace gasped for air. Stepping out of the bath tub, still holding her aloft, the man brought his face to meet hers. His eyes glowed red. She recognised the man from the store. But what she was looking at was no man. He licked his lips and moved them to meet Grace's ear.

"Delicious. I'm going to enjoy feasting on you."

As Daniella fumbled to get her bikini top back on, Duncan was already getting out of the hot tub.

"Grace?" he shouted in to the house. No reply. "Grace?"

As Daniella grabbed her robe from the edge of the tub, all the power went out, plunging them both into darkness.

"Duncan, what's happening?"

Daniella was now trembling with fear, and Duncan himself was terrified for his daughter. That scream was deafening, and definitely not voluntary.

"I don't know sweetheart, but let's go very careful, okay. I've got you."

Duncan led Daniella into the house and felt his way along the wall. The door to the deck was off the kitchen, and soon his hand met the marble work surface. He slid his hand along it, using his other hand to guide Daniella behind him. A shuffling noise came from ahead, and they both stopped where they were.

"What was that?" Daniella asked.

"I'm not sure, but I get the distinct feeling we are not alone."

Another noise from ahead. Followed by a smash, as something hit the floor and shattered. Daniella jumped with fright and gripped onto Duncan's waist.

"It's okay, don't panic," he offered. "I want you to wait here, honey, keep hold of the kitchen counter, and I'm gonna go take a look, okay?"

Daniella was *not* okay with that idea, but she loathed the idea of heading towards the noise even more. She reluctantly nodded and remained with her hands both now clamped onto the counter. The only light in the cabin were a few battery operated flame effect lanterns hanging on the walls which gave a shadowy effect across the floor.

But when do noises ever *not* come from the shadows, Duncan thought. He had always envisioned the prospect of having to face burglars one day. He'd only encountered a fight scenario once before, and it was the night he punched his wife's lab partner. Apart from the horror he witnessed years ago at the store, he had lived a relatively violence free lifestyle.

He could hear Daniella breathing rapidly a few feet behind him, as he reached the doorway. He felt for the wooden frame, and gradually stuck his head out, looking in both directions. As he moved forwards, his bare feet encountered the shattered object, and he leapt from the floor in pain, and landed on his back, clutching his feet. Behind him in the kitchen, he heard a muffled scream from Daniella, and a large scurrying noise. And then nothing.

"Daniella?" he called into the darkness.

Nothing. No breathing, no response.

He felt his feet and found a piece of whatever he had trodden on sticking out of the skin. He pulled it free, and winced as the pain shot through him, and then subsided slightly. As the clouds briefly opened again, the moonlight cast a glow on the fragments of porcelain. The vase in the entrance way had been knocked onto the floor. But knocked by what? That was the question. The clouds removed the extra light once more.

Duncan used the door frame to help him to his feet, and then looked back into the kitchen. Daniella was gone. Now he knew, they were not alone. Something rushed past him, and he spun around. He couldn't see anything, but he could *hear* something. In the direction of the stairs, Duncan could hear whispering. He carefully used the glare of the lanterns to step around the remaining broken elements of the vase on the floor and moved between the shadows towards the staircase in the middle of the cabin. The whispering intensified, and it soon became clear, there were *multiple* voices.

Suddenly, Duncan felt someone rushing up on him from behind, and as he spun around, he was hit full force by an unseen figure, and was thrown a clear thirty feet across the main entrance hall and slammed into the wall next to the lounge entrance with such force, it splintered the wood, and Duncan fell to the floor in a heap. He looked up from the floor, his vision out of focus, his chest in intense pain. He had broken some ribs at the very least. As his eyes tried to make sense of what was in front of him, he could make out a pair of red eyes moving towards him. He attempted to address the figure.

"Wh… What… What do you want?"

Giggling from near the stairs. The figure continued to advance.

"Where's my… my daughter… and… and my wife?"

Breathing was proving very painful for Duncan, but again, the figure continued towards him, and as his eyes focussed some more, he could see another pair of eyes moving down the stairs to join them.

"He looks so puny," said the first figure, although Duncan was unsure as to who he was talking to. "I can't say I'm too impressed. I was hoping for more of a hunt."

The second voice came from beside the first and appeared to be that of a woman.

"No, but the wife looks delicious."

Duncan forced himself to sit up, holding his ribs, but now an anger burning in his chest alongside the pain.

"WHAT HAVE YOU DONE WITH MY FAMILY?" he shouted.

Not speaking directly to Duncan, the woman spoke.

"I'll have Eugene hang the wife from the ceiling. It'll give her more... flavour."

The response sent a shiver right through to Duncan's soul.

The first figure knelt in front of Duncan, and that is when he recognised the face. He looked across to see the woman and recognised her too.

"You were at the store."

His words came out breathy and harsh. The woman growled excitedly in her throat.

"Thought I'd have eyes bigger than my belly," she replied. "But looking at your wife, I can't wait to devour her."

She smiled and the lantern glow glinted off her teeth. Duncan pressed his back to the damaged wall. Her teeth were *pointed*. The eyes, the teeth. These were not normal people. Duncan attempted to stand, but the man rushed him with lightning quickness, grabbed his throat and pinned him against the wall, impaling his back on slivers of broken wood. Duncan tried to scream in pain, but the man's grip on his throat was too tight. He ran his nose along the side of Duncan's neck, sniffing his scent, before looking him directly in the eyes.

"This one is tainted," he said in a gruff, and somewhat disappointed voice.

He let Duncan fall to the floor, choking for air.

"Something has drunk from him already?" asked the confused woman.

The man shook his head.

"No, but he has a scent on him. It is *Lycan*."

The man spat on the floor in disgust, as the woman moved towards Duncan. She leaned over and smelt him too. She immediately stood up and wretched, spitting on the floor also.

"We cannot feast on tainted blood, Dayton," said the woman.

The man, now known as Dayton, nodded and glanced back up the stairs, a smile then spreading across his lips, before looking back at Duncan. He addressed the woman again.

"No. Maybe we can get the smell off him later… for a snack. But he can watch us feast on his women. Bring him upstairs."

Duncan tried to fight it, but the woman was too strong. She lifted him by the throat and used her other arm to lift his body onto her back.

As Dayton led them up the stairs, Duncan's eyes scanned for any sign of Daniella or Grace. He feared that he would not see them alive. And what did Dayton say? He was *tainted*? Tainted by *Lycan*? What did that mean? The entrance hall went dark again, as they moved beyond the glow of the lanterns.

The female threw Duncan to the floor at the entrance to his bedroom, the door closed. He could hear muffled screams from within. Dayton smiled. He looked down at Duncan and then addressed the woman.

"Well Elizabeth, it sounds like Gunter is having fun in there."

"You fucking piece of shit! If anything happens to my family…"

Duncan was cut off by a swift boot to the face. He lay on the floor, spitting the blood from his mouth.

"You would do well to hold your tongue. Before I rip it from your mouth."

Elizabeth opened the door, and there was a glow of candlelight from within. Still dazed from the assault, Duncan felt himself being dragged into the room by Dayton. When he let him go, he was slumped against his own dresser, facing the bed. His eyes bulged in horror at the sight before him.

On his bed, was Grace. She was tied to each corner of the bed by rope, her shirt torn open, and her jeans in tatters. As he focussed his eyes more, he could see large gashes in both her thighs, and a long slit across the top of her right breast, the blood seeping into her bra. The bed sheets were also soaked with blood, and her wrists and ankles were worn bloody from struggling against them. A large, hulking figure was hunched over her right arm, and Grace was screaming through the gag in her mouth.

The anger flowed through Duncan's chest, but he felt too weak to stand. He could feel blood dripping down his own back from the splinters of wood, and he was pretty sure his nose was broken. Grace let out another loud scream, and Gunter roared in protest, and punched Grace square in the face, hard. She immediately became almost silent, and began coughing blood, her gag was now dark red, and a huge stream of blood now trickled from her forehead.

Duncan let out his own scream and lunged forward, but was stopped by Dayton, who held Duncan back against the wall to the side of the bed and forced his head to look at the scene of his daughter on the bed. He was nearly sick at the image in front of him. Gunter was biting Grace's arm, and he appeared to be *drinking her blood*. As he lifted his head, he turned towards Duncan, blood dripping from his pointed teeth, his face stained red to match his eyes. He sniffed the air and stood up towards Duncan.

"You don't want this one yet, Gunter, he's been tainted by a Lycan. Save him until last," Dayton explained.

Duncan gazed down at his helpless daughter. She had been battered and assaulted by some monster, who now had her blood dripping from his mouth. Wait, tainted by a Lycan.?

Garrett!

Could he have been the one they were talking about? His eyes were an intense shade of blue, and he was acting strangely. He must have done something when he opened the door. What had he done to Duncan that protected him from this, mutilation? The sticky residue on his neck!

Duncan tried not to think about what that may have been, but whatever it was, it was keeping him from being potentially eaten.

Elizabeth strolled over towards Grace's spread out body, and leaned in. To Duncan's horror, she ran her tongue along Grace's cheek, licking up the blood, following the trail down her neck and over her chest. As she ran her tongue over the wound on Grace's breast, Grace let out another yelp, and Elizabeth backhanded her across the face. Duncan struggled as much as he could against Dayton, but the grip was too strong, and he was too weak. Elizabeth spoke to Gunter.

"Where's the wife? I like a more vintage Cabernet."

As she smiled, her tongue licked her pointed teeth.

"Mmm, she is in the daughter's room with Eugene. Sounded like they were having a party of their own," replied Gunter.

Elizabeth seemed excited by this idea, and another long, low growl, erupted from her throat.

"YOU STAY THE FUCK AWAY FROM MY WIFE YOU SICK WHORE!"

The words left Duncan's mouth before he could accept he had thought of them. Elizabeth stopped in front of him, and ran her hands down his chest, putting her face close to his.

"I'm going to *fuck* your wife, little man. And then, I'm going to drink her blood."

She ran her tongue over Duncan's face and disappeared out the doorway towards Grace's bedroom. Dayton laughed a low guttural cackle, as Gunter turned back towards Grace, who upon seeing him moving back towards her, began struggling once again. The clouds had cleared, and the moon was now fully visible in the sky, casting even more illumination on the horrors before him. Dayton moved closer to Duncan.

"*You're gonna want to watch this part,*" he whispered.

Gunter ran his long finger nails up Grace's outer thigh, leaving deep scratches as they went, and followed the trail across her belly, up the middle of her chest and he grabbed her by the throat.

"LET HER GO YOU FUCKING SICK FUCK!"

Nobody was paying attention to Duncan's cries of anger and fear.

Gunter smelled Grace's bloody face and turned her head to the side. Duncan watched as his pointed teeth grew longer, and he reared his head back and roared. As he swung his head forwards to bite Grace's neck, a loud bang came from down the corridor, followed by a woman's horrific scream. Gunter stopped millimetres from Grace's neck, and looked towards the hallway, as did Dayton. Crashing and banging echoed through the cabin. Another terrifying scream vibrated the wall against which, Duncan was still being held. Even Grace, through all her pain, had gone silent and was looking towards the doorway.

Then, silence.

"Gunter, go and see what's going on," directed Dayton.

Gunter grunted in the affirmative and headed in the direction of the noises.

CRASH!

A figure came flying through the bedroom window, sending glass and wood across the room. Dayton dropped Duncan to the floor, as whatever had entered the room had leapt onto Gunter and tore him to the ground. Duncan could just make out ripping sounds, growls, and he thought he could see fur. But this was no bear. Dayton growled, and leapt onto the back of the beast, and sunk his teeth into its shoulder. The creature let out a huge howling noise, and reared its head, eyes glowing yellow, teeth snarling, drool dripping from its mouth. It continued to rip into Gunter, blood spraying the walls, the huge mass of the former aggressor being torn to shreds. Dayton continued to bite into the animal with very little effect.

Duncan looked through the broken window to see the moon shining directly onto the wolf-like creature. He broke his gaze on the battle going on before him and moved towards his daughter. He slid the gag from her mouth and embraced her face.

"Dad! Please get me out of here, it burns so badly!"

"Don't worry honey, I've got you, I've got you!"

Duncan untied the restraints, and peeled them from Grace's wounded skin, and she cautiously slid across the blood soaked bed towards him. They moved to edge out of the room, when Dayton was thrown off the back of the beast, and smashed through the dresser, falling to the floor. He got back to his feet and targeted his gaze on Duncan and Grace as they stood in the doorway. As he advanced towards them, another growl came from down the hallway, and the thudding of heavy footsteps.

They turned towards the noise to see a second lumbering fur-clad beast smashing its way through the landing of the cabin, wood and ornaments flying everywhere. Duncan grabbed his daughter, and threw her to the floor to safety, as Dayton lunged on to Duncan. As his teeth plunged into Duncan's neck, the second creature barrelled into both of them and sent all three of them crashing through the side of the cabin and falling to the snow below.

Grace looked over at the remains of Gunter on the floor, to which the first animal was now pawing through, and she slipped through the doorway, and headed down towards her bedroom in search of her mother. As she limped into the room, the sight before her was a bloodbath. Lying in the remains of her bed, was the fourth blood sucker, or what remained of him. His insides had been completely ripped out and strewn all over the room. His face was hanging from his skull, and his arm was lying away from the rest of the body, on the floor. As she turned away in horror, she saw the mangled body of Elizabeth hanging upside down from the shower curtain rail in the bathroom, blood now filling the tub. On the floor near the door to the bathroom, was a blood stained two-piece bikini, and a shredded robe. Grace looked at it, and the evidence before her, and moved as quickly as she could down the stairs, pushing through the pain, and made her way through the front door, the battle upstairs now becoming quieter.

As she trekked through the snow, which was strangely soothing to her skin, she made her way around the corner of the porch and saw the body of her father lying on the ground. She stopped and held her hand to her mouth. His eyes closed, body limp, and skin pale. She knew that it was too late. But further ahead of her, the second wolf was still engaged in battle with Dayton. As Grace moved forward, she fell to the snow as a sudden burning pain surged through her system. It felt like someone had lit a match in her veins and the fire was now working its way through her like an explosion in a tunnel. The pain briefly subsided, but the cry of pain had attracted the attention of the wolf creature. It looked at her with almost sympathetic eyes and was side swiped by Dayton's claw-like nails, sending it crashing to the ground. Dayton leapt upon the creature and began tearing at its fur and flesh.

"NO! LEAVE HER ALONE!" screamed Grace, but Dayton continued.

Then Grace felt a hand on her shoulder. She jumped and fell to the ground. When she looked back up, Duncan was standing in front of her.

His eyes were red, and there were two thin trails of blood on his neck. He smiled down at his daughter and helped her to her feet.

"Stay here Grace," he said calmly.

She stood, leaning on the side of the cabin, as her father sprinted at a speed she didn't think possible towards the battle. Dayton looked over at the sound of Duncan rushing towards him, but it was too late. Duncan leapt into the air and extended his arms as he crashed into Dayton and sent them both tumbling through the snow.

Duncan got to his feet and charged at Dayton again. The pair exchanged punches and swipes, lashing out at each other's faces in a battle of gymnastics and rage. As Grace watched, the wolf creature slowly climbed to its feet, its fur matted with blood. It looked at the scene before it and it uttered a growl. Grace thought she made out the word *husband* but was unsure.

The creature stumbled towards the pair of fighting men, as the onslaught continued. Duncan slashed his fingernails across Dayton's face, but he then ducked below the next swipe, and plunged his own nails directly into Duncan's side, causing him to let out a loud scream of pain. Dayton smiled and retracted the nails, and watched Duncan fall into the snow, which was slowly being turned red around him.

"Not bad, but not good enough."

As Dayton raised his nails to strike once again, a huge furry fist erupted through his chest, showering Duncan with blood and organs. As the arm was retracted, Duncan could see the wolf creature through the cavity in Dayton's chest. He lay back in the snow, as Dayton's mangled corpse fell to the ground too. There was another loud growl as from above, the first wolf creature leapt from the window to land in the snow.

Grace was still mesmerized by the sight before her. Her father had risen from the dead. And there were wolf creatures fighting other creatures in the snow. As the clouds moved back across the moon, and darkness once again covered the land, both wolf creatures began whimpering. The second, injured one, limped back towards Grace, while the first one that had leapt from above, staggered off towards the woods. As the second creature fell to the snow in front of Grace, she noticed the fur began to retract from its body. It began to shrink in size, rapidly, and shrank down to a human sized form. As Duncan staggered across, he found himself collapsed in front of the figure of his wife, lying naked in the snow. Grace stumbled over to the truck, and grabbed a blanket from the back, staggered over, and lay it across her mother.

Daniella woke up gradually, and as she looked up, she saw her daughter looking back at her, and smiled. Her eyes were still yellow, as they looked around to Duncan, who was lying clutching his side, his own eyes, still glowing red. As Grace fell backwards, falling victim to another burning pain sensation, Daniella's face turned to fear. She looked down at her own hands and saw they had not yet reverted to her human form.

She took her index finger, and plunged the nail into her other hand, and drew it across her palm. Hot red blood flowed from the hand, and she held it up to Grace's mouth. Confused and in pain from her own emerging transformation, Grace drank the blood, enthusiastically, until she could absorb no more. She collapsed back into the snow, the burning subsiding, and her breathing becoming more calmed. Daniella turned to Duncan and held her hand out to him.

"No, I won't do it. I can fight this."

Daniella shook her head.

"No, you can't. *We* can."

She thrust the hand forward again, and the blood lust overtook Duncan. He grabbed her hand and plunged his now pointed teeth into the wound, and like his daughter had moments before, drank his wife's blood, until he too, could take no more.

Exhausted, Duncan and Grace slipped into an unconscious state. As Daniella's hand and eyes returned to her own, she glanced back towards the woods and saw Garrett standing next to one of the perimeter trees, draped in a blanket of his own. Daniella smiled towards him, and he smiled back before turning, and heading into the forest. As Daniella looked across at her family, now safe, she too slipped into a deep sleep.

"So, you're telling me your dad was a vampire?"

"Yup."

"And you were turning into a vampire?"

"That's right."

"But your mom, who was a werewolf…"

"…Lycan."

"Sorry, Lycan, saved you with her blood?"

"You got it!

"But what about your Dad? He was already fully transformed. And since when has your mom been a werewolf?"

"That's where it gets complicated."

Max had never been more confused in his life. He had been super excited when Grace had moved back to town. He felt he'd let his opportunity with her slip him by, but now he felt like he was in the middle of an episode of *Buffy the Vampire Slayer*.

"Look, Max, you don't have to get all the ins and outs. You just need to know that I got to have an awesome adventure, and you missed out."

"Good job I did, or I'd have probably been dead. Or drinking my Mom's blood through a straw, or something."

Daniella walked in through the front door.

"Hi Max, how are you doing?"

"I'm good thanks Mrs Silverton, how are you?"

Daniella thought for a moment, and then responded.

"Living in my sister-in-law's shadow, but I'm the super creepy monster, so I could always throw her out a window if I get sick of working with her."

All three laughed at the joke of Grace's Aunt Kathryn flying through the air. Grace turned to her mother.

"How's Dad?"

"He'll be okay. It's going to take him some time, but he will get used to being back. He went to see someone today about a job, but said he was heading to *Sisko's* for a beer."

Grace was worried about her Dad. He hadn't been quite the same since his transformation. Daniella and Grace had dealt quite quickly with what they had become. But Duncan was having more trouble. Being transformed from a human to a vampire, and then to a werewolf/vampire hybrid was really taking its toll on his mind, as well as his physical well-being. But Daniella was confident they could make it work.

"And of course, now Max knows, we have another ally in the fight against supernatural forces!"

Daniella smiled at her own joke.

"When do you start working at your sister-in-law's museum Mrs Silverton?" asked Max.

"Tomorrow night. They're having a 'Friday the 13th' theme night. Apparently they have some special guest investigators coming to spend the night, and they're going to film it for *Discovery+*. Should be fun."

"I think you'll like it, I went while you guys were in Alaska, and it's so cool."

Max was visibly excited. Grace suspected, it was due to the prospect of family and friends discount, and the face he was now in the company of real life supernatural creatures.

"Yeah well we'll see. She says some medallion keeps moving around the place, and it's pretty valuable, so I'm gonna try and see what happens when I lock it in a box overnight. Let's be honest, it's got to be better than working in that massive shopping complex her wife opened. Don't think Duncan would ever forgive me working there. Anyway, I'll see you both later."

Daniella waved as she hung up her coat and went upstairs. Grace turned back to Max.

"How did you manage to convince your folks to move back, anyway?"

"Dad's new boss, Mr Vangorph?"

Max nodded.

"His first name was Dayton."

"It was your Dad's boss who tried to kill him?"

"Yeah, funny huh? Almost as if we were never destined to leave this town after all."

Max pondered that for a minute.

"You know, that's weird. You're the second person that's said that to me this week. Your Aunt Kristin said that to me at the museum when I asked her about her trip last year for the pirate exhibit."

"Yeah it does feel like we belong here somehow. I've never been particularly excited whenever I've gone on vacation or on a field trip in the past."

"Yeah, I wonder why that is?"

They both shrugged their shoulders and flicked on the TV.

Daniella sat on the edge of the bed and slipped out of her shoes. Her feet appeared to no longer be the dainty size fives they used to be. As she rubbed the balls of her feet, her phone rang. As she glanced over, she saw '*Duncan calling*' on the screen.

"Hey honey, how are you?" she answered, attempting to instil upbeat emotion into her husband.

"I don't really know, I'm feeling… uncomfortable."

Daniella tried not to let her concern show in her responses.

"What do you mean, uncomfortable?" she asked.

"I had to leave the bar. Some guy bumped into me as he walked past, and I just felt this immense rage start to build, and I just had to get out of there."

"It's going to be okay, honey. It's going to take a while to figure this out."

"It's not just going to figure itself out though is it?"

Duncan replied, with both sadness and frustration clearly audible in his vocal tone.

"Look, I know some people. They helped me when I first… turned. I wouldn't trust anyone else with this."

"I'm ready to try anything, because if I can't even go for a beer without wanting to either kill someone, or eat them, then there isn't much hope for me."

Daniella knew how he felt. She had felt the same when her affair with the neighbour turned into a life-changing event. But this was different. She wasn't entirely sure what Duncan had become, and she needed help.

"Okay honey, I'll get in touch with them. Are you coming home?"

"Yeah, I'm just going to go for a walk to calm down a little, and then I'll head back. I need my head clear for that interview tomorrow."

As Duncan put the phone down, Daniella placed hers on the bed, and rubbed her eyes with her hands. She knew this was not going to be easy. She felt her own emotions bubbling up, and looking outside, saw a slither of the moon between the clouds.

She stood up and walked across to the wardrobe, opened her side, and reached through the dresses and the shirts to the back. Her fingers felt for a small tag, and pulled, exposing a small cavity in the wall behind the wood. She pulled out a small box and sat back on the bed.

Opening it up, she revealed that inside the box were what appeared to be capsule tablets. She popped one into her mouth, and swallowed, feeling the pill slide down her throat. She placed the others back into the wall, and as it began to take effect, she knelt on the ground.

Her veins became visible throughout her body. To an onlooker, it appeared as though she was 'Hulking out' but in reality, the medicine was suppressing her change. As the feelings passed, and she returned to normal, she went to pick up her phone again, when it began vibrating on its own. She swiped the phone open and answered the incoming call.

"Hi Desmond, I was just about to call you."

"That's certainly a coincidence. I have located the final amulet."

"Really? That's some great work."

"Well… it comes with a surprise too."

"What kind of surprise?"

"The estranged kind."

"Well knowing the powers of that amulet, and knowing you, I think I can work out the surprise part."

"We are probably going to need help examining the amulet. And we had to use the grenade to cover up a crime scene."

"Okay, I'll meet you at the store in about an hour. I'm going to need some help with Duncan, he's having a hard time suppressing his instincts. I'm worried about him."

"Okay well we can discuss it at the store. I'll see you soon."

Daniella put the phone down for a second time, and slipped into her more comfortable shoes, grabbed her keys and headed out of the bedroom. As she walked back down the stairs, she attracted the attention of Grace and Max.

"Hey Mom, you heading out again?"

Daniella nodded.

"I'm going to see some friends about your Dad. He's going to need help."

Grace nodded. She seemed to be the lucky one. All her issues had been reversed, but she wanted to help.

"Anything we can do to help?"

"No thanks sweetie. You and Max have a nice time, and when your Dad gets back, tell him I've gone to find him the help he needs."

"Okay Mom. By the way, any developments in the secret supernatural underworld scene?"

Daniella smirked. She had tried to hide her involvement with Desmond and his team, but Grace had ushered it out of her.

"Desmond has just found a seven hundred year old woman who can't die."

Max's eyes bulged and gave Grace a look that screamed 'did I just hear that right?' before opening his mouth to actually form the words.

Grace held up a hand to stop him and wished her mother luck. As Daniella went to go out the door, she leaned back in, and to wind Max up a little, revealed another detail.

"Oh, and by the way, they've also found the amulet of immortality."

THE KEEPER

The ocean crashed over the pebbles and rocks,
And upon the bows of ships, headed for the docks.
The blue, and the green of the watery beast,
More violent than flame, or a crazed wildebeest.
For the ocean is tempting, and lures people in,
But acts as a graveyard for those with sin.
Our tale begins with a victim of this,
It started fifty years ago, with a simple swift kiss.
You see out on the point where the rocks jut right out,
Into the sea, on the coast, where the waves give some clout,
Stands a tower, so tall, white in colour with a stripe,
Of black round the waist, of the lighthouse type.
The occupant within, was a man of few friends,
And each day without fail, three hundred stairs, he'd ascend.
He'd reach the top, and then check on the light,
And stare out the window, whether day or at night.
The light was his beacon of hope to the world,
And atop of the tower, the state flag was unfurled.
This tower, his domain, where he feels most safe,
One day was the place of sanctuary for a young waif.

One cold lonely night, the wind it did roar,
Came a knock and a whimper, below at the door.
The keeper, a man of caution and fear,
Slowly crept down the stairs, knocks louder as he drew near.
He gazed through the peephole, and standing outside,
Was a young woman in a dress, being battered by the tide.
"Oh, please let me in," came the woman's address,
"A man that is following me, he wishes to possess
My body and soul, and he won't hear my no,
And I'm far from my home and have nowhere to go."
The keeper unsure, but captivated by her face,
Decided to open to the door and allow her access to his place.
She stumbled inside, and fell into his arms,
And one glance at his eyes, and she fell for his charms.
The man who had barely ever spoken to a woman,
As she kissed his cheek, threw out all his notions of caution.
He carried the girl up the stairs to the top,
As he asked for her name, water crashed on the outcrop.
Melinda, her reply, what a beautiful name,
Thought the keeper, she asked his, and he answered the same.
They giggled at such a basic misunderstanding,
But her beauty, to him, was too overwhelming.
He fumbled his words, before finding the right one,
"Victor," he replied as he reached for a bun,
To provide Melinda with some food to eat,
Buns were a rarity for Victor, a special sweet treat.
She accepted this gift with a smile and with thanks,
And was offered some tea, from his secret food bank.
Victor kept everything hidden away,
For once, the lighthouse was broken into during the day.
They took all his clothes, and his food, and his drink,
And painted the walls in slogans, coloured in pink.
'You freak' said the words, on his defaced home,
And this intensified his isolation syndrome.
For when he was a child, and attended his school,
He was just as much of an outcast, the others were cruel.

They teased him and beat him, and tortured him too,
They laughed at his mother who worked at the zoo.
They called her a monkey because of her skin,
And his father was known for his addiction to gin.
You see children are cruel, to all religions and races,
They don't see the harm that they create behind faces.
The damage internal, and like a dark, black hole,
Burrows away under the skin, like a mole.
Victor had dealt with racism most of his life,
And domestic abuse as his dad beat his wife.
One day he had taken his drunken rage too far,
And his mother struck back, hitting him with an iron bar.
She plucked it from the fire, and it glowed with the heat,
But she swung the wrong end in her effort to defeat,
The violence of a man who kept punching her head,
And impaled him with the pointed end, and soon he fell dead.
Horrified by the sight that he saw,
Young Victor screamed loudly and ran out the door.
He found the nearest adult who wasn't blind drunk,
And asked for a policeman, his heart sunk.
As they ran back towards Victor's quaint little house,
Amongst all the adults, he felt like a mouse.
But just as they reached the threshold of the door,
They heard a loud gunshot, and a thud on the floor.
The policeman swung open the door and they saw,
Two bodies, blood flowing all over the floor.
Unable to live with the guilt of her action,
Victor's mother had loaded her abusers' shotgun.
She'd placed the barrel in her mouth, and then pulled the trigger,
And afterwards the children continued to snigger.
Then he was teased as the black orphan boy,
And never again would he ever feel joy.
He locked himself away on his own in the house,
But the sight of his parents haunted this mouse.
He burned down the place, with all his possessions,
And on his sixteenth birthday, found a new obsession.

The vacancy came for the keeper of the light,
And they gave him the job upon first sight.
In truth they cared not for whoever did the job,
But Victor took it on to escape from the mob.
He'd always been a loner, and always abused,
But in his new role as keeper, he was finally amused.
His job had a purpose, to keep sailors safe,
And in his tower kept him from feeling *un*safe.
But tonight, he had company, and she hung on every word,
Despite all his difficulty, and how many he slurred.
The wind howled outside, and the tower grew cold,
The woman, she shivered, and Victor grew bold.
He offered her his coat, and fetched a blanket as well,
Whilst outside, the huge waves continued to swell.
Melinda lay down on the blanket on the floor,
And the coat draped over her, warming her to her core.
She slept, and she slept, and all through the night,
Victor watched over her, until morning's first light.
As they shared breakfast, the sun shining bright,
Melinda described the events of the previous night.
Her companion had been out drinking with a friend,
But as men often do, drank too much in the end.
When Melinda had arrived at the place they had agreed on,
The man was a drunken, stupid, mess of a moron.
She knew she should not have been seeing this man,
And told him her thoughts and turned and she ran.
But the man did not stop with her short tempered words,
He followed her through the streets, stumbling forwards.
He shouted her down, and caught up with his target,
And gripped her arms tight, ripping off her charm bracelet.
He breathed the stench of booze in her terrified face,
And they rolled on the floor and all over the place.
He tore at her dress, determined to get his own way,
But Melinda, she fought, punched his face, and ran away.
She picked up her bracelet, and ran as fast as she could,
Whilst behind her, the moron, exposed his manhood.

"This is what you are missing!" the bastard shouted out,
"Get back here you bitch!" he continued with clout.
But Melinda, she ran, unsure that he was gone,
And saw the lighthouse, and how brightly it shone.
She knew there would be help there, she knew she'd be safe,
But to get there, huge waves she would have to strafe.
They crashed over rocks, and onto the outcrop,
She feared she wouldn't make it and begged the ocean to stop.
But reach it she did, and she banged on the door,
And she ended her story as she sat on the floor.
Victor was captivated with all she had said,
He now felt alive, instead of wishing he was dead.
This woman was perfect, and she confided in him,
But there was one thought that was unsettling him.
At some point, he thought, as he watched a huge wave,
Melinda would leave, and her attention he'd crave.
Luckily for him, she decided to stay,
For as she looked out the window, she saw an affray.
The man who had chased her through the streets last night,
Was beating a homeless man, good Lord, what a sight.
Melinda suggested they help the old man,
And Victor agreed, "I will do what I can."
This woman gave him courage he didn't know he had,
And if he failed, she would leave, and he'd be sad.
So, he marched down the stairs, and flung open the door,
And locked it behind him, Melinda safe, he was sure.
He strolled down the path, splashing water as he went,
And as he locked eyes on the man, he knew what she had meant.
The man was still drunk, and his ramblings offensive,
But when he saw Victor walking, it was the keeper on the defensive.
He left the old man, bloodied and beaten,
And staggered towards Victor, the tale did deepen.
He raised a fist in the air with aggression,
And with the other drank from a flask, another boozy session.
He threw the flask at Victor and off his head it bounced,
And as he protected himself, the moron, he pounced.

The pair of them rolled along the rocky floor,
And behind him, he heard Melinda open the door.
"Go back inside Melinda," Victor shouted,
And with one swift strike, the moron was clouted.
Victor hit him in the side of the head with his own flask,
And he crumpled to the floor, Victor too afraid to ask.
"Sir? Are you alright?" asked the keeper with a tremor,
No reply came from the man, which deepened his terror.
Melinda by this point, retreated inside,
It was too late for the moron, Victor saw, he had died.
He turned on his heels, a tear on his cheek,
He ran into the lighthouse and began to speak.
"No, oh Lord no, I have just killed a man!"
From above, he heard the sound of a knocked over can,
Rolling along the floor and then down the stairs,
Melinda had heard the sound of his woeful prayers.
He climbed up the tower, where she stood waiting by the window,
"You killed the man, I saw you strike the death blow."
Victor was traumatised, this is why he stayed alone,
Melinda disturbed, turned, and reached for the phone.
Victor fearing for his life and for his freedom,
Ran up to her and tore the phone from the woman.
"Please, Miss Melinda, I saved you from him,"
Victor pleaded with the woman, as the daylight started to dim.
"You killed him dead, though a moron he was,
Did not deserve to die," she replied, and then paused.
She saw a new look in the keeper's eyes,
And what she recognised came to her with surprise.
It was a look she had seen in the eyes of the man,
Who had chased her through the streets as she ran.
Her fears were confirmed when Victor said,
"It's not my fault that he found himself dead.
I will protect you Melinda, from now until the end,
And nothing will harm you, you will be my girlfriend."
The events of the last twenty-four hours had caused,
Victor's fragile mind to unfurl, and he thought as he paused.

He closed the door at the top of the tower,
And locked it with the only key and noticed the hour.
"I will keep you safe, and away from the harm,
That others would do us," and he reached for her arm.
She drew away from him, scared for her life,
And reached for the table and picked up a knife.
She held it in front, clear for Victor to see,
But he began to cry, "Look what you've done to me!"
Never before had Melinda witnessed this,
A man losing his mind, and beginning to hiss,
Through the tears and the sight of him pulling his hair,
The man who had saved her last night, no longer there.
He stood firm, and wiped the dew from his face,
And moved over to a chest, an unusual case.
He opened it up and removed a length of rope,
The situation grim, Melinda could no longer cope.
She lunged at Victor, the blade slashing wide,
Missing his arm but penetrating his side.
He screamed out in pain, and he dropped the rope to the floor,
While Melinda attempted to open the door.
Victor looked down at the blood pouring from his hip,
And threw out the rope, causing Melinda to trip.
She fell, hit her head on the corner of the table,
And landed with a thud, she was no longer able,
To escape from the top of the black and white tower,
For Melinda, like the moron, had faced her last hour.
As her blood poured out from the top of her head,
It ran along the wood, turning the floor a dark red.
Victor sat hunched, rocking back and forth quickly,
The sight lay before him was incredibly sickly.
History, it seemed was repeating itself,
Flashbacks to his mum, who couldn't live with herself.
His mind had vacated as his world unravelled,
And now he had lost the thing for which he had battled.
If only he hadn't opened the door,
His first love would not be lying dead on his floor.

He sat staring down at the blood on the ground,
For hours upon hours, as the sun went down.
His face became pale from the loss of his blood,
He knew he had to rectify this situation for good.
He clawed his way up to stand on his feet,
And walked over to where the rope met her feet.
He picked it up from the floor, where he threw it before,
And tied a noose in that rope, before checking the door.
Good, it was locked, nobody else could come in,
And now he would pay for his ultimate sin.
He threw the rope up and around the oak beams,
"My only way out, is this way, it seems."
He spoke so calmly about the action he'd take,
"This is the best thing, for everyone's sake."
He tied off the rope with the use of his ladder,
And as he looked down at the floor, he made himself even madder.
The woman had caused all of his anger and fear,
And never again would he let anyone near.
As the light shone out from the light at the top,
Victor put the noose round his head, and flung himself off,
Of the ladder, and dropped with a sickening crack,
And outside a ship's Captain happened to look back.
As he sailed into the bay, and squinted through the night,
He saw the shadow of Victor hanging in the light.
When the police broke inside the very next day,
The scene was grim, and Victor continued to sway.
They cut him down, and took Melinda away,
But Victor did not leave the lighthouse that day.
His body was thrown into the sea for what he had done,
But his spirit remained, he had not yet gone.
And now every night, the ships in the bay,
See the shadow in the light, of the keeper sway.

And Victor forever, is cursed to stay,
Inside of his lighthouse, swinging away.

INTO DARKNESS

The way the light from the fluorescent fittings glinted off the blade, made James look away sharply. He wasn't one for bright lights. Living in a basement apartment will do that to a man. As he examined the craftsmanship of the handle, the brown, aged leather woven around the top, the perfect curve of the steel as it moved around and down to the first point, he already sensed that this was out of his price range. As many collectibles as James had collected, he had never quite been in a financial slump as he now was, and yet he knew he had to have this piece.

"Okay, so how much is it?" he asked the vendor.

"For a fine Klingon such as yourself? I could part with it for three-thousand."

James choked on his water.

"Dollars?!" he exclaimed.

"No, bars of Gold Pressed Latinum," came the sarcastic reply.

James' expression changed from surprise to acceptance that it was too much. Last month he barely made rent, and nearly had to sell his prized possession, one of the chairs from the set of the *Enterprise-D* Observation Lounge. The vendor seemed to sense this, but his eyes followed another shine from the light to James' waist.

"Hey, what do you have there?" he asked, pointing to the item.

James, confused at first, realised what he was pointing at and removed the dagger from his waist.

"This? I got this from Comic-Con 1994. It's a replica of Worf's dagger from '*Ethics*' where he asks Riker to end his life. Why? You interested?"

James could sense the tables had turned. This was not a replica of Worf's dagger. James had bought this cheap from a cosplayer in the UK and refined it and customised it himself. But this was looking like a worthy loss if it got him the *Bat'leth*.

The vendor nodded and asked to see it close up. James was confident in his work, so handed it over. He seemed convinced. James smiled. He had been making props for years, since *The Next Generation* had started, and he'd gotten pretty good at it.

"It's one of my most prized collectibles. I didn't even wanna take it out today, but it looks so good with the rest of this Klingon uniform. Out of interest, what's it worth to you?"

This was where the battle was won or lost. James could easily make a replacement but had no real idea what the true replica would be worth. It was now that James would see if the guy would be honest or try and scam him. That's why he'd asked *worth to you* rather than simply asking what it was worth.

He turned the blade over in his hand several times, admiring the craftsmanship. The exchange had also attracted the attention of dozens of other people who had come across from other booths to witness what was going on.

"The workmanship is exquisite, and the weight of the handle in comparison to the blade is perfectly balanced. How much did you pay for it?" he asked.

James shook his head.

"I asked you first. Just be assured that it was a lot."

The vendor ran his eyes over it a couple more times, and then announced his offer.

"I'd be willing to give you... eighteen hundred dollars for it, cash in your hand, right now."

James worked very hard to keep his cool but decided to push further.

"Not a chance. You wouldn't budge on the price of the *Bat'leth*, so why should I lower my price to eighteen hundred?"

And the gambit was played. Now to see if the guy would take the bait.

"Okay, fair point. If you let me have the blade, and an extra, say, three hundred, then you can take the *Bat'leth*."

James was close, but that three hundred could really help him with his bills. It was pure addiction to collectibles that had brought him to the convention as it was.

"Straight swap, or no deal. I can get another Bat'leth from someone else, it's only because I'm here and now that I was going to take yours, but if you're not going to be sensible, then hand me back the dagger, and I'll be on my way."

James held his hand out, but the vendor clutched the knife to his chest.

"Fine. Take it. I've got another two at home."

He handed over the large bladed weapon, and immediately reached under the counter to fetch out a safety deposit box. He opened the box, carefully laid the dagger inside, locked it, and put it back again. James had what he wanted, but knew upon further inspection, this guy might notice he'd been conned, so he hung the *Bat'leth* on his back holster and made for the exit. These local conventions were never as good anyway, and the only cast member from any of the shows to show up was Mick Fleetwood, and he only played an alien in one episode, and you didn't even see it was him in the costume.

Jealous eyes watched on as James made his way out of the hall and headed for his car. He loaded the collectible into the back, peeled off his latex forehead piece, and sat himself in the driver's seat. Turning the key in the ignition garnered no response from the engine. James tried again. Nothing. Not even the sound of a concentrated effort. Just the clicking of the key turning and nothing more. Now what was he going to do? He couldn't afford the breakdown cover, he had next to no money saved, and he was ten miles away from home. The bus seemed like the only option, but taking a four foot tall weapon on public transport was a definite no-no. He took as much makeup and prosthetics off as he could and slung them all into the back with the *Bat'leth*, and then fumbled in his pocket for his wallet.

As he fumbled through a few notes, he heard a noise behind him. As he turned around, he was met with a fist to the face, sending him backwards, and as he fell, he caught his head on the wing mirror. He tried to see where the blow had originated, but the assault continued. There were several people, and the kicks were swift and many. James felt at least two ribs cracked as the attackers swung their feet back into his chest repeatedly, and a swift stamp on his head broke his nose.

Finally, the assault relented, and James felt hands rifling through his pockets. Just before he faded into darkness, James heard a familiar voice speak to him.

"I'm not that stupid, you fucking freak."

As the vendor and his chums strolled away with the *Bat'leth*, and James' wallet, a couple of them stayed behind, and smashed every window in the car, and then began kicking in the lights. The last thing James heard, was the clanging of his own dagger landing on the floor next to him as he fell unconscious.

The air was almost vicious on his skin. The cold breeze penetrated each pore and felt like tiny little icicles stabbing the surface. As James walked out of the hospital entrance, it suddenly dawned on him. He had no possessions. All he had on him, were the clothes the police found him in. They had taken his wallet, his keys, his *Bat'leth*. And God knows what had happened to his car. It had been three days since James woke up in the hospital, and the entire time, he remained silent. He blamed himself for the attack at first, because it had been him that had conned the vendor into the switch. He had chosen that moment to gain his confidence and look where it had got him. As the rain began to fall, he started walking in the vague direction of his apartment.

The wind mixed with the harsh rain had James feeling that soon, he would be back in the hospital with pneumonia or hypothermia.

"At least hospital was warm," he muttered aloud.

He didn't remember the last time he had been able to afford the heating in his apartment. The electric heater used too much power, so he spent most of his time snuggled under blankets to save money. But it wasn't the same as a nice warm home.

Walking past the cinema, he could feel groups of eyes on him, this half-dressed Klingon warrior, and heard them start to giggle and tease him.

"Hey, get a load of Captain Nerd!"

"Looks like he's been fed through a woodchipper."

James turned and gave them a brief disparaging look, and they took the hint, and walked into the cinema entrance, asking the cashier for two tickets for *Spider-Man*, and taking one last look at James, giggling as they entered the lobby. James had planned to go to that very cinema two days ago. He was reminded as he fiddled in his pockets, and managed to find the rain soaked, mushed up ticket for *Star Trek : Nemesis*.

"Guess I won't be seeing that now," he muttered under his breath, grimacing at the sharp pain from his broken ribs.

As he rounded the street corner and approached the steps leading down to his apartment, he noticed the gate at the top of those steps was locked. As he wiped the rain away from his eyes, and squinted at the notice on the gate, he felt angry tears mixing with the rain.

The note read…

This is a notice of eviction. Due to your failure to pay the agreed amount of rent during the previous two months, the landlord has seized control of the property. You (the tenant) are no longer allowed to enter the premises without the attendance of the landlord. All goods inside have been seized to recoup the outstanding arrears. Do not attempt to re-enter the property, upon threat of imprisonment.

James slumped to the ground, and placed his face in his hands, forgetting his nose was broken, and causing a sharp pain to shoot through his head.

"AAAARRRGGGHHH!"

A passing delivery boy gave him a quick glance, but continued past, and as James' clothes absorbed more and more rain water, he knew he could not stay here. Gazing down through the window, he saw all his belongings were gone. All his collectibles, prized items. His chair. All were gone. He was pretty sure what the landlord had done was illegal, but he didn't have any way of challenging it. At least, not right now. The only hope he had, was to find his car. So that is what he decided to do.

After three hours of slopping around in the rain, shoes now full of water, James finally made the ten mile trip back to where his car was last seen. And sure enough, the car was there. In a manner of speaking. James stood around eight feet away gazing at the hollowed out shell of the vehicle that used to belong to him. At this point, any ordinary person would have broken down in a heap on the floor. But not James. He just stood there, staring at the burnt out carcass.

Overhead, thunder clapped, and lightning lit up the sky with a purple haze. Through all the emotion in his head, James was distracted by something shiny on the floor near one of the axles. As he walked towards it, the sky lit up again with more flashes of purple light. The closer he got, the more frequent the flashes of purple in the sky, and the rumbling of the thunder became more intense.

James approached the object, and he saw what it was that had caught his eye. It was his dagger. The handle was blackened by the fire that had engulfed the car, but otherwise the blade was undamaged.

James felt an attraction to the blade, almost like magnetism. In his head, there were unusual and strange feelings. He didn't *want* to pick up the knife, but he *needed* to pick it up. The sky was now awash with purple fog, flashes of light, and above him, a large violet cloud was forming. James began to feel a static around his head, and his body began to tingle. Then, as if targeted, there was an immense roar of thunder, and a purple bolt shot out from the fog, striking James directly in the chest as he picked up the knife. The blast sent James hurtling across the car park, and he came to rest over fifty feet from where he started. He felt dazed, and his head was swimming in random thoughts, and as he looked up, he saw the cloud had gone, as did any evidence of a storm. The only constant was the rain, which had never stopped.

James carefully got to his feet and walked to lean on the nearby railing of a bench. His head was full of thoughts that were not his own. It almost felt as though he was a spectator in his own head and was watching a series of horror movies play out in his mind. He saw images of death, flashes of suicides, and blood. So much blood.

He raised his hands either side of his head, and clamped his eyes shut, but the images remained. The level of pain now coursing through his mind was enough to knock a man unconscious, but somehow he remained upright. And then... clarity. James had an image in his mind, and it was the only image in focus. He walked about six feet forwards, knelt, and picked up the dagger, the point dragging along the floor scraping the concrete as he lifted it to his side. His eyes were focused and deep within his iris, was a flash of purple, and then he walked out of the car park at pace and headed off towards down-town.

"Yeah, look if you want the damn thing then just go online and bid for it."

"Surely we can come to some sort of arrangement by buying now. I can make you an excellent offer."

"I'm not interested. This piece will go for three thousand easily at a convention."

"Look, if I give you two thousand, would you trade something from my collection?"

"Look buddy, I've already been burnt once this week, I'm not letting it happen again, sorry."

Craig put the phone down, hard, and went back to the kitchen. The rice was nearly done, and the smell of salted water emanated from the stove.

"God damn cheapskates," he muttered to himself as he drained the water from the rice.

There was a bang from the living room, and the sound of glass breaking. Craig put the saucepan down, wiped his hands, and peered through the doorway. The TV was still on, showing an old rerun of *Knight Rider*. Craig watched as Michael hit the turbo boost button and giggled out loud to himself at how ridiculously unrealistic the landings had been given the angles of the car in the previous shots.

There was another scuffle to the left, and Craig snapped his neck around to find the source. Seeing nothing in the dim light from the TV, he switched on a lamp, and noticed that his figure of the fourth *Doctor Who* was on the floor. Movement in the corner of his eye made him jump, and as his cat ran past his feet, he breathed a sigh of relief.

"God damn it Tom!" he shouted.

He picked the figure back up off the floor, and walked back through the kitchen doorway. As the knife erupted from the back of his throat, Craig's body convulsed violently, his hands knocking cups and plates off the kitchen counter with their movements. The hand connected to the blade pulled it out of Craig's neck and allowed the body to drop to the floor.

As the blood seeped onto the white kitchen tiles, Tom the cat watched from the back of the sofa, hissing at the sight. Craig grasped at his throat with his hands, trying to stem the blood flow, gasping for air, but his eyes bulged as the figure loomed closer once again.

The blade raised in the light of the kitchen, glinted, blood dripping from the tip, and as Craig extended an arm in protest, the blade was plunged down from height into his chest. The blood splattered the kitchen cupboards as the knife repeatedly made its way in and out of Craig's now lifeless body.

There was now no surface in the kitchen untouched by red, and as the knife was removed from Craig's chest for the thirty-second and final time, James stood up, turned, and walked back through the broken window in the front door, a blank facial expression, and a flash of purple in his eyes.

The next morning, the sunlight shattered the sky, no clouds anywhere, just a bright blue canvas. People walking past the TV store glanced at the news bulletin on all the screen, detailing the brutal murder of a local memorabilia vendor.

A low grumble came from the alleyway behind the store, and a rustling from between the garbage bags, that had been spilled from the dumpster. As James pulled himself into a seated position, he found himself completely disorientated. His head was once again swimming with confusion. His vision was off centre, and there was a distinct pain behind his eyes. He couldn't remember where he was, or how he had gotten there, but what he did manage to see sent him into a shockwave of panic. As his eyes managed to focus on his own body, he could see that his clothes were no longer soaked with rain water but soaked with blood. *And it wasn't his own blood.*

He scrambled to his feet, pushing himself back against the wall of the alley, and tore the coat from his body, but it was no good. The blood had seeped through all his clothes. The panic consumed him, and he tore all his clothes from his body, and threw them as far away as he could, before running out into the street, narrowly missing being hit by a car. A sharp pain jabbed him in the ankle as he ran up the opposite curb, and he fell against the wall of the corner Deli. As he looked down, he saw the handle of his Klingon dagger sticking out from his boot.

James' mind was unravelling. He was slipping into darkness and despair. The thoughts bombarding his mind were crushing his own personality and were fighting for control of him and his body.

"NO!" he shouted. "GET OUT! GET OUT OF MY MIND!"

Dozens of people were now standing staring at this apparent crazy man, rambling in the streets. One man offered to help James, but he lashed out and shoved him backwards, and sprinted off down the street once more. He spotted a washing line hanging between two apartment buildings, and scrambled up the fire escape, slipping on steps on every flight as he climbed them. He snatched the washing from the line and as he fought his own body to put the clothes on, he collapsed on the metal plate, and began sobbing uncontrollably.

"What is happening to me? Please… somebody…make it stop!"

James' crying had attracted attention from the owner of the clothes he had just stolen, and watching him, he saw James try and fail to get to his feet again. He offered an olive branch.

"You know, if you'd have asked, I'd have just given you the clothes."

James looked up, and between the images of murder and death, he saw the kind face of an older man, maybe mid-fifties, holding a cup of coffee and leaning out of the window.

"I-I'm... I'm s...s..sorry. I'm not... I'm not... my mind... broken."

The man extended a hand towards James.

"Come on inside, son. You need help. Or at least a coffee."

James looked through his tears, his eyes now swollen to double their usual size. He had no idea what was happening to him, but he needed help. He reached out his own hand, and took the man's, and allowed himself to be led inside the apartment.

"I honestly don't know. One minute, I was standing in front of my car, and then the next... I just don't know."

James sipped his coffee, whilst he explained what he could to the kind man.

"It sounds like you went through a hell of a night, my friend," he replied. "My name is Herman. What's yours?"

"James. My name is James. I think."

"You think? You really did have a bad night," Herman replied.

Suddenly, James began sobbing again.

"What's wrong James?" asked Herman.

But he couldn't answer, his breathing was choked, and he couldn't catch a breath. His eyes began to flash purple, and inside his mind, James was being subjected to increasingly painful images. But these weren't normal images, they were playing out almost like *memories*. Some kind of painful virus was breaching his mind, and he wasn't strong enough to fight it.

In the kitchen, Herman was calling for an ambulance, as James began convulsing on the carpet. As he did so, the blade fell out of his boot onto the carpet. Herman looked at the blade, and the red stain on the sock where it had fallen. Something wasn't right here. Who had he invited into his home? Upon confirmation that the ambulance was on its way, Herman replaced the handset and moved towards James.

"James, can you hear me? James? I've called an ambulance, everything is going to be alright, you just need to hang in there."

He glanced back at the knife and moved his hand towards it. As he touched the handle, he felt a spark of electricity, almost like static shoot into his hand. The pain caused him to stumble back.

As he shook off the niggling pain from the discharge, he noticed that James was now sat bolt upright, looking towards the door. The dagger was now in his hand, gripped tight, knuckles turning white, with the intensity of that grip. Herman attempted to make contact again.

"James, please. Are you alright?"

No answer.

"James, please, put the knife down. The ambulance will be here any minute."

Again, no answer.

Herman looked at James' face, and his eyes. His eyes were glowing purple. Almost like a swirl of mist in each one. And they were darting back and forth, like he was trying to look at a million things at once. Against his better judgement, Herman moved towards James once again. Below, out of the window, he heard the siren of the ambulance arrive at the entrance to the building, thankful there had been one nearby.

Herman extended his arms in peace, as he moved towards James, his grip on the dagger still as strong as it had been, his eyes watching it intently.

"James, the ambulance is here, and they're going to take care of you. Then when all this is over, you can come and see my little shop. I could do with an assistant, maybe I could give you some work."

There was a knock at the door, and the paramedics walked in. Three bodies made their way towards James, but before Herman could warn them about the blade, James had become a possessed man. He leapt to his feet, pushing Herman back onto the floor, and with one swift strike, he flashed the blade across the throat of the nearest paramedic, spraying blood up the wall of Herman's lounge, who was now cowering near the fire escape, watching in terror. As the first body fell to the floor, the other two paramedics tried to tackle James to the floor, each taking a side, but he shook one of them free, and plunged the dagger into the back of the second, and pinned him to the floor, plunging the blade in and out of the poor man's torso. The third paramedic leapt onto James' back and tried to wrestle him off, but he was too strong. The knife continued until thirty-two wounds had been applied. *Thirty-two stab wounds.* What was the significance of that?

James' consciousness momentarily re-emerged and saw what he had done. He shrieked at the top of his lungs and dropped the dagger from his hand. Everything happened in slow motion. The third paramedic slid off him, exhausted, as James glared at the bloody mess before him. However, before the dagger hit the ground, the purple spark reignited, and James snatched the knife from the air, span, and plunged it into the side of the third paramedic's neck.

As the blood continued to spurt, James tackled him to the floor, and continued plunging the blade until it had reached thirty-two. By this point, Herman was scrambling down the fire escape as fast as he could move, screaming for help as he went. Inside the apartment, James had stopped near the first paramedic, still flickering with life. He looked down, and behind the eyes, James was becoming more and more aware of what he was doing. He grasped the sides of his head, but as the imagery intensified, he screamed again, and dropped to the floor, stabbing the man until all three men had the same number of wounds. The carpet was thick with blood.

"What do you mean he doesn't know?" asked the detective.

The sergeant shrugged his shoulders.

"I mean, he doesn't know."

The detective seemed unimpressed by this statement.

"How can he not know that he's killed four people?"

"Look, all he has said to every question that we have asked since we brought him in, is 'I don't know' and 'I'm sorry'."

The detective looked back through the glass at James, who was handcuffed to the table, seemingly chattering to himself.

"What's that? What is he saying?" asked the detective. The sergeant hit the audio switch, and they listened in.

"Pain, so much pain. Too much pain. Why is there so much pain? Death, death. I killed them. But did *I* kill them, so much pain, I can't take any more, please, please make it end."

The two police officers looked at each other, neither one of them able to understand anything that James was saying. They flicked the audio switch off again, and the detective left the room, and entered the interview room, as the sergeant watched from behind the two way mirror. James looked up briefly as he entered the room, and then returned to his mumblings.

"James. My name is Detective Greenwood. I understand you were apprehended at the scene of a triple homicide. Are you aware of that?"

James began picking at his fingernails, nervously, but erratically. He didn't offer an audible answer. Greenwood tried again.

"James, we found a weapon on your possession that we believe was involved in the murder of Craig Birch less than twenty-four hours ago. Can you tell me about that?"

"I-I-I don't know. So much... so much pain. I see them!"

Greenwood saw what he thought was a flash of purple in James' eyes. It was the same experience that Herman had described to the officers when they took his statement.

"What is it, James? What do you see?"

With this question, James' head snapped up and looked directly at the detective. As James began to speak, it became very clear that it was no longer James who was speaking.

"*I see them all. Their pain. All of them. They speak through me because they can no longer speak.*"

Greenwood shifted his chair back a little, disturbed by this turn of events, but also needing more information.

"Who is it that can no longer speak, James?" More flashes of purple, swirling in James' eyes.

"*The five million slain. Their energies are within me. I see all their suffering, their death, their pain. I see it all.*"

Greenwood heard a tap on the glass from behind the mirror and held his hand up for patience.

"What are you?" he asked.

James let out a blood-curdling scream, tears streaming down his face.

"We are the voices of those whose voices were taken away by the betrayer. The one who silenced us. We are the memories of those taken to fuel evil!"

"Who silenced you? Who killed you?"

"She did. The woman of mistrust. She who must be stopped. She will destroy our realm and yours. She must be stopped!"

James' body started to weaken, and he could not stop his sobbing. Again, a tap on the glass from behind Greenwood, and again he held his hand for patience.

"Who is she, James? Who is the woman who must be stopped?"

James garnered his strength again and strained against the handcuffs. He looked at Greenwood, and his head twisted to one side. He did not offer an answer to this question however, so Greenwood tried another question.

"Why do all the victims have thirty-two stab wounds, James? What is the significance of thirty-two?"

Unexpectedly, James began to laugh.

"We are the council of thirty-two."

"What is the council of thirty-two?"

James laughed again.

"Thirty-two control us all. The thirty-two failed to stop her, and now all thirty-two must also die."

"Who is she?"

James laughed again, and this angered Greenwood, who stood up abruptly and repeated the question, raising his voice to a shouting level.

"WHO IS SHE?!"

James stood up with speed, and ripped the handcuffs from the table, raising them above his head. He let out a roar and looked Greenwood directly in the eyes.

"Jasmine."

There was a moment of confusion from Greenwood, and silence from James, but it lasted only a moment. James rushed over the table, and grabbed Greenwood by the throat, thrusting him into the mirror, shattering the glass all over the floor. Greenwood fought to break the grip on his neck, but James' did not weaken.

Officers scrambled into the room, launching themselves at James, and managed to drag him away from the detective, and out of the room.

Greenwood dropped to the floor, choking for air, and holding his neck. The commotion continued in the hallway, as he looked around at the mess. There was a sharp stinging in his back, and as he reached round, he felt a piece of glass protruding from his back. Through gritted teeth, he yanked the glass free, and examined it in his hand.

In the hallway, there were screams of pain, and several different voices. James was putting up quite a fight. As Greenwood began to relax on the floor, the door burst open again, and James came tearing towards him. As he reached Greenwood, he raised the piece of glass, and James ran right onto it, the glass plunging into his heart.

He fell back, and Greenwood sat on the floor, still clutching the piece of glass. When he realised, he dropped it to the floor, letting it shatter amongst the rest, and moved over towards James, who was coughing blood. Greenwood looked over at him, the purple haze now gone from his eyes. James grabbed onto the detective's shirt, and pulled him closer, his breathing becoming more laboured. As Greenwood leaned in, James whispered four words that terrified him.

"She's coming for you."

DYING TO DIE

As the coffin was lowered slowly into the ground, the clouds began to mass in the sky above. The creaking of the wheels in the mechanism was almost deafening. Almost *mocking*. A gentle hand on the shoulder, a reassuring pat on the back, and several hugs later, and Deanna was alone in the cemetery. Her eyes had not moved from the grave of her final child. Of course, everyone else believed *her* to be the child. How could they not. Deanna appeared no more than thirty-five years old, but in reality, she was considerably older.

She watched as the men shovelled the final scoops of earth into the hole, filling the grave, wishing it was her lying in the wooden box, six feet below the ground. She had lived so long, that life and time no longer had any meaning. As the dirt was levelled, she finally turned away and walked towards her car. There was no emotion on her face for the death of her son. No feelings of sadness, or feelings of yearning for his company. Only jealousy, and loathing for whatever force refused to allow her to rest.

She climbed into her car, slammed the door, and sat staring at the steering wheel in front of her. This was one of the nicer cars she had owned, which oddly gave her a little comfort. She usually went under the radar in a family station wagon, or an older saloon, but when her son passed away, she had decided to just splash out, and bought herself a Jaguar XK. Naturally, that meant she had to deal with the sneering looks of her neighbours, who had assumed that she had already cashed in on her 'father's' inheritance money, and despite her protests that she had just been promoted at work, the looks continued.

Her son, Damien, had been seventy-two when he succumbed to cancer. He had been Deanna's fortieth child. She had lost count of the number of times that she had needed to alter her last name over the centuries, but she was growing sick and tired of the never ending onslaught of new jobs, pretending her children were her parents, inventing new and exciting back stories, and quite simply, of being in existence.

She had watched all her children die before her, and each of her twelve husbands go the same way. When Damien had been born, she was not married to his father, Arnold. She had decided that she had been a wife, and a widow too many times, and was just looking for something more casual. But, being the nineteen-twenties, casual relationships were frowned upon, and despite her resistance, Deanna had yet again fallen in love and into the trap of repetition.

She started the engine, and the usual growl came from under the bonnet, which made her smile just for a moment. The one thing she had appreciated through all the different time periods, through the famines, the disasters, and the wars, was the advancement in technology. She had once owned a horse to travel across the country, and now she had the equivalent of two hundred and eighty of those under her right foot. She gripped the steering wheel, feeling the hand stitched leather in her fingers, shifted the car into gear, and slammed the pedal to the floor. The car screeched away, squirrelling with the power, tyres spinning, and massive clouds of smoke pouring into the atmosphere.

Deanna swerved through the cemetery gates sideways and out onto the main road, narrowly missing several cars coming in the opposite direction. She shifted up one gear after the other and glanced down at the speedometer as she gunned through the streets. Another gear change, now one hundred and four miles per hour. A swift down shift, and a haul of the wheel to the right, and she drifted onto the beach front.

Again, her foot planted to the floor, she headed straight, weaving between the traffic.

She cranked the radio up, as *Big Gun* started to play. Her eyes narrowed as she focussed on the road. A truck pulled out in front of her, but there was no change in her demeanour, and as AC/DC continued to scream through the speakers, she yanked the wheel to the right, slammed on the brakes, lifted the handbrake, and almost in slow motion, slid the car underneath the trailer of the truck, spinning three- sixty, and emerging on the other side, once again facing forwards.

The sound of breaking glass, and crumpled metal filled the air behind her, but Deanna did not stop. One glance to her left and she saw her destination. At the next junction, again, she downshifted, and drifted across all four lanes of traffic, and began gunning down the pier. As the road ended, she flew up onto the boardwalk, people diving in every direction, screams filling the air. Deanna continued to accelerate, now hitting ninety-five as she blew past the ring toss game, and the 'Hungry Caterpillar' rollercoaster. Security guards began chasing after the car, but there was no hope for them. Deanna shifted up one more gear, and the car hit one-hundred-twenty, as it smashed through the wooden fence at the end of the pier. The car soared through the air like an arrow fired from a crossbow, and as it began plunging towards the tranquil blue waters, Deanna closed her eyes.

"Here we go again."

The snow was getting more and more intense as the minutes went by and it was now increasingly difficult to see through the windscreen. Perfect. Deanna had chosen so many places to find a way out, and none of them had worked. She should have known when she survived the *Titanic* sinking, that was a sure fire sign that nothing could take her down. As she slid around the next bend, at a ridiculous speed, the truck veered off the road, down an embankment, and started to roll.

Glass and metal smashed, and crunched, until finally the truck came to rest at the edge of a frozen lake. But it hadn't worked.

Deanna kicked open the door to the truck, and climbed out onto the ice, with nothing more than a small cut to her forehead.

"God damn it!" she shouted, and her voice echoed around for miles.

Even the ice refused to crack. Deanna scooted out until she was several metres from the safety of the bank and began jumping up and down with as much force as she could muster, but nothing. The ice was too thick, and with every jump, her frustration was growing and sapping her energy, until finally, she collapsed to her knees, and began to cry. In the background, her truck caught fire, but she didn't notice.

Deanna's mind was now in complete turmoil. She didn't want to live where life no longer had any meaning, and yet she couldn't die. She had tried to end her life over a hundred times now, and not once had she been successful in getting anywhere near death. She had needed to swim for miles after her leap from the pier just to get away from the wreckage of the car, to fool people into believing she was indeed deceased. The sea had refused to claim her, just as the roll down the hill had failed to kill her. Every time she tried to end her life, she had to relocate. An endless cycle of pointless misery.

In the early days, before she really understood what was going on, her families had given her life meaning. Whilst she was devastated as she lost and outlived each one, with the next, she had the chance to live that experience again. But even the joy of family meant nothing now. It wasn't enough. She had lived through so many lifetimes now, that even raising and loving a family meant nothing to her. She was without purpose.

"Perhaps this really is hell, and I've been dead all along," she thought aloud to herself, as she choked back her tears.

Sniffing her nose, and breathing fog into the cool air, she raised herself to her feet. The truck fire was now burning quite intensely and was beginning to have an adverse effect on the ice. Deanna, began to walk back towards the edge of the lake, unaware of the events now in motion. As the heat intensified again, the fuel tank in the truck blew, and the shockwave knocked Deanna off her feet, and sent a thunderous crack straight down the middle of the ice. The vibration reverberated underneath Deanna's body, and as she looked towards the bank, the ice gave way, and she plunged into the freezing waters below.

Instinct began to kick in, and she fought for the surface, losing breath with every motion as the sheer icy grip of the water began to freeze her joints. And then it hit her. This is what she had wanted all along. She stopped fighting, and gradually allowed her lungs to release their air. Her limbs began to freeze up, and she could feel the blood crystallizing in her veins. Perhaps this was it, finally, as painful as it was, this was finally her escape from life.

As she began to fall into a deep sleep, an arm plunged into the water, and wrapped itself around her hair. Pulling hard, but with no reaction from the nearly unconscious Deanna, she was lifted from the icy waters. As she opened her eyes, she found that she was seemingly in an embrace with a young woman. Was this heaven? Had she finally been released from her cursed existence? And then her weary eyes noticed the truck burning in the background, and anger grew within her. She shoved the woman backwards, and coughed up a lungful of icy water, rolling onto her front, and slamming the ground with her fists.

"Hey! Hey are you okay? Take it easy!"

The reassuring tone of the stranger's voice made Deanna even more mad. She didn't want help, she wanted to die. As the woman approached her again, she span and launched a scathing attack on her rescuer.

"You fucking idiot! I didn't want rescuing! I wanted to end it all! There is NOTHING for me in this life, you hear me? NOTHING!"

The stranger held her hands up in a defensive posture and backed away a little as Deanna staggered forwards toward her.

"I have spent centuries trying to release myself from this place, and I might have been within touching distance, and you come along and ruin it! Why won't I just be allowed to die!"

Deanna's emotions got the better of her and she fell back to her knees in the snow, sobbing, and shivering from the realisation that her clothes were seeped in icy water. The strange woman approached cautiously again.

"Listen, I-I'm sorry that you're upset. I saw the smoke from the road, and when I saw you fall in, I just knew I had to pull you out of there."

Deanna looked up, feeling shame at the anger directed towards this woman. As far as she was concerned, she had seen a stranger in trouble, and leapt into action. She had no idea what she had interrupted, and now Deanna felt the need to apologise.

"I'm sorry. You just don't understand what it has been like. I have nothing left here. I-I... thank you."

Slightly confused, but eased that Deanna was starting to calm down, the woman sprinted up the embankment, where Deanna could see a car parked at the side of the road. Moments later, she slid back down, and wrapped a blanket around Deanna's shoulders, and pressed it tight to her body. Deanna nodded in thanks.

"My name is Scarlett. What's yours?"

"Deanna."

"Nice to meet you, Deanna. Now how about we get you somewhere warm, and have you checked out?"

Deanna reluctantly nodded and allowed Scarlett to help her climb back up the embankment, and eased herself slowly into the car.

As Scarlett put the car into drive, Deanna looked back down at the lake, thinking how close she had come to success, and yet again, how something had prevented her from leaving this place. One thing was for sure, the cold had made her very sleepy, and combined with the heat now billowing from the car's air vents, she began to drift off.

"No, no, come on Deanna, I need you to stay awake, you might have hypothermia or some shit."

Scarlett nudged Deanna back into alertness.

"I guess you're just determined to keep me alive, huh?" she asked in what she meant as a scathing tone, but Scarlett took as a joke.

As the car made its way down the snowy road, they passed a road sign, indicating the next town was four miles away. The name of the town meant nothing to her. And although she had never heard of the place before, she allowed herself to slide back towards sleep once more. She was soon shaken out of the daze, however, by a direct question from Scarlett.

"Centuries?"

Deanna paused.

"I'm sorry?"

"You said you'd been trying to end things for *centuries*."

Deanna was now fully aware of just how psychotic she had been on the ice and wondered how much more she had revealed. She decided to try and brush it off.

"Did I? I must have been hallucinating or something. That water was damn cold, I don't even know what I was thinking let alone saying."

Scarlett wasn't biting.

"Bull shit."

Deanna looked over at her rescuer with surprise and a raised eyebrow.

"Don't give me that Dwayne Johnson smoulder, Missy. I heard what you said, and you definitely weren't lying. So, what is up with you?"

Deanna was a little bit taken aback by the directness of the young woman, and a little bit amused by the DJ comparison, one of the many impressions she had managed to perfect over her more recent years.

"Look, I just had a bad day, took my eyes off the road, and then here we are."

Deanna looked back out the window, and Scarlett shook her head again.

"So how many bad days have you had over the last couple of hundred years? Ten, maybe fifteen?"

They both exchanged looks and started laughing with each other. Deanna was unsure if she was being serious or not. But Scarlett offered up some more words.

"Deanna, I don't know if you noticed, but I wasn't surprised by what you said."

She hadn't thought about it, because of the rage she had been in, but Scarlett was right. When Deanna had shouted at her, the expressions on her face didn't move from a slightly concerned look. There was no hint of thought that she may be crazy, or dangerous. Only of concern.

"Actually, I did."

"Well, whether you choose to believe me or not, you're going to find that there are much stranger things going on in this town."

As Deanna looked out of the window, a large blue sign appeared at the roadside.

'*Welcome to Wealdstone*'.

"So, what do you think, Doc? Is she all good?"

The doctor put down his clipboard and folded his arms.

"Yes, I think she is going to be fine. I'd like to run a few more checks in a few days, just to see how she is getting on, but I think you're good to go."

Deanna was trying to count in her mind all the times that a doctor or physician had told her she was going to be fine. It still annoyed the hell out of her every time. With the hypocratic oath rattling around in their brain all the time, they never considered that she didn't want to be fine. Nevertheless, she expressed her gratitude, and her and Scarlett left the building.

"You wanna get something to eat?" offered Scarlett.

Deanna began to feel the cycle repeating again.

"Look, Scarlett, I'm grateful for all you've done, but maybe I should be heading off on my own. I don't want to impose on you any longer."

Scarlett didn't really take any notice of what she had said and gestured for her to get back in the car.

"No, seriously, I think I should go."

Scarlett gestured again. Deanna gave in.

"Okay, fine. Something to eat, and then I'm gone."

Scarlett smiled as she celebrated her victory. As they sat in the car, Deanna turned to her and asked a question she already knew the answer to.

"You always get your way, don't you?"

A wider smile spread across her face as they headed into town.

"So, be honest with me. Was what you said at the lake true?"

Scarlett was talking between mouthfuls of bacon and scrambled eggs, but her eyes were focussed on Deanna.

"Look, as I said..."

"No, no, I want the truth Deanna. Come on, I saved your life. You owe me."

Deanna took a deep breath and lowered her fork to her plate, all her levity gone from her face.

"What is it?" Scarlett asked.

"I just... I don't know what to say to you. Something about you makes me feel like I can trust you, but I don't even know you."

"Yeah, I get that a lot." she replied. "But it isn't me. It's something about this town."

"What do you mean?"

Deanna was now slightly taken off course by that response.

"There are things in this town, that we will never fully understand."

Scarlett's face was now deadly serious.

"Are you really doing the intro to *Ghost Adventures* right now?"

Deanna may have been hundreds of years old, but good TV is good TV. Scarlett burst out laughing.

"Oh, come on, you could have at least finished it!"

The laughing continued, and in the background, the last customer left the diner. With a quick look around, to make sure nobody was listening, Deanna leaned closer and pressed for more details.

"What kind of things?"

Scarlett wiped her mouth, and put her fork down, pushing her plate away.

"Okay, so there have been some seriously weird things happening here. When I was a kid, I saw a vampire."

Deanna's eyebrows raised again.

"A vampire?" she asked.

Scarlett nodded.

"Like... *Angel* style, or *Blade* style?"

Scarlett did not laugh.

"Deanna, I'm serious. I saw like red glowing eyes, and then this girl stepped out of the shadows, and her teeth *grew*. I tried to tell my mother, but by the time she looked, the girl had gone."

"And you think you saw a vampire?"

"There's more. There have been reports of ghosts up at the Highland

Manor House. And when a bunch of Bagans wannabes went up there, one of them ended up dead."

Deanna had to admit, that did intrigue her. Scarlett continued.

"And literally three days ago, there were sightings of some kind of monster rampaging around near the Silverton Shopping District."

"A monster?"

"Well, the witnesses said it was like a bear, but bigger, and it had huge fangs instead of teeth."

"Do you know how ridiculous all this sounds," asked Deanna.

"Well tell me if your story is any less ridiculous."

She had her there. Deanna's story would sound insane under normal circumstances. But she had a feeling that Scarlett would drink this in as fact.

"Okay. But no interruptions. It's a long story, so I'd better start at the beginning."

Scarlett shuffled to get comfortable, and then gestured for Deanna to begin.

"It all started when I was thirty years old."

13th June 1352

"Being thirty years old, was quite frankly, doing well given the time I was born into. I was born in Britain, and I was a weaver. Every morning, I would go and collect my materials and I would return home, and create baskets, or bedding, and sell them at the market. And then I saw him.

I'd been married once before, but you must understand that we were living in a time of the Black Death, and it had swept entire countries to their knees. Everywhere you went, there were bodies in the streets, and sickness at every turn. My first husband had died when I was nineteen, and I'd chosen not to seek another. At least that was the plan originally.

I'd lost my mother and my father to the disease, and it was the village healer who had eased their suffering, and he too had lost his wife and daughter to the deadly plague. I felt a connection with him, and we shared pleasant memories together whenever we had free time.

Unfortunately, there was another woman who desired this man, and she was a practitioner of unearthly ways.

Of course, you must understand that witchcraft and the occult were very much believed and feared. In fact, all throughout history, people have been afraid of the magical and the unknown. But I was a naive woman. I felt that if there were such wonders, that surely they could be used to cure this awful killer disease, and as they hadn't, then they couldn't possibly be real.

I found myself alone in my hut when she confronted me. She warned me away from the healer, and I refused. She warned me again, and a second time I refused. And that is when she spoke words from a language I did not know, and began chanting, and spreading items around my home. I attempted to get her to stop, but she just carried on, and slapped me to the ground when I tried to leave.

When she was done, she moved to the entrance of my hut and turned and spoke to me in English. She said that I was now a cursed woman. I may live in happiness and love with the healer for the rest of his life, but not the rest of mine. I was now doomed to walk the Earth forever more, never dying, never ageing, where I would watch my loved ones come and go, and watch them wither and die, whilst I carried on living.

This woman then left my home, and I never saw her again. I did indeed marry the healer, and we had a short, but wonderful life together, raising two daughters, until his death at just forty-seven. I tried to ignore the fact that I did not seem to be ageing a day, and as our daughters grew, they too became unnerved by the notion that they were beginning to look older than their mother. I lost them both before their time, taken by the same plague.

As everyone around me began to wither and die, just as the woman had predicted, I remained unaltered, and I began to understand the true pain of what she had done.

There was hope for my suffering to end, when there was a terrible storm on the eve of my second daughter's death, and lightning hit our home, setting the building alight. Unfortunately, as I accepted that I was about to die, I closed my eyes. When I woke up, the house was gone, but I was lying in the ruins, almost completely untouched by the flame.

Time, though is a wonderful healer. As I lost one family, I began a new one. I shared the love and lives of many children and husbands. I even had a couple of wives throughout the years. But after each family died away, I was forced to relocate.

A woman who appeared to be thirty years old for over twenty years, tended to raise suspicions after a while. I moved around Britain for three centuries, but before too long, I realised that it was becoming more and more difficult for this to continue. I managed to barter passage to the 'new world' on the *Mayflower*, sailing from Plymouth in 1620. But several issues caused the *Mayflower* and the ship she was travelling with, the *Speedwell*, to turn back twice.

July 1620

It was at the second time of returning to Plymouth, that I met my eighth husband, Desmond. As we disembarked the ship to allow for repairs, I fell into the water off the dock, and he jumped in to rescue me. A common occurrence for me, falling into water, as it seems. I decided not to travel on the *Mayflower* as it left for the third and final time and remained in Plymouth with Desmond.

We were married for a very short time. He was brutally murdered on the Barbican by a gathering of drunken louts, who decided they wanted his money to spend on more drink in the local tavern. When they were done with him, they threw his body into the harbour, and again I suffered the pain of losing a loved one and had also lost my chance of getting away from my home country.

I was beside myself when I discovered that I was pregnant again following Desmond's death. Previously, I had been overjoyed at getting to see my children grow up, but after three centuries, and so many losses, I was distraught. None of my children had been blessed with children of their own, so the added hurt of each family coming to a complete end, was starting to affect my mental state. I seriously considered a dangerous procedure to abort the baby. I found myself locating a man who would attempt the process, but when it came to it, I just couldn't go through with it.

My son was born, and I named him Desmond after his father. But even then, something was missing. I was surrounded by the constant knowledge that I would outlive my son, and I had to try and explain to him how his mother did not age. He thought I was telling him a tall tale and left home at just fifteen. I never saw him again.

I fell into an incredible depression, and it was at this point that I attempted to take my own life for the first time. I walked to a secluded locale known as Ernesettle Creek, and at high tide, I leapt from the bridge over the water. I could feel myself sinking to the bottom of the estuary, and as the water filled my lungs, I felt the pain. You see, although I seem unable to die, I feel every moment of every attempt. I sat at the bottom of the creek for two hours or more, in constant pain of drowning, and yet unable to drown. I walked out of the creek and broke down on the banks. I remember very vividly, screaming into the night air, and I slept underneath the supports of that bridge for weeks, isolated from the world, slipping into a dark place in my mind.

I have spent many years attempting to take my life, as I said. Every time my final family member dies, I attempt to take my life, and whilst it doesn't work, it does make it appear to everyone else that I have gone, and then I relocate and start again.

10th April 1912

It took another quarter of a millennium before I finally managed to leave Great Britain. I had amassed large amounts of wealth over my long and laboured life, and was in the fortunate position to purchase a ticket to sail for New York on the Titanic. I remember boarding the ship, and thinking that perhaps this was a way for me to finally find a new purpose in my life. I was leaving everything behind apart from the suitcase I took with me. And of course, four days later, we all know what happened there. I attempted to end my life twice during the sinking. The first time, as the ship went down, I made my way down to the flooded decks to fade into the water. But unfortunately, a piece of ceiling detached, and I was knocked unconscious, and pulled out of the water by a well meaning gentleman. When I was finally placed into a lifeboat and we rowed away from the ship, I tried to leap into the water, but was restrained by the crew, and despite my protests, they would not let me go.

My life's purpose shifted dramatically during the middle of my life. I guess you could call it some kind of midlife crisis, looking back. But my goal became not to live my life, but to end it. It has consumed me for the last four hundred years. I have shot myself, tried to suffocate myself, even overdoses and car accidents, but as you have seen, either by some refusal of my body to cease function, or by the actions of others, I am not allowed to die.

And here we are, sitting in this diner, after another botched attempt. I honestly don't think this suffering will ever end."

Scarlett sat, leaning forward, head propped up by her hands taking in every word, captivated. It took a moment for her to realise that Deanna had finished speaking.

"That's incredible. You're telling me that you're six hundred and ninety-nine years old?"

Deanna waited for a more enthusiastic response to her tale but nodded reluctantly.

"That's the part you're focusing on?" she asked.

Scarlet sat upright.

"I'm sorry, but it's not every day you meet someone that's nearly three quarters of a millennia old!"

Scarlett was now geed up, but at no point called Deanna out on any detail.

"I've never told anyone my story since Desmond left. I always said I had a medical condition, and then later in life, as my children passed me in age by a considerable amount, I relocated with them, and played the part of their daughter until they died."

"Well yeah sure, you would need to do that. It's a wonder they didn't burn you at Salem."

Deanna raised her eyebrow again, giving Scarlett a 'that's a story for another day' look.

The diner owner was now sweeping the floor and switching off the lights, which was their signal to leave. As they walked outside, Deanna put a hand on Scarlett's shoulder.

"Can I ask you something?" she asked.

"Yeah, sure, anything," Scarlett replied, with a slightly concerned look on her face.

"I want you to help me."

The confused look deepened. "I don't follow."

"I want you to help me die, Scarlett."

"I'm sorry? You want me to help you kill yourself?"

Scarlett was confused, and in disbelief at what she was being asked to do.

"I need help, and if this place is as weird and scary as you say it is, there must be a way here to end this curse."

Scarlett began walking away, shaking her head, and Deanna set off in pursuit.

"Scarlett, wait!"

"No. No, I will not help you kill yourself, no I don't know a way to break your curse, and no I will not try and help you find one!"

Scarlett climbed into her car, slammed the door shut, and drove away, tyres screeching, leaving Deanna stood in an empty car park, beneath a flickering street light.

Deanna was in her second hour of walking the streets. Her mind was filled with the same thoughts that plagued her mind daily. What can I try next? As she turned onto what must have been the hundredth street of the night, she came across a gang of men who appeared to be carrying a body out of a house. As the men closed the van, and re- entered the building, Deanna snuck along the edge of the adjacent buildings, narrowly avoiding the glare from the bus depot floodlights, until she reached the perimeter of the building.

The door appeared to be leading to a small jewellery store. She peered through the window, and could see a light moving around inside, and noticed the glass in the bottom of the door had been broken. She was about to go around the back when she saw light shimmer off an object inside. She checked again, but suspected the men were still in the back, perhaps looking for a safe, and that the unfortunate owner may have been the person loaded into the van.

Deanna carefully stepped through the door, and approached the object, sitting inside an unbroken glass case. Upon closer inspection, she saw it was a kind of amulet. Gold in colour, with green jewels set in a circle around the edge of the piece. As Deanna opened the case, and lifted it up to eye level, the jewel in the centre, previously clear, began to glow yellow. As she held it, the amulet seemed to *call* to her.

Suddenly reminded of her situation, and the dangerous men elsewhere in the store, she started to back up, when she heard a noise from behind her. As she spun around, she saw a man standing in the entrance.

"Who's there?" she asked.

"I hear that you wanted to die?" came the voice from the shadows.

"Excuse me?" replied Deanna.

The figure stepped forward into the light, but before Deanna could see his face, she was hit in the chest by a bullet, seemingly fired from the man in front of her. As she looked down, blood began to pour from the centre of her body. As she looked up again, four more gunshots rang out through the air, striking Deanna in the stomach and shoulder in turn.

Deanna slumped to her knees, pain surging throughout her body. She had been shot before, but something about this felt different. She felt herself drifting away. Surely this wasn't happening. The world started to become fainter, and strangely, she began to panic. She had spent so long trying to end her life, but now that she was on the verge of death, she was terrified. She wanted to stay. Her vision was almost faded to black, as she collapsed to the ground, her head lying on the floor. She made out the faint outline of the man walking towards her.

A bright light appeared before her, and she squinted into it, preparing herself for whatever plain she was to ascend to. As the car smashed through the front of the shop, the advancing man rolled up over the top of the vehicle, smashing the windscreen, and landing with a heavy thump on the floor. The two men in the back room, ran out, saw the carnage, and sprinted out the building through the back door. As Scarlett climbed out of the car and ran towards her, Deanna felt warm relief. But she was continuing to fade away.

"Deanna!" shouted Scarlett. "Can you hear me?"

Deanna's voice was faint and distant.

"Don't want to go... I'm scared."

Scarlett looked around for anything to help, but there was now so much blood pouring from Deanna's body, that she feared she was too late.

"Deanna, I need you to stay with me!"

"I don't want to go anymore."

Deanna's voice now sounded so much like a child, crying to her mother, that tears began to fill Scarlett's eyes. But caught in the glimpse of those eyes, was the amulet that Deanna was still holding. It was glowing with a fury, and the yellow gem was now getting brighter and brighter. As Deanna's life began to fade away, the gem continued to brighten. Scarlett took a risk, and reached into Deanna's hand and removed the amulet, and almost instantly, the gem dimmed. Scarlett looked back towards Deanna, and she saw colour returning to her friend's skin.

Lifting her shirt, she saw the gunshot wounds beginning to heal rapidly. Joy swept over her face.

"Deanna! You're going to be alright!"

She held the amulet tight, as her joy grew, ignoring the movement behind her, and the sound of broken glass crunching. As she heard a gun being cocked, she was too late. She turned around in time to feel the bullets rip through her body.

The man stood, leaning on the car, gun still poised, smoke erupting from the barrel. As he opened the chamber, and reached into his pockets for more bullets, Deanna became more self-aware. However, her confusion was not at the man reloading the gun, nor the fact that she thought she was going to die. It was at the fact that Scarlett had not yet fallen to the ground, and was now stood, staring at her open wounds, and as all three people watched, her wounds began to heal too.

Deanna pulled herself to her feet, and as the man regained his composure, and raised the gun again, she charged at him. He managed to fire another three shots at Deanna, before she hit him, and with his wounds, easily knocked the gun out of his hands, as he rolled to the floor, landing on his front.

She ran back over to Scarlett, who now stood completely healed.

"Woah. That's interesting."

Deanna looked down at the amulet, which was glowing once again. As the man began to stir again behind them, Deanna walked over to the gun and picked it up. But this was no ordinary gun. It was silver in colour, and when she opened the chamber, the bullets within were also silver edged, but hollow inside. They appeared to contain liquid. She handed the gun to Scarlett, grabbed the man by the shoulders, and spun him around. As the street lights hit his face, Deanna staggered back against one of the cabinets.

The face was older, and sported a five 'o' clock shadow, but there was no mistaking it.

"Desmond?" she said, her voice coming out as a whimper.

The man through pained, gritted teeth stood up, and again, propped himself against the car.

"Hello mother."

Scarlett looked on in shock at what was unfolding before her eyes, as Deanna lost strength and slumped down in front of the cabinet.

"But... *how?*" she asked, wide eyed, and barely able to catch her breath.

Desmond knelt in front of his mother, as best as he could given his injuries.

"Well thanks to you, of course."

"But... I don't understand. How can you be here?"

Desmond now seemed to be gaining more strength, and as Scarlett squinted, she saw his wounds were also beginning to heal.

"You filled my head with all that nonsense about never ageing, and how you would have to watch me die! I was fifteen! Do you have any comprehension of how that fractured my young mind? No of course you don't! I spent years trying to find a way to reverse this supposed curse you told me about. But instead, I found myself in the company of the very woman who cursed you."

Deanna shook her head, hoping she was wrong, but already knowing that she wasn't.

"Please tell me she didn't do the same to you?"

Desmond nodded.

"She was a witch, belonging to an ancient clan. She was near death when I found her. She had lived for centuries, but her power was waning. I foolishly thought if I killed her, then you would be set free. However, before I could get near to her, she had enough time and power to curse me too."

Desmond now appeared completely healed, and stood up, and walked out of the front of the store. Deanna followed in pursuit, and Scarlett behind them, still holding both the gun, and the amulet.

"Desmond wait!" Deanna called after him.

"There's nothing you can say mother! You could have just carried on as you'd done with all your other children, and lie to them, but no, you had to tell me the truth. And now I'm no better off than you are!"

Deanna put a hand on his shoulder, but it was batted away.

"My life has been meaningless for over a quarter of a millennia. Had I known that you were still alive, I would have found you!"

Desmond span on his heels, small pieces of shattered glass still falling from his coat to the ground.

"Unlike you, mother, I have not been wasting my life. I have a mission. I am a part of something much bigger than you and me."

Desmond moved his face closer to his mother.

"What do you mean?" she asked.

He pointed at Scarlett.

"That gun was my attempt to release you. As soon as I knew you were in town, I knew I had to find you. When I saw you holding the amulet, I knew it was my chance."

"I don't understand," Scarlett offered. "What exactly is this amulet?"

"It is one of three identical pieces that were cast in the Victorian times by a very powerful coven of witches in England. They enchanted the amulets with the power to give invincibility to whoever held it. Or in my mother's case, remove it."

The realisation of the situation finally fell into place. That explained why Deanna nearly died, and Scarlett did not. Desmond continued his story, now in a much calmer place than he had been moments before.

"Two of them had been destroyed over the last century or so, but this one managed to find its way into Wealdstone. I was tracking it when I saw you, mother."

Deanna was overwhelmed with feelings she had not experienced for centuries. All the time she had been trying to end her own life, her son had been alive too, unable to die, the same as she. But he appeared to have found a purpose. Perhaps it was one in which she could share.

"Desmond, what kind of gun is that? And why are you hunting for mystical jewellery?" she asked.

"The gun is a crafted design to accommodate the bullets that it uses. The bullets are silver encased capsules of holy water. I am part of a small group of people who investigate the supernatural and the paranormal. We started in Victorian England, with our founders Annie Weston and Herman Fredericks. We have policed phenomenon all over the world, including whatever took them from here to the Victorian period."

Scarlett's eyes lit up.

"Are you talking about Herman's Curiosities?" she exclaimed with a huge amount of joy in her voice.

Desmond nodded. Scarlett continued.

"So, you're telling me, they vanished from the bookshop, and ended up in Victorian England?"

Desmond nodded again, before offering his reply to the inevitable question of 'how?'.

"We don't know how they moved not only back through time, but across the world. All we know is there are cracks in time in that building. That's why we had it requisitioned."

"But the place was demolished years ago," Scarlett said, a new confused look across her face.

"Yeah, it's not a bad cover is it really?"

"What do you mean?"

"You'll see."

Deanna was taking in more information than she had gained in the last hundred years. Suddenly she was not the only unusual being in the universe. Suddenly, her life was beginning to have meaning again. She had her son, who was immortal like her. She had a friend who she could freely talk to about all the lives she had led. She reached over and took her son's hand in her own and looked up at his face.

"Desmond, I want to join you. Show me what it is you do."

"I did just try to kill you. Are you sure you're done with trying to end your existence here?"

Deanna knew what she wanted to do.

"You've given me a purpose again."

Scarlett tucked the amulet into her pocket, and as sirens began to be heard in the background, Desmond decided now was the time to leave.

"Then we need to go. Now."

"But what about my car?" Scarlett shouted after them.

"Don't worry about it," replied Desmond as he turned around.

He reached into another pocket and pulled out a round object, which looked a little like a perfume bottle. Scarlett looked at it briefly before forming her usual witty reply.

"We're going to spray them with *Golden Delicious*?"

Desmond gave her a sarcastic look, before pressing a button on top of the object, and launching it into the back window of the car.

"You might want to run."

As the trio sprinted down the street, a massive explosion erupted behind them from the store, obliterating the car and the van outside. As they glanced back, there was very little car left to be identified, and the store was engulfed in flame.

"Now I want one of those," Scarlett said excitedly.

Desmond smiled, and hurried them further down the street, pulling out his smartphone as they walked.

"What are you doing?" asked Deanna.

"Well, I figured I'd better call it in. It's not every day you run into your immortal seven hundred year old mother, with an amulet of immortality."

Deanna smiled at his reply. He really was her son.

A faint voice could be heard answer on the other end.

"Daniella, it's Desmond."

"Hi Desmond, I was just about to call you."

"That's certainly a coincidence. I have located the final amulet."

"Really? That's some great work."

"Well… it comes with a surprise too."

"What kind of surprise?"

"The estranged kind."

"Well knowing the powers of that amulet, and knowing you, I think I can work out the surprise part."

"We are probably going to need help examining the amulet. And we had to use the grenade to cover up a crime scene."

"Okay, I'll meet you at the store in about an hour. I'm going to need some help with Duncan, he's having a hard time suppressing his instincts. I'm worried about him."

"Okay well we can discuss it at the store. I'll see you soon."

Scarlett looked over at Deanna and whispered to her.

"I'm pretty sure you're the surprise."

Deanna held a finger to her lips, expressing the need for quiet.

Deanna turned to Desmond, as he put the phone away.

"Where are we going?" she asked.

He smiled back at her.

"We are going to work."

CONTENT WARNING

Please be aware that the following story contains scenes of extreme violence and sexual assault.
PROCEED WITH CAUTION.

THE LAST TRAIN

Caroline ran as fast as her legs could carry her, but she couldn't escape the barrage of metal and the plumes of smoke. No matter how hard she pumped her legs, she wasn't going anywhere. The fog intensified, and the sound of gunshots filled the air, the flashes from the weaponry blinding her eyes, and yet she could not see where the disturbances were coming from.

Behind her, the wind howled, and the ground vibrated from the canon fire. The violent noises continued, now joined by screams, and cries of terror. The sound of metal penetrating flesh echoed in her ears like banging on the skin of a drum.

The sound of a loud whistle from behind Caroline cut through the rest of the noise like lightning through the sky. She stopped running, and span on her heels, and as she did so, she was narrowly missed by a metal canon ball flying through the air, landing just six feet from her. She lifted her arms to shield herself instinctively, and as she did so, she could make out another large, fast travelling object, barrelling straight for her. Another canon ball whizzed by, and the faint sound of a trumpet could be heard in the distance.

The vibrations in the ground became even more intense, the number of projectiles increasing, the fog now so thick and dense that she couldn't see anyone else, but the cries of pain echoed around the battlefield like the whole world was caught in a bell jar, the sounds having no way to escape. Only the vacuum of death awaiting on the other side.

Immense pain suddenly shot through her left thigh as a bullet tore through the skin. Another through the right knee cap, the bone shattering, Caroline screaming into the cold night air, her breath streaming out, visibly like an icy mist. A third bullet blew through Caroline's left shoulder blade, her voice now adding to the vibrations of the canon fire, her body wanting to crumple, her rifle now falling to the floor. A fourth bullet, fifth and sixth, all through her chest and exploding from her back. As she spluttered blood from her throat, projected from her mouth, number seven, eight, nine and ten ripped through her flesh, two of them through her abdomen, and the other two in her hips.

The bullets stopped, as did the sound of the gunfire. As she waved around in the wind, wanting to collapse into death, but unable to do so, she looked upwards, and a cannon ball blew through her core. And she was gone.

Caroline jumped awake, screaming at the top of her lungs, a cold sweat running down her back. As she came around, she recognised her surroundings. The station was now completely deserted, apart from a small elderly man who had been changing over an advert inside one of the electric bulletin boards. He was now staring at her with a confused look on his face. As Caroline managed to regulate her breathing, she held up a hand to him in apology, and he shook his head before returning to his work.

She put her head in her hands, and rubbed her eyes, her hair matted to her forehead, was brushed back by her cold clammy hands. The maintenance man, locked up the unit, cast her one more glance, and walked out of the concourse. As Caroline stood up and adjusted herself, pulling her skirt back down, and straightening her jacket, she saw him lock up the station entrance, and leave.

Caroline looked around. Everyone had gone now. She had sat down at the bench and had been surrounded by at least twenty or thirty people. How long had she been sat there? When did she fall asleep? Searching around the station for the time, she spotted a digital departures board, but in place of the time, the message *'ERROR'* was displayed.

Frustrated, she sat back down and reached under the bench for her bag. But it was gone. She lunged forward, onto her knees and scoured the floor, but her bag was gone. Somebody must have taken it while she was sleeping.

"FUCK!" she shouted, her vocal chords still strained from her scream upon waking.

Caroline walked towards the now closed branch of *Burger King* to try and spy through the shutters for any sign of life, or just the simple notion of a clock, but just saw glowing lights on the cold fryers behind the counter. The air had dropped at least below freezing, her breath was now erupting from her mouth in fog form. The main building of the station was now locked, and Caroline was stuck on the platform, her only way out now was to climb down onto the tracks and walk.

She guessed it was now around one in the morning, judging by how quiet it was, and the level of darkness, which was severely intimidating for a woman alone, with no means of communication.

She wrapped her jacket as tightly around her as possible, shivering, goosebumps clearly visible in the few dim lights of the station still active. She walked up to the edge of the platform, crossing the yellow line and staring down each direction of the tracks. Nothing but darkness.

"Well, guess there's nothing for it," she muttered to herself.

Caroline sat herself down on the edge of the platform, and gradually, and carefully lowered herself down onto the tracks, landing on the edge of the metal line with a thud, and a crack, as her heel snapped off her shoe, causing her to crash to the ground.

"FUCK FUCK FUUUUUUCK!!!"

Caroline, now raging, rushed to her feet, picked up the broken shoe, and launched it down the track, losing sight of it before hearing it strike the metal in the distance. She slapped her hands to her face, and gripped the skin with frustration, before lowering them and taking a long, deep breath. Looking down at her one clothed foot, and a freezing cold shoeless foot, she began gradually limping down the middle of the tracks, trying to avoid the gaps between the slats at first, but then deciding it was easier to walk between them.

"Who falls asleep, in a train station, at night, and doesn't get woken up by someone going between their legs to steal their bag?" she spoke out loud to herself as she plodded down the tracks.

"I mean seriously? I'm walking down a train line, in the middle of the night, in freezing temperatures, with ONE FUCKING SHOE!"

She carried on stumbling down the tracks, occasionally being blown off centre by the chilling winter breeze, for what seemed like miles. However, just ahead of her, she saw her shoe glinting in the slither of moonlight that was now penetrating the clouds. She bent over, picked it up and put it back on her foot. It was almost comforting, but certainly no warmer. As she took a couple of steps forward, she stopped again, took off the other shoe, and whacked the heel on the edge of the line, sending a clanging noise into the distance as the second heel broke free, leaving Caroline with two flats.

"Much better," she said to herself, smiling at this minor achievement. "Well, if that was here, then I can't have come that far after…"

She stopped speaking, as she turned and saw that there was nothing but tracks, and trees behind her. The station was gone.

Caroline started retracing her steps, picking up pace now she had two balanced shoes on her feet, and jogged for a good five minutes, but even though she should have reached the station by now, still just tracks trailing off into the distance, woods on either side.

A squawk from a crow from behind her, startled her and as she span around, she found herself looking at a mirror image of tracks stretching into the distance, woods on either side. It appeared that Caroline was no longer where she had started.

It had seemed like days when the building finally came into view. Caroline's feet were red from the cold, and sore from the miles she had walked. She had no idea where she was, or where the town had seemingly disappeared to. There was no way off the tracks, as the woodlands on either side were so thick and dense, and themselves, seemingly stretching on for miles. But she had finally come upon some kind of structure, and as she approached the edge of what looked like another platform, she realised it was an old train station.

As she slowly ascended the ramp leading up to the concourse, she noticed that there were lights on, but not electrically powered lights, they were gas lanterns. There were black wrought iron benches scattered about the wooden framed floor, which as it moved further inland, joined onto a concrete structure.

Caroline searched for some kind of exit, but there didn't appear to be any visible doorways away from the station. There was an empty waiting room to the left, and a closed eatery on the right. The station master's office was facing the tracks, but the door was locked.

"Where the hell am I?" she asked herself.

What she didn't expect, was a response.

"The question is, *when* are you?"

Caroline nearly jumped out of her skin and launched her back against the nearest wall. The voice had been raspy and came through whispered breath.

"Oh, come on, you've never jumped like that before," came the voice again.

As Caroline squinted into the shadows, a figure emerged. A tall woman, roughly six feet tall, with bright red long hair, wearing a long dark brown trench coat moved into the flickering gas light. She was wearing a dark red open necked shirt beneath the coat, and long black boots. She blew out a long stream of cigarette smoke, and flicked ash from a lit smoke onto the floor, which seemed to vanish as soon as it touched the wood.

"Who the fuck are you?"

Caroline blurted the words out without really thinking, but being in the business of company takeovers, she was used to having a hostile defence. As strange as it was, although she had never seen this woman before, she seemed somewhat familiar.

"Ah, Caroline. If that's who you are this time. Don't make me explain my life story again. You've tried it your way, and it hasn't worked. You need to come back home."

A puzzled expression moved across Caroline's face as the woman moved closer.

"I have no idea who you are, but you had better not come any closer."

"Or what? You'll hit me with one of your flats?"

The woman snapped her fingers, and Caroline heard the faint sound of rumbling, and a distant whistle.

"What's that sound?" asked Caroline, amazed at the stupidity of the question which has the world's most obvious answer.

The woman rolled her eyes in response, and as she turned around, an old steam train arrived in the station.

"Get on... *Caroline*."

The woman gestured for her to climb on board the train, and as she did so, the door to the carriage opened as if someone had turned the handle and pushed it open. And the way she spoke Caroline's name, suggested she didn't believe it *was* her name.

"There is no way I'm getting on a haunted train with a walking fashion crisis and being driven to some kind of doom."

At this point, Caroline was beginning to think she was dreaming again, after all her last one had been incredibly vivid. But what threw her off guard was the next sentence from the mysterious woman.

"It wasn't a dream... *Caroline*."

Caroline stopped smirking. Her lips formulated a response, but nothing came out. In her head she was thinking, 'what does she mean not a dream' and 'why does she keep saying my name like it's not real?'.

"Because it wasn't a dream... *Caroline*, and because it isn't your real name... *Caroline*."

"How do you keep doing that?"

"Doing what? Hearing your mind?"

Caroline nodded.

The woman laughed.

"I'll let you figure that out... *Caroline*."

"Can you stop saying my name like that!" snapped Caroline. "And just what the hell do I call you?"

The woman thought for a moment.

"For the purposes of this, let's go with... *Jasmine.*"

"Really? You're going for what... the porn star look, so you pick a Hollywood name?"

Jasmine laughed.

"Something like that. Hey why not? I haven't been a pornstar or a movie star yet."

The puzzled look returned to Caroline's face, but she felt a pull towards the train.

"So, what's with the train?" she asked, hesitantly.

"This train? This train, Caroline, is the *last train.*"

"The last train for what?"

Jasmine sighed and rolled her eyes again.

"*Your* last train. The last train you will be boarding No more trains. Finito. After this train, there will be no more trains. Get it?"

Caroline shook her head but was now filled with an inner fear. Jasmine, however, was fed up, and anger started to spread across her face, and Caroline was sure she just grew another few inches in height.

"I'm not getting on any train with..."

Caroline was cut off as Jasmine thrust her arm forwards towards Caroline, who felt an invisible grip on her throat, and she was lifted off the ground. She grappled at the invisible hands around her neck, as she was lifted towards the train, and as Jasmine swept her arm aside, Caroline was propelled through the air, through the carriage door, and slammed into a seat. The door slammed, and the train let out a whistle before lurching into life and pulling out of the station. Caroline watched as Jasmine stood on the platform, and her eyes glowed purple as the train left her behind. The train began picking up speed. Caroline looked around the carriage, but it was empty. She stood up, but the carriage shook, and she fell back into the seat. Another toot of the whistle. Caroline's heart leapt into her mouth. The train seemed to be going faster and faster. Too fast for a train of this variety.

Again, Caroline stood up, and made her way to the door to the next carriage. As she opened it and walked through, a massive gust of wind blew through her, and knocked her backwards. She fell, and hit her head on the floor, and as she slipped into unconsciousness, she thought she could see daylight, and heard Jasmine's voice in her head.

"*This is your last train.*"

As Caroline woke up, she instinctively reached for the back of her head, but her hand met no hair. Scared she sat bolt upright, and found herself lying in a bed, sunlight streaming in through a set of ornate double French doors. She felt her head all over and moved her hands down her face. She did not recognise the feelings. Disorientated and incredibly confused, she threw the covers aside and launched herself towards the dresser opposite.

She had been surprised how little distance there was to the floor, and when she reached the mirror, she realised why. Staring back at her, was the face of a tall, muscular man. Bald, with olive skin. Caroline ran her hands all over the face of the person staring back at her, and her brain began to burn. Then, like lightning in her mind, the name 'Marco' appeared almost like subtitles in her mind. Then she spotted another figure in the mirror behind her. Lying in the bed that she had just climbed out of, was a sleeping woman, long black hair cascading over her shoulder, exposed out of the covers.

Caroline turned around as the woman stirred in the sunlight. She opened her eyes and looked Caroline up and down.

"You're looking particularly ravishing today my love," said the woman.

Caroline was taken aback, and yet felt validation at the same time.

"Says the stunning creature lying in my bed," replied Caroline, without even thinking, and in the deep voice of a man. "I hope I didn't tire you out."

Who was this person? It was as if Caroline was a spectator in her own mind, and yet she was actively doing everything, the speech, the movements, and she was feeling the emotions and feelings of the body she was in.

"Not so much that I couldn't enjoy your touch this morning," the woman replied, and she sat up in bed, allowing the covers to slip down her body, revealing her smooth, olive skin to match that of Marco's body.

As she ran her hands over her bare breasts, Caroline felt aroused, and moved towards the woman she now knew instinctively, was called Bella.

She *knew* the woman.

It was not a simple case of knowing of her, or who she was by association, she *knew* her. As Marco and Bella intertwined their bodies between the covers, she felt every second of the experience. The delicate kisses, the hands exploring her masculine chest, the thrusting of both of their hips. And yet during the whole time, she felt like she was observing through someone else's eyes. The thing she was having the most trouble with, was the memories she had of this place.

As Bella stood from the bed and walked towards the shower in the en- suite, Caroline felt Marco's eyes follow her every move. As she closed the door part way, Caroline began reviewing the situation aloud to herself.

"I feel such love and lust for this woman, and I remember the first time we made love, on the beach under the moonlight. I remember how Bella had been the one to propose on the floor in the middle of our favourite restaurant on Valentine's Day three years ago. And I remember how..."

Caroline stopped herself as she remembered an awful detail. On the night stand beside her, Marco's phone vibrated, and she felt a smile spread over her face, as she read the message.

'*I'm waiting for you lover, are you done with your wife yet?*'

As Caroline saw the words, she felt horrified... and yet deeply satisfied at the same time. She felt Marco turn his head and lean back to peak through the bathroom door. Bella stood beneath the waterfall cascading from the shower, and watched as it flowed over her chest, and down her body to the floor.

But Caroline felt impatience. She was *eager* to leave the house and go to this other woman. Marco had been cheating on Bella, his wife, with another woman.

Angela.

The woman was called Angela. Marco had met her whilst shopping for an anniversary present for Bella. It had been so incredibly fast. At ten a.m. Marco had been asking Angela's opinion on an anniversary gift for his loving wife, and by ten-thirty, they were fucking in the store room of the jewellery store.

Caroline could feel her personality slipping away, and feeling more and more of Marco's feelings and memories, and less of her own. She remembered getting on the train, and something about broken heels... and then... nothing.

She felt Marco typing a reply and felt pride at how happy it made him. *'That depends. Have you finished fucking your husband too?'*

Caroline smiled as she felt him hit send. Angela was an incredible lover, and just thinking about her in comparison to Bella, felt like comparing a VW Beetle to a Ferrari.

But this moment of brief humour was shattered when an almighty crash came from downstairs. Marco sat bolt upright and reached for his shorts. Quickly sliding them on, he heard Bella call out from the shower asking what the noise was. He didn't answer but moved to investigate. Caroline's personality was overcome with a sense of impending doom. She knew what was coming next but couldn't quite focus on the details. Nevertheless, Marco's movements continued.

As he reached the bedroom door, it was kicked open, smacking him in the face and sending him falling backwards onto the floor, hitting his head on the bedpost. Somebody grabbed him by the scruff of the neck, picked him up and pushed him face down onto the bed, and held him there. Several other men moved into the bedroom, two of them headed into the bathroom. Marco could hear Bella screaming and fought against the grip of the man holding him, successfully breaking free, only to be punched hard in the jaw, by another man behind him, and falling back to the bed, where the second man held him down again.

Marco and Caroline watched as the two men dragged Bella out of the bathroom by her hair, his wife still completely naked, and they slammed her up against the wall, one man holding her by the throat.

"Who are you! What the fuck are you doing here?!" Marco called out.

Another blow to the head. And then a voice that Caroline recognised immediately.

"Well, Marco, I thought you pay my wife a visit so often, that I would pay a visit to yours!"

Marco's head was turned to the side so he could see Bella, still held against the wall by the two henchmen. Angela's husband walked up to Bella and drew a gun from his jacket pocket. He ran the barrel down the side of Bella's face. She screamed and fought, and the husband whipped the gun across her face. Marco struggled against his captor as blood began trickling down from Bella's nose, running faster down her face as the blood mixed with the shower water, but he was kicked in the stomach for his troubles.

"Now, Mrs Caglieri, I'm going to do to you, what your husband has been doing with my wife. Of course, I don't think you will like it as much as she does. Sorry, as much as she *did*."

Marco's face turned to horror, as the husband held up a mobile phone towards him, on which was the message he had just sent.

"This is what you caused Marco."

He scrolled to the side and showed Marco a photograph. It was of Angela. She was hanging from a roof beam in her house, her clothes torn and bloodied, and four bullet holes in her chest, one in her head.

Marco stopped struggling and felt terror in the pit of his stomach.

"Shall we begin?" the husband asked Marco, and then repeated the question to Bella.

She looked over at her husband with pure fear in her eyes. In the back of Marco's mind, Caroline tried to close her eyes, but was forced to watch on.

The husband grabbed Bella's hair and threw her forward on to the bed. He directed his men to tie her limbs to the bedpost at the top. She kicked and screamed and received another smack to the face. The husband stepped back and removed his jacket and slipped his belt free. As he climbed onto the bed to the side of Marco, all he and Caroline could do, was watch.

The bed rocked violently as the husband of Angela thrust into his wife repeatedly. Her screams died down after five minutes, and as Marco watched, his face full of tears, he saw his wife's empty eyes. Then, the husband let out a loud groan, and the movement stopped. He climbed off the bed and re-zipped his jeans. Marco saw his wife trembling, face soaked and red with tears.

"Please," he choked through his tears. "Please let her go."

The husband looked at him, then back at Bella.

"You're right. She has suffered enough."

He turned to walk out the door, putting his jacket back on in the process. Two of the men walked out of the room, and the one holding Marco also left. Marco collapsed onto the floor when the husband moved back into the room.

"But you haven't."

He raised his gun, and as Bella looked into Marco's eyes, the husband unloaded ten bullets into her body, each one like a knife into Marco's chest. The blood spattered the bed and the walls, the shots ringing out in Caroline's mind. She now remembered everything.

Marco felt hands lift him to his feet, where he hung in their arms, limp, staring at the bloody corpse of his wife. And then the searing pain in his belly. As he looked down, a knife was buried in his body. He followed the handle, held by the hand of the husband. Their eyes met, and the husband leaned forward and whispered into Marco's ear.

"*Wake up, Caroline.*"

Caroline snapped awake and sat bolt upright again. She was back on the train, and it was moving at pace. Sat on a seat in front of her, was Jasmine.

"Welcome back."

"What… What…"

"What was that?" Jasmine offered to finish the question.

Caroline nodded.

"That was your last time around."

Jasmine stood up and moved over to Caroline, helping her to her feet, and moving her onto the adjacent seat.

"My… my last time around?"

"That's right. You needed to observe the pain of being unable to stop your loved one being hurt, through your own actions."

Caroline had now caught her breath.

"But... I remembered everything. Every action, every feeling, every memory. I knew everything about Marco's entire life up to that point."

Jasmine nodded.

"That's because you were Marco." Caroline shook her head.

"That's not possible," she said.

Jasmine, again looked impatient. She stood up and pointed to the next door.

"Well maybe you should try walking through this one next."

Caroline looked at the door, and through the glass, she thought she could see a bustling market place. Jasmine spoke again.

"This, is where we met the first time."

Caroline stood up and moved to stand in front of the door.

"What do you mean the first time?" she asked.

Jasmine smiled.

"Let's just say this isn't the first time that I have had to... refresh your memory."

Caroline looked back at the door, and as it swung open, she felt another wave of familiarity. She felt herself step through it, and a cold chill move through her body, and felt her eyes close. As her eyes opened again, she was indeed standing in a busy marketplace, and seemed to be a little closer to the ground.

As before, she was aware of her surroundings, and knew why she was in the market. She was now in the body of a young adult, no more than fifteen or sixteen years old. Sixteen. The question was answered by her own memory almost instantly. She walked forwards and returned to the fruit and vegetable stall that the boy worked on for an old grocer and his family. Caroline remembered that he was trying to earn money to buy medicine for his mother who was sick.

Then she remembered that same scenario had occurred before. Was she now remembering another past life? She had a vague memory of trying to earn money so she could help her family buy medicine, then an angry man.

Goldsmith.

She remembered the name. And then, an image of an axe swinging towards her head. No. The head of a man. An assistant. Then nothing.

"Caleb!"

A voice called out, and Caroline responded as if that was her name. Well, the boy's name. The voice had come from the mother of the grocer's family. She was calling for the boy to help a customer pack their potatoes and cabbages. Caleb ran over and started packing the vegetables for the old lady, when Caroline sensed an approaching figure. Caleb didn't turn around though, so Caroline was forced to continue facing forward.

A scream emanated from the crowd, and as Caleb turned, he saw a woman standing before him, holding two knives. She knelt in front of him and looked into his eyes.

"I wonder how many lives you've lived. I guess one more won't hurt."

The woman raised the two knives, and as the crowd watched on, she plunged one knife into Caleb's heart, and one into her own.

The boy fell to the floor, clutching his chest, and within seconds, he was dead, as was the woman. A pool of blood formed beneath both of their bodies, the blood mixing as it met. The crowd ran in all directions, screaming for help. But Caroline now felt herself looking down on Caleb's body. She was no longer a part of him. As she watched the body, the distance between her and the boy was increasing, until she found herself holding onto railings, on a balcony on the next building along, looking back down on the market.

Caroline felt a hand grip hers, and that is when she noticed her own hand was lost in that of the woman. The woman was now of a different appearance.

It was Jasmine.

Caroline looked down, and her hand was now that of an infant. Jasmine held a finger to her lips, and said nothing, leading Caroline through the building, apparently not triggering any response from any of the people inside. Jasmine said nothing until they reached the street. She came to a halt, the two of them now facing the market entrance, watching the commotion unfold within.

Jasmine then began to speak.

"Your time has come my young friend. You've served your purpose and taken on your suffering with pride. But we have other plans for you now."

Caroline now began to feel as though Caroline was not her name after all. Jasmine continued.

"You, my young child, are a pain wraith."

Caroline responded, speaking with a child's voice, but with the authority of an adult, decades older.

"A pain wraith? What does this mean please?"

Jasmine smiled.

"You were birthed in another realm. You are a pain wraith. Our sole purpose during our childhood is to experience all forms of pain and suffering. From our very creation until our maturity, our sole purpose is to exist in agony. Where we come from, there is no physical form. We exist outside of normal dimensions."

The child seemed to understand and nodded. The pair began to walk slowly through the streets.

"How long have I been here?" Caroline asked.

"You were birthed centuries ago. You have been on Earth for three of those centuries. Do you remember your previous hosts?"

Caroline nodded.

"I remember a man named Goldsmith. And an axe. I think I was killed."

Jasmine nodded again.

"That was your first host. The first host is designed to introduce you to the earthly representation of pain. In our realm, we experience pain in ethereal form, before moving into the physical."

"How many lives have I had in this physical form?"

"Since you came here, you have been thirty-one people, both male and female, child, and adult. I cut your most recent form a little short because you have now reached maturity."

"What does that mean?" Caroline was now slipping away and felt herself becoming someone else.

"When we reach maturity, and we have suffered enough, we are gifted with the ability to remain in the physical world, but with powerful abilities."

The pair stopped walking as they reached the top of a gradual hill. They were gazing out onto the ocean, looking at an island less than a mile off the coast.

"Abilities?" asked Caroline.

Jasmine nodded. She knelt beside the child.

"You see that island there?"

Caroline nodded.

"Close your eyes."

Caroline obliged.

"Now I want you to visualise yourself floating on the breeze and flying above the ocean. You become one with the wind. You bathe in the heat of the sun as you move above the waves. You focus on a beautiful oak tree, and as you return to the ground, you see a bird nesting in its branches. The bird stumbles from its nest and falls to the ground."

Caroline heard a thump in front of her. She opened her eyes.

In front of her, on the ground was a robin. Dead. At the base of a large oak tree. As Caroline turned around, she found herself looking back at the mainland. They were now on the island.

"How did I do that?" she asked.

Jasmine smiled.

"This is just the beginning of what you will be able to do. Soon, I will teach you to do things like this."

As Caroline watched, Jasmine grew to ten feet tall, and morphed into a swirl of black smoke, before morphing into a bright red, horned beast, resembling the devil. Whilst the image was disturbing, it didn't seem to faze the small child. She watched as Jasmine's enormous hand reached down and picked her up and placed her onto the thickest branch in the tree, before becoming a swirl of black smoke again, and reappearing on the branch next to her.

"That was incredible. How do I even learn to do these things?" she asked.

Jasmine's face became serious, and she held the child's hand, and looked deep into her eyes.

"I will teach you all you need to know, but you must understand that there are rules."

Caroline looked confused.

"Rules? But I thought you said I was to be free?"

Jasmine nodded but did not break her gaze.

"You are indeed to be free, to move from body to body as you please, to manipulate things around you, and to create your own paradise. But you cannot interfere with time."

"What do you mean?" said the child, although now suddenly seeming to have a much deeper voice.

Her hand now also looked bigger. Jasmine smiled at her and held her face with her free hand.

"You are maturing fast, young daughter. It is time for your first life as a free woman."

Before either Jasmine or Caroline could say another word, Jasmine snapped her fingers, and Caroline was whisked away, her body tumbling through the air, everything rushing besides her, like an aeroplane thundering through the sky, and she became immersed in a blinding light. When she woke up, she was once again sat in the train, next to Jasmine.

She looked over at her.

"You're my mother?"

Jasmine nodded and reached to hold her hand.

"My name... my name is... Ariella."

Jasmine beamed a smile and nodded again, tightening her grip on Caroline's hand.

"I lost you around a century after that. You decided that you knew better and started interfering with other people's lives. You broke the rules."

Ariella was now beginning to fill with rage. She pulled her hand free as all her memories came flooding back, the train seeming to slow down with each one that returned.

"I remember! I remember you telling me that I could not interfere with time. You didn't say anything about not living a happy life with the person I loved!"

Jasmine's smile faded, and she looked around as the train slowed again. Her daughter's rant continued, and Ariella stood slowly, her rage continuing.

"I remember, mother dearest, that you tried to take me back to our realm against my wishes! I remember that you murdered the man I loved! I REMEMBER that you SLAUGHTERED my CHILDREN in their BEDS!"

As Ariella became more intensely angry, the train's brakes began to grip the wheels, slowing the train down to almost a crawl, and as her anger grew further, Jasmine shrunk back into her seat, and Ariella began to rise from the floor.

"And I remember, dear mother, that you told me that what is done is done! That we could not go back and change the past! BUT THAT WASN'T TRUE WAS IT?!"

Ariella was now roughly three feet off the floor, and the train ground to a stop, sending Jasmine flying down the carriage, where she crashed through the next door. Ariella flew after her through the air and passed into the next and final carriage.

Jasmine looked up to find that she was now floating above a planet in the vastness of space. Ariella was floating besides her. She gripped her mother's throat with her own invisible force and directed her gaze towards the planet below.

"Recognise this mother?" she asked.

Her eyes were now glowing the deepest purple, casting light upon her mother's face.

"This planet was a thriving salvation for mankind, and I killed them all! All because of you! I spent centuries trying to atone for a simple mistake. You killed my family, and I escaped you. I helped my friend in my next life, and you forced me to kill him too! I slaughtered his family, because you told me I couldn't change the past and I had to correct it! I KILLED THE ENTIRE HUMAN RACE!"

Her grip on her mother intensified, and despite her incredible powers of her own, Jasmine could not break free. Her daughter's anger was too intense. Her gaze was turned back towards her daughter.

"But I learnt something from these humans, mother."

Ariella snapped her mother's gaze towards a small ship in the distance. As Jasmine tried to focus on it, she saw the word '*Raven*' on the hull and could make out two figures moving through the window.

"You see that human inside The *Raven*? He is called Mace. Watch what he does next."

Jasmine watched in pain, as she observed the ship fly into the sun around which the planet was orbiting. She felt a sharp pain in her core and heard the screams of her daughter echo across time and space. She watched as a violet stream of energy cascaded from the sun, and the planet below faded away.

There was a huge flash of light, almost like the dawn of creation. Jasmine clamped her eyes shut, and when the light subsided, she found herself standing on top of a hill, overlooking a road. The moon was high in the sky, and Ariella was sat on a rock watching the road.

"Mace taught me something. He was prepared to fly his ship into the sun to rid the universe of me, rather than survive and find a way to continue his species. He thought that destroying me could save anyone else from suffering the way I had made the humans suffer. I had grown so obsessed with putting right a mistake that you told me was irreversible, that even the people I had killed and sent to our realm figured out a way to break my grip and warn him. Fly them home. All their home had left was their sun. That's what they kept telling him. Fly the ship into the sun, and poof! Everything returns as it was."

"Ariella, I never meant to hurt you. I only wanted the best for you."

Ariella stood up, the anger building again. She turned towards her mother, fists clenched.

"You wanted to control me, the way you controlled my brothers!" she screamed.

"Your... brothers?" Jasmine said in reply, uncertain just how much her daughter was now remembering.

"Oh yes, I remember my brothers. They found love in different time periods, and you didn't like that they had such freedom. You dragged them back to our realm and chained them up like DOGS!"

"They were going to reveal our existence, I couldn't allow that!" Jasmine shouted through choked tears.

"THEY WERE IN LOVE!" Ariella screamed back. "I was so out of my mind because of all your lies, and all the lives that I had taken, I tried to hide my memories! Every single body I moved through, I lost more of my memories, more details of my previous lives!"

She collapsed to the ground, as below them, a car narrowly avoided crashing into a truck coming the other way. Ariella glanced down and chuckled to herself.

"Alex. I killed him the first time round, you know. I told him all about you, and how you taught me to change form, inhabit bodies, and that we couldn't go back in time. Then I took his body and used it to kill twelve people. When I woke up and found myself here again, I remembered everything, and that's when I realised that time has no meaning to us. You lied. I had a chance to fix everything I had done. So, I let him go. Then I went back and made the right choice. I didn't change the lottery results. John didn't win the lottery, and his life fell apart, just as it was meant to."

Ariella now started to cry.

"But there was one thing I couldn't change. You see, no matter how much I tried, I couldn't go back to where I met the man I loved. Every time I tried, I ended up somewhere else. I could get close, but every time I tried to jump back into that body, it was like something was stopping me."

Jasmine was looking down, her jaw clenched. She stood up and held out her arms.

"I'm sorry Ariella. I thought when you died in that sun, that I'd lost you. I had to remove that memory. I was constantly reminded wherever I went, whichever realm I was in, that you were gone, and yet he never would be!"

"That was NOT your choice to make! You pulled him from existence! You murdered *five million* pain wraiths to use their power to alter the fabric of existence to remove *one man*! When I knew what you had done, I moved into Caroline's body, and blocked out all my memories. I didn't want to know what I had lived with. I wanted to live as a human, in peace, and move through life freely."

Ariella lifted her mother from the ground again and thrust her backwards with force. She flew through the train door, smashing it off its hinges, the glass flying everywhere, as she continued through the air, through one door, and through another, eventually bursting out the back of the train, and careering down the tracks, eventually coming to a stop over a hundred metres from the back of the train.

Ariella stepped down from the locomotive, and looked around the side of the carriages to the front of the train. Directly in front of it, was a large purple haze. From within it, screams and cries of pain could be heard echoing through time. She turned back to face her mother.

"You were going to drag me back, and chain me up like Dara and Leda! You were going to take my freedom as well!"

Jasmine slowly regained her footing.

"There was nothing left for you here!"

Ariella marched further towards Jasmine, fists balled once again.

"That's because you had taken it!"

"I had to! You were beyond my control! You expose our realm, and you put us ALL in danger. Do you really think these humans can be trusted not to destroy our home, the way they are destroying their own? You are a LIABILITY!"

Jasmine attempted to grip Ariella's body, but she fought back, and it was Jasmine who weakened first.

"I can do whatever I want to mother. I was granted my freedom, and you tried to take it from me. For all those lives you took. I can make amends. You cannot. It is you who will face our punishments, not me."

Jasmine's eyes began to bulge as her form was squeezed by an invisible grip, and with one swift gesture of her hands, she was thrown back through the train, each carriage collapsing to rubble as she passed through them, until she burst through the front of the cab and into the purple haze, landing within it like falling into an oil slick.

As she lay captured and gradually being pulled back into her realm, glowing threads of matter emerged from the haze, and wrapped themselves around Jasmine's body, pulling her in. She fought against them, but more appeared and took hold. Her face glowed red, and her eyes burned violet. She raised a hand towards her daughter.

"You will not destroy our realm, daughter. I will return!" Ariella looked back with tears streaming down her face.

"This was not my last train ride mother. It was yours. Enjoy your eternal suffering."

And with a final scream of terror, Jasmine disappeared through the haze, and in a blast of purple light, the train was gone, and Ariella found herself sat on a bench in the train station where it all started. People moved around her, and as she looked up at the clock, it read nine-thirty. She smiled to herself and picked up her bag from under the bench. As she went to walk towards the train, which was now pulling into the station, she bumped into a man who was also running for it.

"Oh, I'm so sorry, please do excuse me."

The man reached down and picked up Ariella's bag and handed it back to her.

"That's okay, don't worry about it," she replied. She was captured in the man's gaze.

He too seemed rather taken with her.

"Sorry, I don't mean to stare, but you are rather beautiful."

Ariella was a little taken aback but felt a smile moving across her face.

"Umm, thank you. That's very kind of you."

"I know it's forward, but would you like to maybe get a coffee sometime?" asked the man.

"Yeah, I think I'd like that. I'm Caroline."

"Nice to meet you. I'm Arthur."

CLOWNING AROUND

I was paralysed with fear. I couldn't move more than a twitch from my toes, and my eyes were fixed dead ahead. I felt a cold sweat run down my back and could feel it beading up on my forehead. As the evil creature looked back at me, I feared that I was completely at its mercy.

The music started, and each of the children started dancing around the chairs, each eagerly looking back at the sound system, waiting for the music to stop, and sticking as close to the chairs as possible. The second Julia hit the button, they dived into a seat, one of the smaller kids missing out and landing on their butt on the floor, with a bit of a thud. Julia carted the kid off to the side and introduced…it.

I've never been able to deal with clowns. Ever since I was a little kid, I've been absolutely terrified of them. I was diagnosed with a variation of Coulrophobia when I was five. My mother had thrown a birthday party for me and hired a clown. When he didn't come out of the bathroom for about an hour, I made the mistake of wandering in, and found him dead on the floor, eyes wide open, in full make up, staring right back at me. Ever since then, they have been my number one fear. Even more than spiders.

And let's be honest, Stephen King wasn't exactly much help.

As he began dancing around, and playing with the balloons, he glanced up at me, and my heart started pounding almost to bursting point. This was not my idea of fun, and as soon as he looked away, I made every effort to slide along the wall, and into the kitchen. It wasn't until I was on the other side of the wall that I began to breathe again.

"Jesus Christ."

I was panting slightly, and Julia rushed over to hand me a glass of water.

"Thank you."

"Look, if you're that scared of them, then why did you come?" she asked me.

I thought about it for a moment, but the reason was obvious to me.

"Because it's the only way I get to see my son, that's why."

Joe was the only reason I ever did anything outside of work. His mother and I had never really been the best parents. I met Julia when I was seventeen, and she really wasn't interested. In fact, she couldn't have made her point any clearer. But I was determined, and she was the sexiest girl I'd ever seen. I spent the next two and a half years trying to convince her to even take a second glance at me. My luck came at a Halloween party that year, when I was sat in one of the bedrooms at the house the party was being held in, basking in my misery, when she walked in, completely wasted, and sat on the bed next to me. She's made it very clear since, that she had been looking for the captain of the basketball team, but I'm confident she didn't know where she was going.

She ended up kissing me first, and being the desperate little shit I was, I did nothing to stop it. We never went any further than what my mother always described as 'heavy petting' but at the St Patrick's Day party the following year, it happened again. After two parties of her initiating the intimacy, and then nothing coming of it, at the third attempt, at a Christmas party, I made the move.

She wandered over to me, this time, having only had one drink, and we walked outside. We chatted and she told me about how her Dad had been beating her mother, and how he had finally been arrested and locked up. I told her about how long I had wanted to spend time with her, and how much those two drunken encounters had really meant, and we ended up kissing again. I led her to my car, and the rest as they say is history.

We got engaged three years later, but the relationship was a turbulent one. I was spending a lot of time working for my Dad's shipping firm, and she was at medical school. This all meant that the time we were spending together, it was all sex and dating, but no real intimacy.

When Julia found out she was pregnant, she hit the roof. Neither one of us had been responsible, and were both equally to blame, and yet somehow, it was all my fault. I had ruined her career, and now her body was going to be destroyed. Her father suggested she have the baby terminated, but she refused, which I was relieved about.

That was when I realised that she was just scared. She was young to be having a child, and especially with all her studies. I offered to remain with her and give up my job, to help us both prepare for the arrival, and she agreed.

Every night we argued. I was bringing in minimum wage from working in a fast food place to stay near her, and she was finding it harder and harder to concentrate at school. We broke up before Joe was born. I wasn't there at the birth, and it killed me. Julia dropped out of medical school after getting involved with a bad crowd. She started taking drugs, and drinking a lot, but wouldn't let me see Joe. Eventually, she was forced to clean up her act when she was arrested for drugs offences, and she went back to study accounting. Our relationship, however, remained fractured.

I only got to see my son when it suited her. I couldn't afford to try for custody of Joe, I'd burnt my bridges with my old man, and he was now working with my brother, and so every chance I got to see him, I took it with both hands.

Julia would taunt me any time I saw him, by sending a clown doll in his rucksack. She knew how traumatised I was over clowns, and still she taunted me. I often think about her, and how different our lives would have been if we had both made more of an effort to make it work. I still miss her.

A massive bang came from the lounge, and Julia poked her head around the corner, reporting an exploded balloon, and nothing more.

"I don't know why you needed to hire a clown, Julia."

"Well kids like clowns," she replied.

I begged to differ.

"Couldn't you get a milder version?" I asked.

"Milder? How do you have a mild clown?"

She was now giggling at me.

"You know, more Krusty the Clown, and less Pennywise."

Even mentioning the name of that monster made me shudder. The rest of the party went with almost no hitches. One of Joe's friends decided to climb a bookcase, and ended up landing in the birthday cake, which did not impress the birthday boy. Or Julia. As everybody left, I felt a distinct tap on the shoulder. I turned around and standing before me was the clown, staring right back at me.

I staggered backwards, and fell backwards, tripping over a discarded dumper truck, and crashing through one of the plastic tables, sending glasses and plates everywhere. Joe looked at me with embarrassment, and the clown looked confused.

"I only wanted to know where the bathroom was," the clown said.

Joe walked over to him, and pointed him in the right direction, before walking over to me.

"You know Dad, you're pretty old to be scared of a man in makeup."

"Fear doesn't have an age, Joe. You can be ninety and still scared of things."

"Yeah, scared of death, scared of peeing your pants, scared of not being able to pee your pants."

Joe continued to reel off a list of sarcastic remarks, while in the background, I heard the toilet flush. Moments later, the man emerged, thankfully without his wig and makeup.

"Sorry if I gave you a fright buddy," he said. "Your friend here has only just told me about your clown phobia."

I gave Julia a scathing look and turned back to the man. "That's okay, it's just something I'm trying to deal with."

He nodded, patted me on the shoulder and left.

"So, Lance, do you need to pay a visit to the little boys room too?" asked Julia, with a smirk growing ever wider on her face.

Joe started laughing, but I wasn't amused.

"No thank you. Come on Joe, let's get out of here before I have an aneurysm."

I sat in the bar, watching the game on the TV. After the latest slanging match with Julia, I decided a stiff drink or five was in order. Me and Joe had enjoyed a birthday McDonalds before I returned him home. I seemed to be the only one watching, but as Manchester United scored their eighth goal, and the Southampton players sat down on the pitch, I figured the game had kind of lost its interest.

"Hey Lance, you're out a bit late aren't you?"

I was in this place so often these days, that the bartender knew me on a first name basis.

"Yeah Barry. Had another encounter with the ex."

Barry nodded understandingly. This was the fourth time this month I had needed a pick-me-up. Or five.

"You're surely not driving back to Wealdstone tonight? I mean you're not in much state to drive, even if it is only a rental car."

I looked down at my watch, and sure enough, it had gone eleven.

"I guess I'll be sleeping in the car then," came my reply.

Barry went away and came back with the local newspaper. He opened the page and pointed at an advertisement.

"This place re-opened last week, cheap rates, and not far from here."

I read the advert.

WE'RE BACK!

Cheap rates, weekly discount, rooms from just $14 per night! Bigger and better than ever, book your room now!

THE CLOWN HOTEL

My eyes bulged when I read the name of the place. America was huge, and yet my son had to live in a town with the hotel modelled on my number one fear.

"No fucking way."

My reply stunned Barry a little.

"Well, it's the only hotel still operating. Out of season now you know," he said in defence.

"Barry, no offence, but are you afraid of anything? You know, like phobias?"

Barry thought for a minute.

"Snakes. I hate snakes. I'm with *Indiana Jones* on this one. Slimy little bastards. No thank you."

"Well imagine the only hotel in town was the 'Snake Hotel' and there were pictures of snakes and toy snakes and all sorts of snake related things in there. What would you do?"

He thought for a moment, before nodding. "I'd drive the six hours back to Wealdstone."

"Exactly."

Thinking I'd won my argument, Barry came back.

"But I haven't been drinking for the last two hours."

Damn it. He had a point. I looked up at the TV and as Manchester United hit their ninth goal, I conceded the point.

"I just can't do it Barry. They terrify me."

"Well why don't you call the hotel, book a room, but ask them to remove any clown related items from your room?"

I hadn't thought about that. Given my half drunken state, although it still terrified me, even being in the same building as clowns, if they weren't in my room, I should be able to make it.

Barry made the call, and booked the room for me, and I said my goodnight to him and left the bar.

I stood in the car park staring up at the building before me. I was going to be in for quite an intense night. The exterior was dark red brick, and the entrance was crafted in the design of the entrance to a big top. There was a clown standing on either side, I guessed made of fibreglass. But what added the creepiness factor was the fact that directly behind the hotel, was the town cemetery. In my slightly inebriated state, I got further than I otherwise would have done, and managed to walk through the entrance, albeit sideways on, to avoid any contact with those monstrous creations.

The reception was something else.

I counted approximately forty clown figures, figurines, posters and souvenirs. There was even a clown motif in the carpet. Thankfully, the individual on the reception desk, was not dressed as a clown. Despite my focus not being as sharp as usual, the fear had crept in, and it was everything I could do to get my words out.

"Erm… I'm… I have a room booked. Clown free."

The receptionist looked about as interested in me as I look if someone puts *Love Island* on the TV. She reached under the counter and pulled out a key, with a large clown keyring hanging from it. The look on my face told her everything she needed to know. She retracted the key, snapped the clown from it, and handed it back.

"Room forty-one, fourth floor, first on the left."

"Thank… thank you."

My head was spinning, sweat now dripping from my forehead. A fact that did not go unnoticed.

"Hey! Take the service lift through that door, and you'll skip most of them."

I nodded towards the receptionist in a thankful manner and tried not to look at any of the figurines lined up along the desk.

"If you need anything else, it'll have to wait until morning. I'm off. Sleep tight."

She picked up her bag and coat and walked out the doors. I kept my hand in front of my eyes, looking only at the floor and walked through the door marked 'Staff Only'. Thankfully there were no clowns in the staff area, and I was able to see where I was going.

I was in a large, white passageway, showing images on the walls of the hotel during its lifetime. From the looks of the images, the place had only recently been marketed in this bizarre way and was being modelled after a motel in Nevada. The service lift was directly ahead, so I wasted no time in pressing the button, and eagerly waited for the doors to open.

I heard shuffling noises behind me but suspected that the noise was being caused by a rat or a mouse. The kitchen was off to the right, and with everyone gone, it was prime time for a rodent snacking session.

The ding from the lift sounded out, and as the doors opened, I rushed inside, pressing the button for the fourth floor. As the doors closed, I could have sworn I saw a shadow moving in the kitchen. Perhaps one of the kitchen staff on their way out, I thought. The doors clunked shut, and I leaned against the back wall, closed my eyes, and took a deep breath.

"It's only fake ones. They aren't real. Just breathe."

I opened my eyes as the lift passed the second floor and turned to my right only to see a six foot clown staring back at me.

I flew backwards into the wall of the elevator with such force that I shook the entire vehicle. My hands clamped against the wall, as I stared intently at the life-sized figure standing in a cardboard box, amongst which were more figurines, probably from display on their way to storage.

The clown was of Victorian clothing and stared directly ahead at the lift doors. It's nose was red, as one would expect, and the frills around its neck just kept reminding me of that damn Pennywise. I think I speak for the entire planet when I say that fictional monster is responsible for many nightmares.

As the lift passed the third floor, I closed my eyes again. The familiar ding sounded out, signalling our arrival at the fourth floor. I opened my eyes and froze in my place.

The clown was now facing me. It's plastic eyes bore into my own.

"It...it...it must have shifted from... from the lift movements."

I tried to reassure myself of how this had happened, and gradually slipped out of the lift, my eyes never leaving it's face for a second. As the doors closed before me, the figure turned again, and through the final slit in the doors, I saw it turn forwards once more.

I was now very much on edge, either from the booze or the genuine fear of something more happening here. As I gazed around the hallway, the lights were dim, but it was clear the obsession continued here. The wallpaper was red and white striped, and every picture or painting was of a clown either performing, or face on portraits. And to make matters worse, there was another of the six foot replica clowns standing to the left hand side of every door to every room, like an army of undead soldiers.

There was however, one positive element. The clown next to my room had been removed, and I was only seven or eight feet away. I took another deep breath and slipped the key card into the door, and the second it clicked, I flew inside, slamming the door shut behind me.

I sat on the floor behind the door for at least fifteen minutes, taking deep breaths, and trying to compose myself. I was exhausted, and my eyes were stinging from the sweat. I looked around the room, and sure enough, as requested, everything to do with clowns had been removed, except the carpet which obviously wasn't an option. However, this was mostly covered with rugs, so I felt more at ease.

I meandered over to the window, which was open, the breeze moving the net curtain around, and was dismayed at what I saw. My room, naturally, had a bird's eye view of the cemetery. Every grave and headstone was facing the hotel.

"I should have slept in the car," I said aloud to myself.

I shut the window and closed the curtains. Big top curtains. Seriously. Who the hell decides to theme a hotel after something as ridiculous as clowns? I hadn't bothered bringing my bag up from the car, knowing I'd probably leave something behind at a random point of terror, so I slipped off my shirt, and shoes, and lay down on the bed. The room was silent. Perfect conditions under normal circumstances. I switched off the light, and lay there, head on the pillow, and tried to give in to my exhaustion.

An hour passed, and still I hadn't managed to join the land of nod. I turned to lie on my back. Letting out a heavy sigh, my mind began to wander back towards the graveyard.

"Stop it, you fucking wimp," I said to myself aloud. "You're nearly thirty years old!"

I hadn't been expecting a response of any kind, but when it came, it chilled me to the bone.

From the doorway, I heard a distinct laugh.

Shivers reverberated through my entire body. I lay there still as a corpse and listening intently.

"*Hahaha,*" came the laugh a second time.

I closed my eyes again and tried to picture a drunken couple making their way to their room down the hallway. Oddly, that did seem to ease my mind slightly.

KNOCK KNOCK.

I sat bolt upright in bed as the door shuddered with the force of the knock. I didn't move. I didn't dare. My mind was racing faster than my heart. The sweat was back, and to the side of the bed, the window clicked open again, sending a breeze billowing through the room, curtains flying in the wind.

KNOCK, KNOCK, KNOCK.

The noise came again.

"Who...Who's... Who's there?"

I managed to get the words out of my mouth. No reply.

I slid towards the window, and clicked it shut once more. But standing in the middle of the graves directly in front of the window, looking up, was a clown. I was frozen at the window, and the clown tilted it's head to one side and began to smile. As it did so, the door knocked again, and I heard the laughing outside once more. As a reflex, my head snapped towards the door, to find that it was completely open. I hadn't heard it open, but there it was. I shot my gaze back out of the window, and the clown was gone. Pulling the curtains closed, and facing the doorway again, I reached for my shirt and put it back on.

I was *terrified to my core.*

I found myself shuffling towards the door. It felt like an eternity to reach it, and as I put my hand on the door, the laughing started again. It sounded like it was coming from down the hall, so I slowly stuck my head out and looked down the corridor.

There was nobody there. And I mean *nobody.*

All the clowns were gone.

Then suddenly, from behind me, more laughter. I flew out of my room, pressing myself back against the wall in the corridor. More giggling from *inside* my room. As I stared up and down the hallway, I noticed a shadow from inside the room. As I focused more closely, the shadow figure appeared to move through the window from *outside.* As it walked into the light, I recognised it instantly. The clown from the graveyard was now standing in my room, next to my bed.

It began laughing, the smile on its face widening.

More laughter came but this time from my right, and I turned in that direction to be met with three clowns staring at me from the end of the hallway near the service lift. The clown in the middle was the one from the lift, in the Victorian gear.

As my stomach churned, I began backing up down the hallway. As I did so, their laughing intensified, and the three clowns began moving towards me, and the faster I backed up, the faster they moved, until they were sprinting. The fourth clown from my room joined them. I screamed out loud.

"HELP! SOMEBODY HELP ME PLEASE!"

I tripped over a raised section of carpet, and clattered to the floor, the clowns almost upon me. I burst into tears and covered my head, screaming louder than I'd ever screamed before, waiting for the attack.

But it never came.

I slowly lifted my arms from my head, and the clowns were gone. Looking around the hallway, all the clowns were back at the entrance to each door.

I was breathing so rapidly, my head was spinning, and it took all my strength to drag myself along the carpet back to my room. The door, still open, I peered inside, but there was nothing in there. I left the door open, climbed to my feet, and edged towards the window. Looking outside, everything was as it had been before.

I collapsed back on the bed, trying to rationalise what had occurred. My blood was cold, and my skin clammy all over. I closed my eyes and continued to take deep breaths once more until my heart rate eased.

And then the door slammed shut.

I sat bolt upright again and was face to face with the clown from the graveyard. It stood at the bottom of my bed staring at me, this time with a serious face.

"Please," I muttered. "Please don't hurt me!"

The clown cocked it's head to one side, and a confused look spread over its face.

"I don't have any intention of hurting you."

I was staggered by its voice. I had not expected a reply. In fact, I had expected death.

"Wh-What do you want?" I asked, my voice trembling, but more with interest than fear.

The clown smiled, and the fear was back.

"You need to go to your son."

The fear intensified.

"What did you say?"

The clown walked towards me. The smile no longer appeared terrifying, but somehow had morphed into a caring smile. I was completely disarmed by this.

"You must go to your son. Now."

The clown stopped a foot away from me.

"Your son is in danger."

The fear of this monstrous entity had gone. The mention of Joe had my complete attention, and all my senses were focused on this, and nothing else.

"What do you mean? Where is he?"

The clown said nothing but turned and pointed out of the window towards the graveyard.

"Go to your son, and then go down there. You will have your answers."

I looked out the window, which was now fully open again, but when I looked back at the clown, he was gone. I jumped off the bed, and looked back out the window, and saw the clown walking towards one of the gravestones. He turned back and looked at me, pointing to the car park.

I cannot explain what came over me next. It was as if a roadmap had appeared in my mind, like somebody else was inside there, and was planning my every move. I grabbed the key to the room, and ran out the door, slamming it behind me, and sprinted for the normal lift.

Every clown on the floor was now pointing towards that lift.

As I entered it, I slammed my hand on the ground floor button repeatedly until the doors closed. The descent of the lift seemed to take an eternity, and as I emerged, the clowns in reception, were all pointing outside, reiterating the fact I needed to leave. As I made it outside, the two standing either side of the entrance, pointed up and to the right. As I followed their gaze, I could see smoke, and an ominous glow in the sky.

Again, I cannot explain it, but I knew what it was immediately. I threw myself into the car, started the engine and span my way out of the car park.

As I pulled up outside Julia's house, the flames were now shooting out of the roof. There were sirens in the distance, but nobody close enough. I ran up the path, and as I approached the front door, the lounge windows blew out, showering me in shards of broken glass. From inside, I heard coughing. I summed up all my courage and kicked the door in, and the heat hit me like a freight train. I grabbed a coat from the coat stand near the door and threw it over my head.

"JOE?" I shouted as loud as I could but got no reply. "JULIA?"

Again, no reply.

I moved forward and headed straight up the stairs towards Joe's room. The fire was at its most intense up here, and the closer I got to Joe's bedroom, the more I realised the fire was coming from Julia's. I heard the coughing again.

"JOE?" I shouted over the loud sound of the crackling fire.

"Dad?"

A faint voice came from Joe's room, and I pushed my way through the debris and into the room. Part of the ceiling had collapsed onto the bed, and Joe was trapped beneath it.

"JOE!"

I threw the coat over my son and wrestled with the chunks of ceiling. As the rubble slid off the edge of the bed, it punched a hole in the floor, and I just managed to catch my son before he too fell through the hole.

"Come on, we need to get out of here now!"

I carried him, covered in the coat out of his room.

"What about Mom?" he asked.

I hesitated for a moment, but I looked him in the eyes and gave him my reply.

"I'm gonna get you outside, and then come back for your Mom, okay?"

He nodded, and we made our way down the stairs. As we pushed through the front door, the fire engines arrived in the street, and all the neighbours were now outside, watching in horror. I put Joe down and headed back inside to look for Julia.

As I reached the door to her bedroom, I could smell something that gave me a good indication that this was not going to be a successful rescue. I couldn't get very close to the door because of the intensity of the heat and the flames. As I squinted through the smoke, I saw the clown from the hotel. He looked inside the room, and then looked back at me. He shook his head, and I knew she was dead. I threw the coat back over my head, and headed out the door just as the firemen started going in.

Joe ran up to me and threw himself into my arms, and I held him tight.

"Mom?" he asked.

All I could do was shake my head.

"I'm sorry Joe."

I could feel his tears coming through my shirt against my hot skin. I looked at all the fire trucks and people now watching and standing just to the left of the truck nearest us, was the clown. He nodded his head, and smiled at me, and then walked away, disappearing into the crowds.

I stood reading the gravestones and found myself nodding as I read the words. Joe stood beside me, confused, and trying to comprehend.

"I don't understand, Dad. How did the clowns know?"

I read the words again. The gravestones were not graves, but memorials.

Here lie the memories of the fifty three miners lost to the deadly fire of eighteen-eighty-two. Lost in the mines at Frankland Hill on the fateful day of September sixteenth, when a ruptured gas main was ignited by the lanterns of the workers. All workers perished. We present this monument, and series of memorials in their honour. Lest we forget.

"They weren't clowns son, they just looked like clowns.""What do you mean?"

"Your house, where is it?" I asked my son.

"We live on Frankland Hill," he replied.

"There is an old mine under the housing estate. These men lost their lives in a fire. I think they were trying to warn me because they had suffered a similar fate."

Joe contemplated this for a minute.

"They told you to save my life."

I nodded and held him close.

"Come on son, let's get out of here."

As we walked out of the cemetery, I saw up in the window of my hotel room, the clown, looking down. As I smiled at him, the clown image disappeared, and was replaced by an ordinary man. He held up a hand to wave, and I waved back. As we reached the car, I looked back at the entrance to the hotel, and all the clowns. I didn't feel fear anymore. Joe noticed me looking.

"What is it Dad?"

I smiled to myself and looked at him.

"Nothing. But I don't think I'm afraid of clowns anymore."

CALL OF THE SERPENTS

The sky swirled with a green haze, mingled with the clouds, forming a whirlwind of deep emerald light. Below, the waves crashed onto the rocks, foam from the surge reaching high over the outcrops and up into the air. Inside the cavern, there were a chorus of screams, both earthly and unearthly. Echoing around each chamber, the sounds lifted and fell with the waves. Each rock pool and water based tunnel was bubbling with fury, and as the ground began to shake, chunks of rock fell from above, landing with the force of a meteorite.

The sound of pounding footsteps joined the symphony of screams, sand, and rock crunching underfoot, added to the sound of heavy, fast breathing. Kristin flew down each tunnel, the golden glow behind her charging in pursuit. Looking back, she saw disembodied hands grip the walls, and mangled water bloated bodies using them to launch themselves forward.

She ducked, narrowly missing a chunk of the roof landing on her head. She reached the pool through which she had previously swam, but as she dangled her legs into the bubbling water to jump in and swim through, hands reached up from within and began grabbing at her thighs, scratching her skin as they did so.

She screamed and fought them, kicking and slapping the hands away.

Beneath the water she saw the dead eyes in the faces of Alex and Steve as their hands continued to grasp at her flesh. She freed her legs, now bleeding from the scratches, and got back to her feet, but it was too late. The crew had emerged into the chamber. They crawled along the walls, and the ground, screams getting ever louder. More began rising from the pools around her, and she backed up against the rocks, nowhere to go, and nobody to save her.

"Stay the fuck away!" she screamed.

The crew amassed in front of her and stopped. The mangled and twisted form of Augustin Pereyra staggered forwards, his face mere millimetres from Kristin's. His cold dead breath was putrid, and Kristin closed her eyes tight in response. As his bony fingers reached into her wetsuit, her entire being tightened in fear, the slimy feeling not a pleasant one.

As the hand retracted, it held within it, the two medallions Kristin had taken. She opened her eyes and Augustin walked back through the crowd. She began to feel a slight feeling of relief. But it was not to be. As the Captain vanished out of sight, the hoards moved in, and began tearing Kristin to pieces. Shredding the wetsuit, pawing at her skin, their bony nails tearing open the flesh. Her screams were drowned out in the noise of those of the crew, and as she was dragged down into the bubbling water, it ran red. And deep under the red ocean, the dead hands dragged Kristin down to the depths, her hands desperately reaching for the surface, and she vanished into the dark abyss.

Kristin launched herself upright in bed, gasping for breath, and clutching at her throat. Her head was dripping with sweat, and the bed covers were soaked too. Her eyes bulging with fear, she felt Kathryn stir next to her.

"Hey, hey, what is it?" she asked, worried and placing her hands on the shoulders of her wife.

Kristin gasped for more air, but her breathing gradually calmed, and she allowed herself to begin relaxing her muscles.

"You okay?" Kathryn asked again if she was alright.

Kristin nodded.

"I'm fine. Bad dream."

"Are you sure?"

Kathryn looked extremely concerned. Kristin nodded again.

"Yeah, no it's fine. I'm fine. Let's just get back to sleep."

Kathryn leaned over, placed a delicate kiss on her head, and returned to the pillow. Kristin lay back down, but sleep would not come to her so easily. From outside, she could hear the waves lapping at the shore, almost taunting her. She reached over the edge of the bed and opened her bag. Shimmering in the pale moonlight from the window, was the whisper of gold. She stared at that medallion, and almost felt it calling to her. Her head pounded, and her heart began to race again.

She shut her bag, and turned over, clutching the pillow in her arms. She felt a comforting hand from Kathryn on her arm as she rolled over to cuddle her, and she had to admit, she did feel more at ease. She closed her eyes but didn't sleep. And for the next four hours, the scenes from her nightmare played out over and over in her mind, until the sun shone through the window the next morning.

The smell of freshly roasted coffee filled the air, but Kristin's demeanour had not improved. Kathryn had noticed it too, and she was becoming less than impressed.

"Are you going to actually smile on this vacation?" she asked as she took a sip from her cup.

Kristin shot her wife a look that said she wasn't helping her mood.

"I'm trying, just didn't get much sleep last night," she replied.

"Yeah, neither did I in the end. Kept worrying about you fidgeting. I could tell something wasn't right."

Kristin sighed and held her hand.

"It's nothing that can't be solved by a lovely day out," she said and forced a smile.

"I thought you'd have loved the surprise, but now I'm thinking I made a mistake." Kathryn again displayed a look of concern.

The surprise she was referring to, was the fact that following their shotgun wedding in Wealdstone, Kathryn had booked a whirlwind honeymoon in the Bahamas, but not informed her new wife, and as they had boarded the plane, Kristin had made her concerns very vocally.

"No, it's fine. It's just. I went through a lot here last year, and it just brings back bad memories."

Kathryn began to pick up on what she was referring to. She hadn't said a lot following her return with the piece for the museum. Only that things had not gone according to plan, and she was lucky to make it back.

"You know, you can talk to me about this. I mean hell, you completely freaked out about how everything happened to me while you were away getting the damn thing. But you never told me the details."

Kristin thought about it, and Kathryn was right. She wasn't sure how she was going to take it but owed it to her partner that she didn't keep any secrets.

"Okay, but not here. Let's go down to the beach and find somewhere secluded where it will be just the two of us."

Kathryn's eyebrow raised in curiosity.

"You know usually on a honeymoon, that is said in a very different context," she hinted.

Kristin gave her *that* look, and Kathryn held her hands up in defence.

"Okay, okay, let's go. But I want some one on one time later. Honeymooning in the Bahamas is not an opportunity to be squandered!"

The pair of them shared a laugh as they finished their coffees and headed out into the warm Atlantic air.

"Fuck me."

The initial response from Kathryn was quite direct. Kristin waited for her to expand on her statement. She had remained quiet throughout the entire storytelling process, other than an occasional hand on the knee.

"No wonder you were so traumatised. Is this why you're having nightmares?"

Kristin nodded and shrugged her shoulders.

"I think it's being back in the Bahamas. I mean, does it not feel like a twisted fate to you? We could have stayed on any island in the Bahamas, and yet you chose New Providence, where Nassau is located. And it's off the coast of Nassau that we found the wreck of the *Sapphire Serpent*."

Kathryn could understand where she was coming from. It did seem symbolic. She had often thought the same about her encounter with serial killer John Martin. He had escaped from a prison transport, but he had gone straight back to the house he had lived in and committed his most heinous crimes, to meet his end.

"So, what do you think you're supposed to do here?" she asked Kristin.

"I think I'm meant to bring the gold back."

Kathryn changed her expression. The medallion from the *Serpent* had proven to be one of the most popular exhibits in the museum, and she was reluctant to consider letting it go.

"But you only have one, the other is back home, and it's making us an awful lot of money. It practically paid for this trip."

Kristin became annoyed at this remark.

"Money is not as important as my mental state, Kathryn. This is seriously screwing with my mind!"

"Yeah, says the woman who refused to let me back out of opening the museum after I was nearly killed there. What about my mental state?"

Kristin stood up to leave.

"Look, I'm not arguing with you. The bottom line is that I need to fix this, and I can't do it alone!"

Kathryn stood up and held her wife's hands in her own. She knew she was being unreasonable and attempted to reassure her.

"Okay, fine. I'm sorry I yelled, but how do we get the other medallion here. We're making a lot of money, but it isn't enough to keep jetting back and forth."

Kristin had already figured this out.

"It's okay. I was hanging out with Max just after the wedding. He was showing quite an interest in the pirate exhibit. I could call him and get him to FedEx it to the hotel. I'll bribe him with a year of free movies at the shopping district."

Kathryn grew a wry smile.

"You know, now we're married, technically your money should be my money. You make a lot more than I do, and you already named the district after me anyway."

Kristin laughed.

"Yeah, who doesn't want to rebuild half their empire when it blows up! Besides, I own the development site, not the stores. If one goes out of business, I lose rent. And it's a nice name."

"Spoken like a true financial advisor."

They giggled between themselves, but their levity was short lived, when they heard a large amount of activity coming from the main beach.

"I wonder what that's all about?" asked Kathryn.

They both went around the corner of the rocks they had climbed over to get their privacy and stopped in their tracks when they saw what the fuss was all about.

"How the fuck did *that* get there?" Kathryn yelled.

Kristin felt sick to her stomach and said nothing.

Directly in front of them, in the middle of the beach, surrounded by tourists, was the wreck of the *Sapphire Serpent*.

"Don't shout at me! I didn't bring the fucking thing here!"

Kathryn slammed the hotel room door behind her, as Kristin marched up to the dressing table and slammed her fists down onto the wooden surface in anger.

"I didn't say you brought the fucking thing, I said you brought *me*!"

"Well God forbid I should want to do something special for the one person in my life who means the most to me!"

Kristin hung her head in defeat. She was arguing over something that they hadn't had any control over. Kathryn continued her argument.

"Besides, if someone had bothered to confide in me what they had gone through, then maybe I would have chosen Hawaii!"

"Alright, enough!"

Kristin held up a hand in peace.

"I'm sorry. I know it isn't your fault. But don't you find it slightly coincidental that somehow the wreck of this cursed ship somehow manages to unstick itself and seemingly sail forty-five miles inland, just as we arrive on the island?"

Kathryn nodded and sat on the edge of the bed.

"I'm guessing that somehow, unearthly forces were involved. If that ship was as buried in the rock as you say, to travel this far is definitely not possible with any form of help from our realm."

Kristin grabbed her phone, as it beeped with an alert for a text message. It was from Max.

"Max has sent the other medallion out here. He says there was some weird activity going on at the museum with it. Daniella tried locking it in a box overnight, but it managed to find its way back to the display case."

Kathryn had a thought that perhaps while they had been arguing, more details had emerged regarding the circumstances surrounding the *Serpent*. She reached for the TV remote and flicked on the news channel. Kristin joined her wife on the bed and they both watched together, as the report came live from the beach. The reporter was getting pretty windswept, as the breeze had turned itself up a notch or two, and the sky had now darkened with clouds.

The exact circumstances behind this incredible mystery are still mostly unknown. We are aware through sightings of members of the public who had been out wakeboarding, that the ship appeared to be travelling under its own power, despite the condition she is now known to be in. There were no known storms in the area at the time, and it is not known how this ship, previously believed to be a myth,

has made its way to where it now lies. Investigators have found no
evidence of the legendary haul the ship was meant to be carrying,
and from the size of the hole in the side of the ship, if this treasure
was real, it had surely spilled out into the ocean, never to be seen
again.

The report cut off when the camera lost its live feed, and moments later, all of the power went out in the hotel. The TV went dark, and the ceiling fans came to a stop. Outside, the weather was now becoming increasingly volatile, and the waves were now crashing onto the shore.

Kathryn stood up and walked to the door, and out onto the balcony at the front of the hotel. The waves were now pounding the hull of the *Sapphire Serpent*, the ship however, refusing to budge. People began scattering, as the tide appeared to be coming in, at an alarmingly fast rate. The clouds darkened in response, until they were almost black. Kristin began feeling very uneasy. Too many elements of what were happening brought her dream back into focus.

Kathryn reached towards her wife to reassure her, when from the other side of the room, a vibrating noise became audible. They both looked in that direction, and Kathryn put her arm across Kristin to keep her back and moved forward to investigate.

"Kat, don't!"

Kristin pleaded, but Kathryn held her arm out again to protect her and continued to move towards the source of the rumbling. She tracked the sound down to the edge of the bed, and Kristin's handbag. As she got closer, and the wind howled further, the vibrating sound became louder and more intense. Opening the bag, she saw the medallion in the bottom of the bag, shaking directly in the centre, everything else in the bag having moved away from it. The gold flipped over repeatedly, and Kathryn jumped back, startled at the movement. Then, suddenly, the medallion was still, and the vibration stopped.

Kathryn stood up, and moved her gaze from the bag, turning to her wife.

"Hey Kris..."

Kristin was being held by her throat, around six feet in the air by what Kathryn could only describe as a rotten corpse. The skin was hanging from the bones by the tendons, discoloured, almost grey. The clothes were shredded, and the hair scarce and twisted. Kristin was choking, and despite the sight in front of her Kathryn felt the need to act, and act now.

"HEY! CAPTAIN ASSHOLE!"

The words left her mouth before she knew they had even formed, and the pirate corpse snapped its head in her direction instantly. Kathryn reached into the bag and grabbed the medallion, holding it up in the air. The creature threw Kristin into the wall of the room, and she fell crumpled in a heap, unconscious, but breathing. The beastly figure began moving towards Kathryn.

"Oh shit, that did it."

She moved as far back as she could, until she was up against the bathroom door, the creature still moving towards her, leaving a trail of water behind it. Kathryn had no options open to her. She gripped the gold coin and prepared to launch it through the air.

"You want it? Go fucking get it!"

She fired the coin through the air, but as it reached the mid-way point, it stopped and hung above the bed for a moment, before turning and heading right into the pirate's hand, clinking against the bones as it did so. It looked down at the shimmering treasure in its hand, and then returned it's gaze to Kathryn and continued to move towards her.

"You've got what you wanted, what more do you need?"

Kathryn's voice was now becoming more panicked, and she attempted to break past the figure, but it grabbed her by the throat, as it had done to Kristin, and she felt herself raised from the ground. She was pushed back and held against the bathroom door, her legs dangling above the ground. The creature moved its haggard decaying face to hers, and to her astonishment, began to speak.

"Dónde está el otro?"

It's breath smelt salty and putrid, but as Kathryn struggled to breath, the creature intensified its grip and asked again.

"Dónde está el otro?"

Kathryn began to lose her grip on consciousness. She didn't understand the language being spoken to her and tried to convey this to the monster currently choking her to death, but was unable to move.

Her arms and legs were tingling, and her head was spinning. The creature shouted the phrase once more.

Dónde está el otro!?"

"ABANDONA ESTE LUGAR!"

The pirate spun around, releasing its grip on Kathryn, and she fell to the floor gasping for air. In the doorway was the outline of a man, but Kathryn could not make out any discerning features. Again, the man spoke in Spanish to the pirate demon.

"Estás desterrado de este lugar!"

The man thrust a crucifix into the air, and the pirate spirit let out a long scream, opening its mouth as wide as its face, before collapsing into the floor as a body of water, splashing everywhere as it vanished.

The man ran over to Kathryn and helped her to sit up against the door. She squinted and could just make out the image of a man she faintly recognised but couldn't quite place.

"What did you say to it?" she asked, still unsure that she was awake and not having a nightmare.

The man helped lift her up and onto the bed.

"I told him to leave this place, and that he was banished from here. You should be safe in this room for now. But he will be back."

In the corner near the entrance to the room, Kristin began to stir. The man leaned down and helped her up and lay her alongside Kathryn on the bed. While Kathryn had not been able to place the face, Kristin did.

"John Slater?"

The man smiled and nodded.

"Nice to know I still have fans somewhere."

Kathryn was now becoming more aware.

"Sorry, who are you?"

John's face slumped a little. He hadn't exactly been a world famous celebrity, but it was unusual for people not to recognise him in the States. Kristin answered for him.

"Babe, this is John Slater. He used to host Extreme Investigations on Channel Six. You know, the ghost show."

Now she remembered where she had seen his face before.

"Oh yeah, you guys were meant to come film at the museum and then didn't show up."

John hung his head a little.

"Yeah, I apologise for that, but we lost a member of our crew after an investigation in Wealdstone, so we had to pull out. Given the level of activity you reported at the Stevenson house, we felt it was a bad idea to do two investigations in the city that killed my friend."

Kristin suddenly came to life, as she remembered reading the news articles about the death of Hector Lanzini.

"That was at Highland Manor, right?" she asked.

John nodded.

"One of the most active locations we had ever investigated. We had some communication on one of our devices that suggested Hector was in danger, but we were so stoked about getting such amazing evidence, that we ignored the warnings. The next day, we found him gone. He went back to the Manor, alone, and we found him dead on the front porch."

Kathryn was then distracted, by the sight of a figure standing outside their door. Kristin and John followed her gaze and saw the apparition of another pirate ghoul looking back at them.

"What is with these things?" asked Kathryn. "I gave them the stupid medallion back, why won't they leave?"

Kristin and John moved towards the door. It appeared the words John had laid down, were working. At least for now.

"Because they know we have the other one."

John turned to look at Kristin.

"You mean you didn't bring it with you?"

"No, we only had the one I always keep with me. I didn't know we were coming here for our honeymoon. The other one is on its way here from the museum."

A glance outside revealed another two pirate figures standing at different points on the balcony, each more harrowing than the last.

"What can we do to get rid of these things? The medallion won't be here until tomorrow."

Kathryn's face again expressed panic. She had seen a lot of paranormal activity since she had bought the museum, but as of yet, none had threatened her life. John stood firm in the doorway and repeated the words he had spoken to the Captain of the crew moments before. As the wind howled, the figures blew away as watery mist.

Kristin tapped him on the shoulder.

"Hey, how do you know Spanish?" she asked.

John's face looked reflective as he answered.

"Hector taught me. We did a series of investigations in Mexico, and a couple on the Costa del Sol in Spain, and I kept making an ass of myself, so he taught me."

"I'm guessing the chief spectre was asking me for the other medallion then?" interrupted Kathryn.

John nodded.

"I don't think they're going to leave you alone until they get it. And even then, we may have to take precautions."

A thought then occurred to Kristin.

"Not that I'm ungrateful or anything, but where did you come from?"

John laughed.

"I live here. I moved out here when Channel Six paid me off and cancelled the show. The idea was to make a spin-off with a different network and start by investigating the legend of the *Sapphire Serpent*. I'd heard you had found a medallion, so I decided I'd try to find it too. What I didn't realise was that Steve and Frank had tried it too. A little detail I only discovered when I happened to be walking by you earlier."

As a clap of thunder rattled the sky, almost as if on cue, Kristin had an overwhelming sense of remorse and guilt. But then came a realisation.

"Don't you think it's a little suspicious that you investigate Highland Manor, with Frank as your fellow investigator, and Steve at the time, being the caretaker, only for them both to end up out here with me? And now for you to be here too, as we show up here?"

John shook his head.

"Not really, no. I believe that the spirits, and demons are all able to interconnect somehow. Investigating as many places as I have, things become attached to you, and you carry them with you. This was always due to be played out."

The thunder intensified, and the rain began to pound the roof. Kathryn decided this was enough reminiscing, and it was time to act.

"Well, we can't stay cooped up here for the next twelve hours until the package arrives, so what are we going to do?" she demanded.

"Actually, this is the safest place to be. They can't enter for now, and I can fortify the thresholds with a couple of blessings, and we have a view of the ship. I think this is the safest we can be given the circumstances."

John had seemingly taken charge of the situation, and while she was glad for his help, Kathryn couldn't help but think he had an ulterior motive. Nevertheless, as it became darker, and the weather shot up another notch, they agreed to take watch overnight, and John carried out his blessings, reading them from his phone. The power still hadn't come back on by the time night fell, and so they ordered some candles to be sent up to the room, and they sat in the glow of the flame, until they fell asleep, John watching out.

Kristin woke in the middle of the night, to the sound of John snoring in the corner of the room. Some night watchmen he was. She climbed out of bed and looked at her watch. Three a.m. Nearly time for her shift anyway. She stood up and walked over to the window. The weather had seemingly calmed slightly, the wind not quite as strong. As she was about to move away and get a drink of water, she spotted something emanating from inside the ship.

A deep green glow was visible, and the longer she looked at it, the more drawn she was to it. Suddenly, a pulse of light erupted from the ship, and flew across the sky until it reached Kristin. She swayed from the effect, and then stood still. Under the power of some kind of unseen force, she felt herself moving, and within moments, she was outside. She felt as if she was being pulled along a conveyor belt, aware of what she was doing, but in her trance-like state, unable to stop it.

Kristin's hair was whipped around in the wind as it once again intensified. As she continued to effectively sleep-walk to the beach, the sea was still crashing all around the boat. The glow was still as intense as before, and appeared to be coming from the hold, and shining through the hole in the side. As she approached the water, she was met by two police officers who were guarding the entrance to the sand.

"Excuse me Miss, but you cannot enter the beach. Health and safety reasons."

Kristin's gaze did not break from the ship's ominous green glow. The officers did not seem aware of it. The second officer then reached out towards Kristin.

"Miss, did you hear us?" he spoke.

Whatever unseen force was pulling Kristin towards the *Serpent*, reappeared as the two officers were lifted from the ground as if by magic, and as their faces contorted in shock, their necks were jerked sharply to the side, and their necks cracked, the sickening sound lost in the howling wind, their bodies then dropped to the floor. As Kristin stepped her first foot onto the beach, the water began to part, creating a path through the waves. Inside her mind, she was screaming at herself to turn back, but her body couldn't respond. As she moved further down the path, the water closed in behind her.

Kathryn smacked her phone as she was stirred from her sleep, the sound of it vibrating on the night stand irritating her. The phone ceased to obey her random punches, and so she picked it up and swiped across the screen to answer it.

"This better be fucking important," was her sleep deprived response.

"Mrs Silverton! It's gone!"

Kathryn began to wake up a little more, and in the corner, she heard John begin to stir too.

"Who is this?" she asked, still not a hundred percent sure.

"It's Max! Look, I went to pack up the medallion yesterday evening, and I even arranged for it to be collected, but when I went to get it from the museum, the medallion was gone!"

A cold chill ran right through Kathryn's body.

"How is that possible?" she asked in panic.

"I don't know, but it can't be a coincidence, right?"

John's face in the candle light became a concern when Kathryn noticed his eyes bulging. When she turned to her left and saw the door open, and Kristin gone, she too engaged her panic mode.

"Listen Max, I have to go."

She slammed the phone down on the bed, and she looked at John.

"Where the fuck did she go?" she shouted.

"I've no idea! Who was on the phone?"

"It was my niece's friend. He says the medallion has disappeared!"

John jumped to his feet.

"That can't be a coincidence right?"

"No, considering Kristin told me Max had already sent it via courier this morning, and now she's gone."

They both looked outside, and John shouted out loud.

"There she is!"

Kathryn joined him in the window, and sure enough, Kristin was walking between the waves somehow, towards the hull of the ship. There was a mysterious green glow coming from the ship, and it glinted off something in Kristin's hand.

"Tell me that isn't the medallion?" she asked John.

He rummaged through his rucksack, and pulled out a pair of binoculars, bringing them up to his eyes. The medallion was sat in the palm of Kristin's hand.

"I'm afraid so."

"We need to go after her!" Kathryn shouted and went to run out of the door.

"WAIT!" John shouted after her.

The instant Kathryn ran out of the room, three pirate spirits materialised in front of her. John went after her, only for a fourth to appear in front of him and plunge its hand into his chest. The sound of bones cracking echoed all around them, as his face twisted in agony. The ghoul in question was the Captain who had threatened the group before. He lifted John into the air, as the blood began to trickle from his mouth. Kathryn watched on in horror, backing up towards the room. The Captain looked up at John's contorted expression and spat words from his void of a mouth.

"Bienvenido al infierno."

A violent jerk forward from the decaying arm, another loud crunch, and the pirate Captain removed his arm from John's chest, and the body fell to a crumpled heap on the floor. Kathryn let out a whimper, as John's eyes looked back at her from the ground, the trio of figures still very much blocking her way. The Captain began moving towards her, blood dripping from his arm. John's blood. Kathryn desperately tried to remember the phrase John had used to keep the spirits out of the hotel room. As she watched Kristin approach the opening in the hull of the *Serpent*, it came to her, and she screamed it as loud as she could.

"ESTÁS DESTERRADO DE ESTE LUGAR!"

With a shriek of pain from the figures, they all once more collapsed into the ground in a watery splash. Kathryn took the opportunity, and after giving one final glance at John's now lifeless body, she sprinted towards the beach.

As Kristin walked into the hole in the side of the ship, she felt her mind being released, and she fell to the floor. She looked around her, and when she realised she was indeed inside the *Sapphire Serpent*, she immediately turned to run. As she did so, hands appeared from the wooden floor of the hold and reached up towards her, the hands giving way to bony arms, until there were full skeletal pirate figures standing in the way. Kristin stopped and fell back and felt something solid in her palm.

"What the fuck?" she asked herself.

She opened her hand, and within it, was the second medallion. Her mouth opened in shock. She had no idea how the coin had made its way to her. As far as she knew, it was in a packing box making its way from the US. She held a firm grip on it, as she stared back at the ghostly creatures before her. Through the gap in the hull, she saw the waves crashing, but no water entered the vessel. As she looked closer, the ship appeared to be *moving*. She decided now was as good a time as any to talk to ghosts and stood up and faced them directly.

"What do you want?"

A low rumbling sound, and the ship vibrated. They were definitely moving. It felt like the ship was grinding along the sand beneath them.

"I said, what the fuck do you want?!"

A loud clunking noise came from her left, and as she turned in that direction, she saw the Captain standing before her. Kristin addressed him directly.

"Why am I here?" she asked.

And to her surprise, she received a response in English.

"You took the treasure Señora."

Kristin looked down at the medallion in her hand, still with no recollection of taking it from the museum. The Captain continued, as he approached her.

"You took the treasure, and now you must give it back."

"What do you mean? Here, take it!"

Kristin threw the medallion towards the Captain, and he caught it, like a magnet attracting a piece of iron.

"There! You have it! Let me go!"

The Captain shook his head, the remnants of flesh dangling from his chin as he did so.

"You took the cursed gold, now you too are cursed."

The other pirate ghouls began to approach her, closing the distance between her and any form of safety. She shrank back, and now her dreams were beginning to become more vivid in her mind. The ship began to rise and drop, and Kristin knew now that the ship was at sea. How, she had no idea, but whatever force brought the ship to Nassau, was now seemingly returning it to where it came from.

"No! You can't take me with you! You have your treasure, why can't you rest in peace?!"

The Captain let out a low deep laugh, which took her by surprise.

"We cannot rest Señora, we can never rest! She will not let us rest!"

"Who won't let you rest?"

"If we cannot rest, then you shall not rest either!"

The figure of Augustin Pereyra swept towards her, seemingly to float on the air, and as he reached her, his bony arm stretched out towards her face.

"Get the fuck away from her you sack of bony shit!"

Pereyra swirled around to see the image of something that terrified him to his very core. Kathryn was standing where the pirate guards had stood, but alongside her was a woman who he thought long gone.

"No... it cannot be!"

Kristin was overcome with relief at the sight of her wife, but she did not see what Augustin saw. Standing next to Kathryn was the image of the woman who cursed the crew, hundreds of years before. Augustin staggered backwards, the ship still being thrown about by the waves.

The woman began to move towards him, as Kathryn did the same. The spirit was almost mimicking her movements, like they were spiritually attached somehow. The closer Kathryn got, the closer the woman got, and they both reached out their hands. The ship seemingly turned, as it swung to port, and Kristin did everything she could to hold on. She saw behind Kathryn, through the hole, that the beach was again in sight. Somehow, Kathryn was steering the ship back.

But it wasn't Kathryn, it was the dead woman, with hands now outstretched towards Augustin, seemingly had a grip over his throat. The woman let out a low guttural growl towards him as she got nearer. His dead eyes bulged in terror, as Kristin watched on.

What was happening? How was Kathryn doing all of this?

"Kathryn! How are you doing this?" she called out, but her wife did not respond.

Her eyes had turned black, and her voice was not her own. She addressed the Captain, but the voice was deeper, and *darker.*

"You will never rest, Augustin. You will remain forever cursed!"

"I am sorry Sophia! Forever, I ask for forgiveness!"

Kathryn placed her hand on the skeleton chest of Augustin. The voice became deeper again, and Kathryn began to rise from the floor, much to Kristin's surprise.

"You could have helped us. You did not. You allowed your first mate to murder your family, and you can NEVER be redeemed from that!"

Kristin was clamped to the wall in sheer terror, as Kathryn thrust her hand into the chest of the pirate Captain, and his face began twisting in agony, Kathryn's face defiant and contorted with rage. The Captain let out a scream of pain, getting louder and louder with every passing second.

As the ship ran aground once more, Kristin was thrown along the deck, and slid out of the ship through the hole, landing in the water with a heavy splash.

As the scream from Augustin went almost supersonic, his form dissolved, and Kathryn returned to the ground gently. She emerged from the ship as Kristin staggered onto the shore, and she walked through the waves, the water moving apart before her. Kristin shuffled back on the sand, and as Kathryn reached the feet of her wife, she smiled, and collapsed to the floor, landing softly in the sand. In her place was the woman that Augustin had been so fearful of, but up until now, Kristin had not seen.

"You are safe now."

The voice, although deep, was now comforting. Kristin felt no fear from this spirit.

"Thank you," she replied.

The woman, Sophia, nodded, smiled, and then turned and headed back toward the ship. Kristin scrambled over to Kathryn, who had now begun to wake up from her trance.

"Babe, are you okay?" she asked, the sea water still dripping from her hair down her face.

Kathryn nodded, but apparently had no idea where she was.

"What happened?" she asked.

"It's a long story," replied Kristin. "And to be honest, I'm not sure I know the full story."

She looked back towards the ship, but the *Sapphire Serpent* was gone.

Max was beyond excited. These were the stories he lived for. Daniella on the other hand, had a more concerned look on her face. She knew first-hand how dangerous the supernatural world could be.

"So, she was his wife?" asked Max with glee, and a hint of disbelief.

Kathryn nodded.

"Augustin Pereyra was a notorious pirate Captain, and he had kept his family secret, and sent them away on board another ship. He was ashamed for his reputation and had banished them from his company. When his crew began to pillage the *Cortana*, he didn't realise they were on board. He was too ashamed to stop his first mate from slaughtering the children, and he left his wife to die."

Daniella shook her head in sadness.

"To be betrayed like that is the worst kind of pain someone could feel."

From the corner of the bar, a woman chuckled at Daniella's statement, but they ignored her.

"So why was the Captain after you Kristin?" asked Grace, who until this point had remained silently fascinated by the whole affair.

"He wanted the medallions back, and I think he wanted companionship. He had spent an eternity cursed for what he had done, and the guilt had consumed him in life, and in death."

Daniella nodded in an understanding manner.

"I couldn't believe it when I saw you on the CCTV taking the medallion out of the packing box, Kristin. You looked like you were possessed. They must have known you were going to the Bahamas and you took it without knowing."

Kristin still had no memory of the events but nodded in agreement.

"I think I was. Something about that gold, had an attraction, that I just can't explain. It had to go back to where it came from."

The group continued to sip their drinks, and converse until their glasses were empty.

"How's Duncan getting on?" asked Kathryn.

Daniella shook her head, and Grace lowered hers.

"Not great, I'm afraid. He did a little damage to the shopping district last night, Kristin."

Kristin chuckled to herself.

"I think I should probably just shut that place down! It's been the cause of nothing but trouble since I opened it!"

Kathryn had a more concerned look on her face.

"Where is he now?" she asked.

"He's in a safe place. A friend of mine took care of it. It seems to be the only place he can be right now, until we figure out just what he's capable of."

The group nodded in sympathy. It was Grace who broke the silence.

"We'd better go and see how he's doing, Mom."

Daniella nodded in agreement, and they said their goodbyes. Kathryn took Kristin's hand and placed a gentle kiss on top.

"I'm pretty exhausted too. Wanna head back home?"

Kristin nodded.

"Yeah in a sec. I'd better go settle the bill. You head out, and I'll catch you up."

Kathryn picked up her bag and coat, and followed Daniella, Max, and Grace out of the bar. Kristin approached the bar and signalled for the person to get her cheque.

"You don't know the half of pain."

Kristin was a little confused at the sentence. She looked at the woman sat at the bar, eyes focussed on her empty glass.

"I'm sorry?" she asked.

"Nothing. There is more pain in this world and the next than anyone can imagine."

The bartender refilled the woman's glass.

"Are you okay?" Kristin asked her.

The woman laughed.

"I lost my daughter. She sent me away a long time ago."

The woman was clearly drunk, and from the looks of her, had been in a rough scrap. Her coat was torn, and her shirt was hanging open. Kristin was concerned she had been assaulted. The woman's bra was clearly visible, and her inebriated state would make her a prime target for creeps.

"I'm so sorry to hear that. Do you need any help?"

Again, the woman laughed.

"I will be fine. I will find her. And then everything will be fine."

The bartender brought Kristin the bill, and she handed over her credit card.

"If you're sure, this can be a rough neighbourhood at night."

The bartender returned the card, and Kristin thanked him.

"I can take care of myself, but thank you..."

She waited for Kristin to offer her name, but it took her a moment to realise.

"Oh! Sorry, Kristin. My name is Kristin." "Pleased to meet you Kristin."

The woman offered her hand and Kristin shook it. "My name is Jasmine."

EPILOGUE

As she brought the book to a close, the light in the lantern flickered in an invisible breeze. She did not realise that she had been sat in the chair for hours, and as she placed the volume back on the shelf, she felt eyes on her.

There were now no more lights on in the building. It appeared that the librarian had left, and she had been forgotten, consumed by the tales of horror, and left to her own devices. As the rain continued to cascade down the enormous windows, she picked up the lantern and made her way out of the darkest corner of the library, but she found nobody.

With each step, her shadow was cast against the huge stone walls, wavering in the simulated candle flame. She thought for a moment, that she could hear the sound of whispering, but dismissed it as an after effect of what she had been reading.

She continued forward until she reached a rope, across the top of a set of stairs. A sign hung on the rope. It read *'No entry under any circumstances by staff or patrons.'* She moved to walk past it, but a voice called out to her from below. She stopped in her tracks and waited to see if she heard it again.

She did.

The whispers intensified, and despite all her better instincts, she unhooked the velvet rope, and moved beyond it, hooking it back in behind her. As she descended the stone steps, her footsteps echoed below. She heard the voice call out for her again.

"Ariella…"

She moved further down the staircase, and at the bottom, she found not a basement, but a large wooden door. The whispering had become constant. She could make out some of the words, but not all.

"Wake up… I'm coming… Ariella…"

Curiosity got the better of her, and she placed the lantern on the floor, as its battery began to die. Her hand reached out, and she could feel the cold metal of the doorknob in her hand, and it sent a chill up her arm and throughout the rest of her body.

As she turned the doorknob, a wave of energy washed over her, and her head lost all cohesion. She felt herself falling, and yet she remained standing. The door swung open, and she looked through it, and was blinded by a purple light.

Ariella threw up her arms to shield her eyes, but her arms were no longer there. In their place were two strands of deep violet energy, twisting and shifting in front of her. As she lowered her head, she saw her body was also made of the purple ribbons, and she felt herself floating.

The library had now been replaced by a vast empty space, filled with other ribbons of light, and strands of violet and mauve twisting and cascading through the void. Screaming echoed around her, and as much as she wanted to cover her ears, there were no longer any ears to cover.

In the distance, Ariella could see a more defined shape moving towards her. She tried to move forwards but could go no further. The figure moved closer, and multiple strands of violet began to blend until they formed a humanoid shape.

Ariella was now consumed in this realm of screams, and as this new entity approached, she recognised the face instantly. Jasmine's face honed into view, and became twisted in anger, her eyes glowing brightly, lightning strikes crashing all around her. As she raised her fists into the void, she brought them down with a force that ripped through Ariella's twisting form, and she felt an incredible burst of pain, and the realm itself seemed to implode before her, before another enormous flash of purple light.

Ariella woke with a startled cry, sweat dripping from her forehead. She felt a comforting arm on her shoulder as she lifted her head from the bed. Her breathing was beginning to slow down, but not quite to normal levels.

"Are you okay?" came a concerned voice.

Looking around, Ariella was very confused as to where she was and who the voice belonged to. The room was not familiar to her but felt like home. The last thing she had remembered was holding her daughter's hand and walking towards her favourite store. She remembered standing outside Herman's Curiosities, and hearing a loud screech, pushing Annie out of the way, and then... nothing.

"Hey, are you okay?" The voice came again. A soft, and sweetly spoken female voice.

"Yeah. Yeah, I'm fine."

Ariella's voice was deep, huskier than before, and very definitely male. It would appear she had moved bodies again.

"Sam, are you sure you're okay? Bad dream?"

The woman raised herself to her elbows and pulled Ariella's shoulder towards her. The woman was beautiful, and as the memories of her new host began to return to her, she remembered that this was 'Sam's' wife, Sadie.

In the corner of the room, she could see a police badge glinting on the dresser, and a gun, holstered on the back of a chair. Interesting upgrade. But what about Annie? That would have to wait. Her dreams had revealed something deeply unsettling. She was coming for her, and she would not stop at anything.

"Yeah. It was a bad dream. I'm fine."

Reassured, the woman lay back down and rolled over.

"Good, then go back to sleep, honey. You've got work in a few hours."

Within moments, the woman was asleep, a low snore audible in the dim light. Ariella, now 'Sam', lay back down, but she knew there would be no sleep. She had seen warning signs, both in her dreams, and through Sam's memories.

Jasmine was coming.

AFTERWORD

I have, over the years, thanked many people from all aspects and avenues of my life in the backs of my books. Sometimes, even mentioning famous people who have inspired me, despite I knew all too well that they would never see it. But, it was my book and I could say what I wanted to!

Now the series is coming to an end, I would like to unify my acknowledgements across the board into this one message. Particularly as I have even more people to thank years after the first book hit websites!

First and foremost, I must thank my incredible wife, Charlotte. Without her, I simply do not know where I would be, not just with my writing but in my life. I was starting to give up on almost everything when I met her, and she quickly became my rock, my confidante, and more importantly, my best friend. It is with her that I was able to start a family, and in February 2022, we welcomed little Molly Rose Adams into the world. They are both my world, and entire universe and I simply cannot imagine anywhere in the multiverse where we aren't all together.

Naturally, the next in line for thanks and appreciation would be my parents, Shirley and Vince Adams. Particularly since my introduction to various forms of social media in the last few years, I have come across far too many stories of unhappy childhoods, and lack of support from families of many people in my life. I, fortunately, am certainly not one of them. My mother and father have never once put me down, attempted to dissuade me from doing anything or making any significant life changes. They have shown me nothing but unconditional love, support, and at times, financial help. They continue to be a beacon of light in my life, and are devoted to my little family completely. If there was a blueprint on how to parent a child, these two would have written it.

That support flows down the family chain, and emanates from my sister, Francesca too. When we were younger, we did not get on. Always hitting each other, shouting at each other, and making each other unhappy and angry almost every day. But as we have gotten older, our bond has strengthened, and she has been there for me, Charlotte and Molly every step of the way. It has even reached the point where we left our home in Plymouth, and moved to Dorset, just a matter of streets away from each other! Her other half, Anthony, is a tower of strength for her, and their two children Jack and Isabelle are the jewels in their little family. It is a joy to be in their company, and their unique place on the autistic spectrum makes them extra loveable, and always fun to be around, because they adore companionship. I'm proud to be their uncle.

My grandparents played a vital role in my early life. My grandfather, William Henry Griffiths, for whom the first book is dedicated, was my best friend. I would see him every fortnight growing up, and he would always have a happy and yet powerful aura around him. He was a huge imposing figure in stature, but was as kind as could be. There were always miniature bars of chocolate in a tin waiting for me and Francesca; and a couple of quid pocket money. His death in 2005 devastated me, and in truth, 18 years later, still resonates within me. I miss him dearly.

My other grandparents, Marlene and Dave are a force of encouragement and love. Nobody fucks with my Nan. Not if they know what is good for them. I remember distinctly her glaring at my soon to be mother-in-law at our wedding when the registrar spoke the words 'if anyone knows of any reason why these two should not be married, speak now.' It was definitely a 'don't fuck with me' look. And of course my Grandad is nothing but a funny cuddle teddy bear, even now. His humour always cuts through any tension or discomfort, as bad as his jokes are, and I was proud to ask him to be my best man at my wedding, where he made the customary jokes, and I was blessed that he accepted.

I never had a job that I truly loved, until I moved to Ilfracombe in North Devon about a year and a half after my maternal grandfather died. I spent 10 months hunting for a job to no avail, before being told that whole time, the fruit and veg shop next door had been looking for someone! And so in the September of 2008, I began what would turn out to be 8 years working for the Norman family. That family made me feel like one of my own. I owe a debt of gratitude to Pam Norman for being my extra grandmother, Trevor and Sarah Norman for showing me such kindness, support and friendship, and Paula Hobman and her family for being like a crazy aunt and always cheering me up. I miss working for them, and being around them all the time, but they left an everlasting mark on my life that I will always carry with me.

Charlotte's Great Uncle Richard Oliver, and his daughter Nancy, have become two of our strongest connections. They have always backed us with whatever choices we made, and helped us along the way. They exude love and support, and at certain times, I'm not sure what we would have done without them. I simply cannot accurately place into words, what the two of them mean, but I like to think that they know.

And finally, I would like to take a minute or two to mention some of the people I have met in recent years through the wonders of the online community.

I joined Flare in 2023, a peer support group for those dealing with mental health issues and physical disabilities. It is a place to talk together, support others, and build a friendly safe community in the often toxic world of the internet. Founded by Robyn, Josh and Emma, it has gone from strength to strength and in doing so, I gained some very good friends. Like many friends, we have our differences, but the benefit they have given to my life has helped me develop my persona, particularly through their support of my social media presence and helping me to be more outgoing through mentoring and doing my own livestreams. Robyn in particular was instrumental in that, and for someone who has gone through so much in her short life, she gives so much more.

In the same timeframe, I met Chantel. Much like my Nan, you don't fuck with Chantel. She is fierce, devoted and loving in a way that makes her a very treasured individual. I have given her cause to digitally slap me in the face numerous times, but I have never stopped admiring her and the person she has become through the adversity she has battled through. I hope we remain friends for a long time to come.

BookTok's community changed me for the better. I met some wonderful author friends, and not only are they kind and supportive and funny, they are extremely talented writers and designers.

RD Baker is one of my closest author friends. Which is no mean feat considering she lives in Australia! I had never read either a fantasy or spicy book until I was enraptured by her book *Shadow and the Draw*. The world building was so well done and yet I was able to follow it all! I have since joined her ARC team and anticipate every book she writes with rising enthusiasm. She is also an incredible advocate for indie authors, and kindness across the world. If you haven't read her books before, what are you doing with your life?!?!

Next up is someone who I came across during a giveaway she was doing on TikTok. Alexia Mulle-Rushbrook very kindly sent me a free copy of her dystopian sci-fi The Minority Rule, and once I read it, I immediately bought the rest of the trilogy, devouring each book. They were simply wonderful, and I was happy to become part of her ARC team for the more recent release *They Call Me Angel*, which was her best work to date. She is a kind and giving person, and we chat often through direct messages, and always support each other on TikTok.

And no thanks would be complete without the presence of Christian Francis. I came across him when I saw one of his many videos on TikTok offering advice to indie authors like me, and everything the man said made perfect sense, and I followed it often. I particularly enjoyed his video on writing a scary scene which I may have coerced into a particular chapter of *Frame of Mind*, so this is me giving him credit! He also very kindly was the man behind this redesign of *The Dark Corner* series, and I will never forget the time, effort and resources he provided to me for that task. As if that wasn't enough, he designed the covers for my other series *The Frozen Planet Trilogy*, and created the amazing *myindiebookshelf.com* which champions indie authors, giving them a platform to showcase their work and link people exactly where to find them. And let's not forget that his books are fucking awesome. Disturbing… but fucking awesome.

Well, I have rambled on long enough. It's almost as if I was reciting my life story at times, I know, but with this being the best version of my work out there, I wanted to really get the message across.

Arnold Schwarzenegger says often that people are free to call him many things, but don't ever call him a self-made man. Because he has had help from people all his life, and without them, he wouldn't be who he is today. And that sums up perfectly how I feel. Without all the people I mentioned above, I wouldn't be who I am today.

I have written many books since my debut, and I am proud of most of them. While *The Dark Corner* series comes to an end, other journeys begin, and I am happy to say I don't see me stopping typing away anytime soon. So thank you for joining me on the journey, and I hope we can go on many more adventures together as the years go by.

Oh and one more thing…

It is possible to make no mistakes and still lose. That is not failure, that is life. I feel too many people forget that, particularly in this industry.

Take care, and see you in Sisko's.

David W. Adams
November 2023

ABOUT THE AUTHOR

David was born in 1988 in Wolverhampton, England. He spent most of his youth growing up in nearby Telford, where he attended the prestigious Thomas Telford School. However, unsure of which direction he wished his life to go in, he left higher education during sixth form, in order to get a job and pay his way. He has spent most of his life since, working in retail.

In 2007, following the death of his grandfather William Henry Griffiths a couple of years earlier, David's family relocated to the North Devon coastal town of Ilfracombe, where he got a job in local greengrocers, Normans Fruit & Veg as a general assistant, and spent 8 happy years there. In 2014, David met Charlotte, and in 2016, relocated to Plymouth to live with her as she continued her University studies.

In 2018, the pair were married, and currently reside on the Isle of Portland, Dorset.

The first published works of David's, was *The Dark Corner*. It was a compilation of short haunting stories which he wrote to help him escape the reality of the Coronavirus pandemic in early-mid 2020. However, it was not until January 2021, that he made the decision to publish.

From there… *The Dark Corner Literary Universe* was spawned….

You can follow David on TikTok @davidwadams.author.

tiktok.com/@davidwadams.author

amazon.com/stores/author/B08VHD911S

9 781916 582392